STOLEN LEGACIES

STOLEN LEGACIES

Aditya Banerjee

This is a work of fiction. Names, characters, business, events, and incidents are the products of the author's imagination. Any resemblance to actual persons, living or dead, or actual events is purely coincidental.

Copyright © 2021 Aditya Banerjee
All rights reserved. This book or any portion thereof may not be reproduced or used in any manner whatsoever without the express written permission of the publisher except for the use of brief quotations in a book review.

ISBN: 978-1-7773578-2-5 (paperback)
ISBN: 978-1-7773578-3-2 (Electronic book)

To those who write their own music.

Table of Contents

1. Introduction · 1
2. The Scandal · 3
3. New Beginnings · · · · · · · · · · · · · · · · · · · 48
4. The Archives · 82
5. Secrets · 121
6. Mist · 172
7. Providence · 208
8. Entrapment · 266
9. Deception · 313
10. The System · 347
11. The Visitor · 373
12. Epilogue · 393

About the Author · · · · · · · · · · · · · · · · · · · 401

1

Introduction

When India gained independence in 1947, nearly half of its land and a quarter of its population were part of 550 princely states. While the rulers of some large princely states like Jaipur and Gwalior were rich and affluent, those belonging to the lesser known and smaller states resembled large landlords overseeing their ancestral domains. The size of their land holdings and estates varied greatly, and postindependence many of them, unable to change with the times, saw their fortunes dwindle quite rapidly.

The privy purse was a payment made to the ruling families of the erstwhile princely states as part of their agreements to integrate with India after its independence. The sum was intended to cover all expenses of the former ruling families. The rulers surrendered their sovereignty, and as a quid pro quo, they were granted, in addition to these privy purses, other privileges such as retaining their titles like raja or maharaja. In 1971, an amendment to the Indian constitution abolished the privy purse, and the ruling families lost their allowances, their titles, and all the privileges that came with them.

Our mystery is set in the midseventies, nearly three decades after India's independence and a few years after the privy purse had been abolished. Our story follows the decline in fortunes of one such estate, Surinampur, in the state of Bengal in the east coast of India. Most of the story takes place there and in the eastern city of Calcutta on the Bay of Bengal.

2

The Scandal

Manik Bose knew that there was something wrong the moment he walked into the building. He was in early, as always. But something was different today. He could sense it as soon as he walked into the gates of the compound, even before reaching the building. The parking lot was full. He could see a flurry of new cars in the VIP section. He immediately recognized the one belonging to Tarun Roy, the owner of the *New Eastern Herald*. Usually Tarun came to the office only when there was an important meeting or during a major festival to celebrate with his employees. Manik did not recognize the other cars, but from their makes and models, he knew that the owners were rich and influential. The chauffeurs were cleaning the cars—not that they needed much polishing.

As he walked through the gates, past the parking lot, and into the building, he was greeted with cautious glances and could immediately sense that people were looking at him and speaking to one another in whispers. The receptionist told him that he was expected in the editor's office and that he should go there right away. As he started climbing the stairs, he saw people quickly walking past him, some nodding, others with serious looks on their faces. As he reached the second floor, where his desk was, he realized that he was not the only one who had been summoned to the editor's office. He saw his boss, Harish, hurrying past the desks, heading to the same place.

Once he reached his desk, he left his bag and looked around to see if anyone would let him know what was going on. He sensed that it was probably related to the editorial that had appeared over the weekend, the one that he and Harish had written. It was on how land was being acquired by builders from the state government and private landowners at throwaway prices. These companies were building factories and housing colonies and selling them back to private buyers and to the government at higher prices. The editorial had questioned whether this whole process was transparent and whether any middlemen were facilitating these transactions. In a country where approvals and licenses took several months, the process in this case was being completed in a matter of weeks, seemingly without any oversight.

Harish Mishra had worked on the story for almost a year. He had taken Manik on board to help him with the research and to mentor him. When Manik joined the *New Eastern Herald* a year and a half back, he was assigned some minor projects and stories, as was the case for new recruits. He collaborated with another senior journalist on an article on labor laws and their impact on the workforce. Harish was impressed with the research that Manik had done on that piece. Harish then asked his editor to put Manik on the land story. He did not regret it. Manik was a quick learner. He was thorough, respectful, and at the same time not afraid to ask difficult questions when needed. What impressed Harish most was Manik's work ethic. He was always on time, worked late when needed, and showed initiative in taking on tasks.

All that was far from their minds on this January morning in 1974. Following the publication of the article, there was a flurry of meetings among the editor and other senior management. They had underestimated the impact it would have on the business community, politicians, and, most importantly, the owners of the *New Eastern Herald*. They had known that the article was going to be controversial, but not to the point where the paper's reputation would be questioned. Manik was initially surprised by the reaction, and then he started getting worried. Before leaving the night before, he had recalled his conversation with Harish. It bothered him that Harish, who had worked as a senior journalist in many newspapers and had been one of the first reporters to join the paper a decade ago, was apprehensive about what was going to happen.

Before leaving, he had called Manik to his desk to let him know what was going on.

"Manik, I think you may have sensed that all is not well following the publication of our article."

"Did we do something wrong?" Manik asked thoughtfully.

"No. But it seems the article has rubbed some influential people the wrong way."

"But was there something wrong or incorrect in the article? It was an opinion piece on the editorial page. What exactly is the issue, sir?"

Harish was lost in thought, and Manik didn't know if he had caught his question. Just before he started repeating it, Harish looked at him and asked him to sit down. It was evident that his boss wanted to have a long conversation with him. Manik had never seen Harish this worried, ever, in the months they had worked together. He also knew that Harish was a well-respected journalist and was seen as someone who could write controversial articles.

"Manik, the problem is that this article seems to have caused some issues with the owners of the paper."

The *New Eastern Herald* was owned by the Roy family. Sarat Roy, who was the founder, had started the newspaper more than a decade ago, and now his son, Tarun Roy, was tasked with looking after the paper, making decisions, and moving things forward. The Roys owned a number of companies, and the paper was not the largest part of their business empire. They spent most of their time at the two steel mills they owned. Apart from the mills and the paper, they had a construction company, a cement plant, and a film production house. All the businesses were in and around Calcutta, and each one of them was profitable. They wanted to expand to other cities in Bengal and, eventually, the rest of India. For the most part, they left the day-to-day running of the newspaper to the managing editor, Swaroop Pal.

Swaroop had been there since the beginning and was an effective leader. He understood that a new newspaper would need good journalists and reporters to get off to a good start. He also understood the business side of things. He made sure that the paper catered to the needs of the advertisers. His main focus was to expand readership. It was here that he had succeeded the most. In the span of a decade, he had increased the circulation of the paper many times over, and now it was the top regional daily in English in terms of circulation and third if one counted the national dailies in Bengal. The owners were happy to give him the independence he needed and were extremely pleased with where he had taken the paper since it started. With a staff of over six hundred employees, he had managed to build a solid reputation for the paper among its readers. The owners had promised him that they would consider taking the paper national in the next five years. With a growing English-speaking population in India, things looked good, provided they could maintain their current growth.

Manik had rarely spoken to Swaroop. He knew that Swaroop was the first one to get to work every day and the last one to leave. Swaroop knew everyone's name and made it a point to greet them by name whenever he spoke to them or met them. Much of the reputation of the paper was built around Swaroop and the senior journalists he had hired. Most of them were hand-picked by him and poached from other papers. Harish had been working for a national daily when Swaroop approached him to join the *New Eastern Herald*. He sold him the dream of starting something new and growing with it. It was not a disappointment. Everyone who started when the paper was founded was in a senior position. Swaroop and the Roys made sure they retained the best-performing talent.

Harish was now the most senior journalist in the paper and was close to retirement. He had written about a wide range of topics, mostly around business ventures and politics. When he took on the story on the land acquisition deals, Harish was excited. He knew that this was probably going to be one of his last high-profile stories before retiring. He wanted to leave on a high, and this story showed a lot of promise. As he spoke to Manik, Harish wanted to let him know what was going on behind the scenes in the various meetings and discussions.

"Manik, I just came back from Swaroop's office. We have a meeting tomorrow morning with the owners. They want to talk to us about the article."

"What problems has it caused for the owners exactly?"

"It seems some clients of their other businesses are not too happy with the general premise of the article. They are threatening to take their business elsewhere, and from what I have heard, even contemplating legal action against the paper."

"I am guessing this is because the clients of the steel mills and the cement plant are builders and real estate companies, and the threat is coming from those businesses?"

"Yes. Swaroop is also worried that it will affect the paper's reputation and, of course, advertising revenues. As you know, a big chunk of the ad revenue comes from builders and construction companies."

"Yes, sir. But what exactly do they want us to do?"

"The Roys—I don't know. We will know tomorrow, once we meet them. I know what Swaroop wants us to do."

"What's that, sir?"

"Write a follow-up article, some sort of retraction to smooth things over."

Manik was quiet. He knew that this didn't sit well with Harish either, and he could see that his boss was wrestling with it.

"Do you think we should print a retraction?"

"No. But we may have to. I don't know. I don't want to preempt anything before talking to the Roys."

"What do you think we should do, sir?"

"Nothing. If it were left up to me, I wouldn't do anything."

Manik was pleased to hear that. But he also knew that they probably wouldn't have much of a choice if Swaroop and the Roys wanted them to write a retraction.

"You know, Manik, what bothers me is that it has irked the businesses to the point that they are threatening to sue. That means that whatever we have written is somewhat true or that they know that we won't find any evidence to back up our opinion piece because the system is corrupt."

"Sir, why is this such a big deal if we just asked questions without naming names? The article did not mention any specific company."

"Well, there are only three large construction companies in the city, and all of them get steel and cement from the plants that the Roys own. They obviously see it as some sort of betrayal on the Roys' part to question their business practices when the owners of the paper are benefiting from the very industries whose practices are being questioned. You have to look at it from their point of view."

"Right."

"When we meet tomorrow, be prepared to answer all the questions regarding the article. Please feel free to convey your thoughts. I have known Sarat Roy for a long time, and he appreciates candor and direct answers. Tarun, on the other hand, as you know, can be a bit of a bully. If he does raise his voice, which I doubt he will do in front of his father, don't worry too much about it. Deep down, he is a good guy and is reasonable."

"What about Swaroop?" Manik asked.

"What about him?"

"Where does he stand in all of this? He *did* agree to publish the article."

"Yes. But ultimately it was our article and our content. Don't worry too much about Swaroop. He is worried about what the Roys will ask us to do. But he will also try to back us up if needed. It's getting late, and we have a long day tomorrow. Good night. Get some rest."

"Yes, sir."

As he walked out of the building that night, Manik couldn't help but wonder about his year and a half at the *New Eastern Herald*. Overall, it had been an enriching experience. Initially he had had some misgivings about joining a regional newspaper. But in the end, he didn't have much of a choice. When he graduated from college, jobs were hard to come by. He had worked in a print shop for a few months to get by. He had applied to all the national dailies. Some of them politely refused, while others didn't bother sending a reply. His graduating class was having a hard time finding jobs. Although India's economy was growing, it wasn't growing fast enough to absorb the large volume of graduates each year. The early seventies were particularly challenging for the country as a whole. New businesses were having a hard time raising capital. When he got the call back from the *New Eastern Herald*, he was excited. There were three rounds of interviews over a four-week period. When he finally got selected, he was ecstatic. This was his first real job, and he was off to a great start.

The paper was full of young men and women trying to make their mark. The new employees were paired up with senior journalists and reporters who acted as their mentors. Manik had initially been assigned to someone else, but after six months he ended up with Harish. They had a good working relationship, and Harish took the time to explain things properly. He was a good mentor and gave Manik the freedom to do his tasks his own way, in his own time. As long as the tasks were completed on time, Harish didn't bother him. What Manik really valued was that during their time together working on the article, Harish probed him and asked him questions and wanted his input and opinion. They didn't always agree, but Manik liked the fact that Harish always asked his opinion. He had grown to respect Harish not only as a journalist but also as a person.

When Manik and Harish started working together on the article that was creating all the issues, it didn't seem like it would be controversial to the point that readers would question the reputation of the paper itself. Manik was convinced the readers did not have the same misgivings about the article. Many of them probably agreed with its content. Although it was an opinion piece, Harish had made sure that it was well researched and had been careful not to mention names of companies or people. The idea was to question the system itself. Land in and around Calcutta was being appropriated by industrialists and businessmen to build factories and residential apartments. Most of the land belonged to the government, but some of the land close to the city, in prime locations, belonged to private owners. Many of them were middle-class families who were being coerced into selling their land at prices lower than their market value. Once the land had been acquired, the businesses would then build apartments and offices and then sell them back to private owners or even the government at much higher prices.

This entire process was being done with the help of so-called "consultants" or middlemen who were making lots of money in the process. Also disturbing was that some of the land was just being plain taken away if the owners failed to show up or prove that they owned the property. The government had tasked the builders with finding the owners of the land, and if no one came forward, there were advertisements posted in the regional and national dailies. After ninety days the builder would appropriate the land for a fee to the government. Needless to say, this fee was much less than the actual value of the land itself. The government was happy that their coffers were getting filled, and it simply did not have the manpower to administer this whole process, nor the resources to ensure that the entire process was transparent. There was of course the whole issue of whether senior government officials and politicians were gaining from all of this.

The article was meant to question this entire process and also force the government to make it more transparent and fairer. Manik and Harish thought that when they asked Swaroop to approve the article for publication, they would be complimented on their work and research. They had conducted interviews with some of the private landowners, contractors who worked at the building sites, and workers in some of the businesses acquiring the land, and they had also managed to question some ex-employees of the rogue "consultants." They were able to follow the money trail and figure out the commissions being made by the middlemen and the exorbitant profits that the builders were making in the whole process. But when Swaroop saw all this, he was worried. Manik recalled the conversation in Swaroop's office the day before the article was approved for printing.

"Harish, this is a good article. But most of your information has been obtained by word of mouth. Is there any paper trail that proves any of this?" Swaroop asked.

"No. But there wouldn't be. Folks involved in this want to make sure that nothing is recorded officially, except for the paperwork needed buy and sell the land and apartments. But that's not where the corruption is. It's the way the land is being acquired and the price at which it is being sold back once the construction has been completed."

"Why would our readers be interested in this?"

"The taxpayers are getting a raw deal. Many of these buildings are being bought back by the government at exorbitant prices for offices and low-cost housing."

"So why haven't there been any court cases?" Swaroop pressed further.

"It's because most of the land belongs to folks who cannot afford a long, drawn-out legal battle. The builders know how to coerce them, and their tactics are not always above board."

"What about the police?"

"For that to happen, someone has to register a case with a specific complaint. Otherwise the police won't investigate."

"And why do you think we should carry this?" Swaroop continued.

"As a newspaper we have an obligation to question the establishment and expose any wrongdoings. In this case we are simply asking the government to review their process and sharing our view with the readers that something is not right," Harish pleaded.

Swaroop took another look at the article and started reading it again. Harish and Manik looked at each other, keeping quiet.

"All right. Please leave this with me. Let me think about it, and I will let you know in a couple of days" Swaroop said.

True to his word, after a couple of days, Swaroop asked Manik and Harish to make some cosmetic changes to the article and then gave his nod to get it printed on the weekend editorial page. Swaroop's first inkling that the article might have hit a nerve came on Monday morning, when one of the builders called him up directly and threatened to cancel his advertising contract with the paper. This was followed by a subsequent call from one of the senior managers at the steel plant that the Roys owned, asking him if he had gotten the article approved by either of the owners before printing it. He hadn't. He didn't need to. Swaroop was the managing editor, and the Roys had given him the freedom to judge what content would be published and what wouldn't. But the calls made him nervous. Then in the afternoon, he got a similar call along the same lines from the cement plant that was one of the main suppliers to the builders. He knew that this had ruffled enough feathers that he would be getting a call from Roys soon enough.

Finally, in the evening, Tarun Roy called Swaroop and summoned him to his father's residence. The meeting was short, polite, and direct. The Roys instructed Swaroop to talk to the journalists who had written the article and collect all the evidence and research they had acquired and send it to their lawyers. They also asked Swaroop to have them present during their visit to the office the following day. Both father and son coming to the *Herald* building for an official meeting on the same day was a very rare occurrence. Manik was not aware of all the details, but when Harish told him that the owners and Swaroop wanted to talk to them, he knew that it was important. He had discussed the matter with his friends Subodh and Avik. They worked at the paper as well and lived in the same apartment building. All of them had started working at the paper a few weeks apart, and over the course of eighteen months, they had become good friends. Both Subodh and Avik were worried about Manik, and they told him to do what was needed to keep his job. They all knew that jobs were hard to come by, and if indeed Manik were to leave under these circumstances, it would be difficult for him to find another job.

Manik was mulling over all this while waiting to be called into Tarun Roy's office. He was sitting outside in a large waiting area on the top floor of the building. Unlike the two other floors, where most of the staff worked, this floor was dedicated to upper management. There were a few spacious offices, some conference rooms, a large reception area, a storage room, a library, and a small tearoom for the staff who worked on this floor. Manik had only come to this floor a few times, to use the library. As he sat there waiting to be called in, he marveled at how impressive the offices were. Each one of them looked new, although this was an old building. The paper had moved into its current establishment well before Manik joined. The current building met the expanding needs of the paper and was in a nice locality in the outskirts of Calcutta. The building used to be a run-down state government office. The Roys bought it and completely renovated it. The three-story building was surrounded by a garden. The campus was an oasis in an otherwise industrial part of town. When Manik joined, he made the decision to rent a place that was walking distance from the office. It helped, of course, that other colleagues were in the same apartment building. He did not have to worry about the morning and evening commutes that everyone else living in the city was always complaining about.

His gaze turned toward the secretaries who were sitting behind their desks outside Tarun's office. They didn't have much of a friendly disposition, or perhaps they knew what was going to happen in the meeting and were keeping their distance. He recognized Rajan, Swaroop's trusted secretary. He was well-known to the senior staff and well connected. The other secretaries were the ones who were visiting because the Roys were there. Tarun Roy always had at least one or more assistant accompany him everywhere. Manik did not know them.

The other floors of the office were loud with the printing press, cafeteria, and courtyard on the ground floor and the news desk on the second floor with all the journalists and the clickety-clack sounds of hundreds of typewriters. The top floor was eerily quiet. It was well insulated from what was happening in the rest of the building. Manik often wondered whether the décor on this floor where the owners had their offices was meant to be dark and imposing by design. He did enjoy going to the library. One thing he admired about the Roys was that they spent money and resources on the paper. They had state-of-the-art printing machines, typewriters, and photocopiers. The library was stacked with the latest journals and books, and employees could make suggestions for new additions and subscriptions.

Finally, after waiting for an hour or so, he saw Swaroop and Harish coming out of Tarun's office, along with other senior journalists and some people who looked like lawyers, though Manik wasn't sure. Harish walked up to him with a worried look on his face.

"The Roys will be calling us in in ten minutes or so."

"Yes, sir."

"We were just talking to the legal team."

"How did it go?" Manik asked, not sure if he really wanted to know the answer.

"I am not sure. I think they are trying to figure out if they can leave this matter outside the courts. One encouraging sign is that the lawyers mentioned that since we did not name names and it was an opinion piece, it would be hard to file any serious case around the article."

"That's good, isn't it?" Manik asked, sounding a bit relieved.

"I think Tarun is more worried about the impact on the rest of the businesses and the overall reputation of the paper."

"I can understand the financial implications if other businesses pull their advertisements. But why the reputation of the paper? Aren't we supposed to ask these questions?" Manik asked.

"Ideally, yes. But we live in the real world, with business imperatives and conflicts. Let's just stay positive and see what the Roys have to say."

"Yes, sir."

After a few minutes, Tarun Roy's secretary came up to them and took them to his office. As they entered, they could see Sarat Roy sitting in an armchair by the large window at one end of the room. Sitting beside him was Swaroop. Tarun was sitting behind his desk. The three men looked very different from one another in their appearance and their mannerisms. Sarat Roy was old and slow, and his movements seemed deliberate. The glasses and walking stick made him look older. He was dressed in traditional white Bengali attire. He was known as someone who spoke softly and slowly. His face and mannerisms were serious, but he had an affectionate look on his face. His short stature and thin frame hid a confident and successful man.

Swaroop looked like someone who had the weight of the world on his shoulders. He was overweight, smoked like a chimney, and although his attire was expensive, it seemed unkempt. Each action seemed hurried, and he was known to have a nervous disposition.

Tarun Roy was young, dressed in a dark suit, stoic, and looked like someone in a hurry. His appearance and attire were polished, and he spoke English without any accent. His tall, athletic built made him look imposing. He motioned them over to come and sit across from him.

Manik had been to this room only once in his eighteen months on the job. It was an impressive and imposing office. It was sparsely used, since the Roys never really came to the office. Tarun got up from behind the desk and came to where Manik and Harish were sitting, moving toward the other side of the window so that he could face all four of them. It was Swaroop who broke the silence.

"This is Manik Bose. He has been with us for a year and half. He worked with Harish on the article."

Tarun and Sarat acknowledged Manik with a nod. The other people in the room knew one another fairly well. Tarun looked at Manik and started speaking.

"Thank you, Swaroop. I would have liked to meet you under more pleasing circumstances. I am guessing you know who we are?"

"Yes, sir" Manik replied.

Tarun shifted his gaze to address both Harish and Manik.

"The article that you wrote got us into trouble. Harish, you have been here for a long time. I can't imagine that you wouldn't have guessed what would happen once this was printed."

"I knew the article would be controversial. But I didn't realize it would have the effect that it did," Harish replied.

"What about you, Swaroop?" asked Tarun.

"I agree with Harish. I gave the final approval to have this printed. But honestly, I did not realize that it would come to this," Swaroop replied.

Manik kept quiet, and Tarun didn't ask him anything. He thought it was probably because he was too junior or too new to have any opinion on all this. He was surprised to see that Tarun did most of the talking while Sarat sat quietly with a distant look on his face. Tarun looked at Harish and addressed him directly.

"My father, Swaroop, and I have given it some thought. I think we need to minimize the fallout from this. I certainly don't want to go to the courts. I also don't want the paper's reputation to be tarnished in any way."

Manik wondered about the last point. If indeed there was any truth in the article, then why would it hurt the paper's reputation? In fact, readers would be interested in finding out more about what was going on with these land deals and appropriations. He understood that the businesses involved would probably not want their names dragged into this. But the readers would be fine. Again, he decided to keep quiet and respond only if asked.

"Harish, we would like you and Manik to write a follow-up opinion piece on the weekend editorial page. It doesn't have to come across as a retraction. But essentially it should leave the readers with the impression that the previous article was one side of the story and the follow-up is another point of view."

It was Swaroop who replied first.

"If we do that, readers will know that we have been pressured into writing a retraction. We should not insult their intelligence."

"We won't. You are all journalists. I expect you to use all your language skills to make it sound otherwise," Tarun said.

Manik could sense from Harish's look that he was both sad and angry. He wanted desperately to defend the work and the content of the article. But he had done that already in meetings with the Roys and the lawyers with no apparent success.

Swaroop also sensed Harish's displeasure and tried to change the topic. "What about the lawyers?"

"What about them?" Tarun asked with a surprised look on his face.

"Do we need to run the article by them to get their approval?"

"I will ask them. That's probably a good idea. I will let you know by tomorrow."

Manik could sense Harish's dejection. They had worked hard on the story, and to be accused rather than applauded for it for reasons beyond their control was grossly unfair.

Tarun sensed that and with a gentler voice addressed Harish, Swaroop, and Manik.

"Please try to understand that we have other businesses. They are much larger, and the profits from those businesses have helped this newspaper as well."

They all knew that was true. Despite it being the smallest and least profitable of all their business holdings, the Roys had always valued the paper. They had poured money into it and had been willing to take a loss for many years as it established itself.

Harish finally broke his silence. "I will start working on the new article right away. I will have it ready before the weekend. I will send it to you and Swaroop. I will leave it up to you to make a call on whether it needs to be sent to the lawyers."

"Thank you, Harish," Tarun said.

"I do have one request. Let's not drag Manik's name into any of this. He helped me with the original article, but I don't want any of this to reflect badly on him. He is just starting out and deserves better."

"Agreed," Tarun replied before Manik could protest in any way.

Manik felt bad about how things were turning out for Harish. He did appreciate Harish's gesture in trying to keep him out of the controversy surrounding the article. But at the same time, he felt that he needed to stand by Harish.

Before he could start speaking, Tarun walked back behind his desk and looked at Harish and Manik. "I think that's all I wanted to discuss. Is there anything else you want to add?"

"No, sir," Harish replied before Manik could say anything. He sensed that Harish wanted to leave the room as soon as he could. He felt the same way. They both got up shook hands with Tarun and looked toward Sarat, who had been quiet throughout the conversation. Sarat had let his son do all the talking, sitting in his chair with his hands resting on a walking stick while listening to the entire exchange between Tarun,

Swaroop, and Harish. It was hard for them to judge whether the elder Roy felt any differently.

As they were leaving the room, he gently nodded toward Harish and Manik. Tarun had asked Swaroop to stay back. Once they were back on the floor and at their desks, Harish turned to Manik. "Let's go to the cafeteria. We need to talk."

"Sure, sir," Manik replied.

They could hear that the clickety-clack sound of the typewriters on some of the desks had stopped; their colleagues were looking at them. They knew something was wrong but did not have all the details. Some of them came over, and Manik could sense that most of them were worried about Harish. So were Manik's friends Subodh and Avik. He could sense that they were looking at him and wanted to know what was going on. They wanted to come over and talk to him but waited for the group to disperse first. Once the group went back to their desks, Harish turned to Manik.

"Give me a few minutes. I have to make a quick call to my wife at home. She is stressed out about this. I need to let her know where things stand, and then I will meet you downstairs." Harish headed over to the phone desk at the end of the hall. He did not want to use the phone at his own desk. This was understandable. He wanted some privacy, and it was impossible with the layout of all the desks, typewriters, and phones in the open offices not to overhear conversations.

Once Harish left, Manik started walking toward the stairs to head to the cafeteria. Before he could get there, he was confronted by Subodh and Avik. He could see the worried look on their faces. He quickly told them what had happened. They told him that they would wait for him in the evening, and they would all walk back together. He nodded and made his way down the stairs into the cafeteria. Only a few people were there. It was between breakfast and lunch. Most of the people who were there were either taking a break or having a smoke. Manik had come to know all of them by their faces. Some nodded; others smiled back at him. He didn't know how much the rest of the folks in the paper knew about what was going on. He was fairly sure that most of the senior journalists knew what was going on, while the others were mostly guessing. The folks in the other departments probably didn't care that much. Manik found a table near a window in one corner of the cafeteria. It was easy to find empty tables at this time, and he didn't mind the emptiness. He wanted to be left alone. He ordered some tea for Harish and himself, and just as he was about to sit down, he saw Harish heading over to his table. Once they sat down,

Manik could see that Harish was now somewhat calmer than before. Perhaps the chat with his wife had helped.

"Have you ordered something?"

"Yes, sir. Tea for both of us."

"Do you want a cigarette?"

"Not right now," Manik replied.

"Do you mind if I smoke?" Harish asked as he brought out a pack.

"Not at all."

Once he started smoking, Harish pointed to the other end of the hallway.

"You know when we first moved into the building, our desks were on this floor. That year the heavy rains flooded the grounds outside, and some of the water came into this area. It damaged typewriters, files, phones. Then Swaroop decided to move us upstairs."

Before Manik could speak, their tea arrived. He could sense that Harish had something other than the article on his mind.

"Sir, I appreciate your offer to keep my name off the next article. But I don't mind if we work on it together."

"It will be a lousy article. The whole point of it will be calm the feathers we have ruffled without sounding like we are issuing an apology or a retraction."

"I do want to thank you for trying to keep my name clear of this."

"Oh. That's the least I could do. I know how these things work, Manik. You are just starting out now. I don't know how the chips will fall once this is all said and done. But I don't want you to be saddled with it for too long. In any case, you will see that in a few weeks, people will forget and move on to other things. The focus now is on avoiding any litigation. As you may have guessed from the meeting upstairs, the Roys want to make sure that their other businesses are not impacted by this."

"What about the paper's reputation?"

"What about it?"

"Tarun Roy said he is worried about that as well."

"You really think that's the case?"

"No, sir."

"We shouldn't underestimate the intelligence of our readers. They will eventually know what happened. That's what I think, anyway. There's something else I wanted to talk to you about, Manik."

"What, sir?"

As Harish took his time finishing his cigarette, Manik sensed that what was coming next was not something he wanted to hear. Harish took another sip from his cup.

"You know that I am close to my retirement, right?"

"Yes, sir. You told me another year and half."

"Yes. Well, all this may have just hastened the process."

"How so?"

"I have had several meetings with Swaroop over the last couple of days. Once this is all done, I will be taking an early retirement. A few weeks, and then I am done."

"But do you want to?"

"Are you asking me if I am being forced to?"

"Yes, sir."

"Not in so many words—or that directly. The Roys are good people. They are not the kind of people who would scream and shout and blame their employees and fire them. But in speaking with Swaroop, it is quite evident that they need a fall guy. If I retire early, they can tell their corporate clients—discreetly, of course—that it has been dealt with."

"But you said yourself that this will blow over in a few weeks. So why do you need to do this?" Manik asked in an agitated voice.

"Yes, from the readers' point of view, that is correct. But as I said before, this has nothing to do with the public."

"I still think it is unfair," Manik said, visibly unimpressed.

"As you get older, you will see that there are times when fairness takes a back seat and you just have to accept things as they are."

"Still, it doesn't seem right, sir." Manik wasn't happy with this sort of defeatist attitude. But he understood what Harish was talking about.

"There is one more thing, Manik. I have asked Swaroop to pair you up with another senior journalist, and you will be working with him starting tomorrow. I don't know who it is. But Swaroop will assign you to someone. He will talk to you about it later today."

Based on their conversation, Manik had guessed that this was going to happen. He felt sad about Harish. He had had a stellar career with lots of success, awards, and accolades. To end his career like this would definitely leave a stain on his reputation. They sat in silence for some time. While Harish gazed out the window, Manik could see the tired look on his face. Harish looked his age, and somehow this article and its aftermath were starting to take their toll on his mannerisms and confidence. He was trying to hide it as much as he could.

"Don't worry, Manik. I will still be around for the next few weeks. We can still meet up and chat. But I want you to look past this and worry about your own future."

"Yes, sir. Thank you for all this."

"No. It's the least I could have done. For what it's worth, I should be the one apologizing to you for all this mess. I should have seen it coming. Anyway, I need to head back to my desk. I will let you finish your tea, and we can meet up later for lunch. Please don't forget to pass by Swaroop's office later today."

"Sure, sir."

As Harish walked away, Manik couldn't help but wonder if there was something they could have done differently. None of them could have predicted this outcome. He was also sad that he would no longer be working with Harish. He wondered what Swaroop had planned for him. While he was thinking about all this and trying to finish his tea, he realized that someone had come over to his table and was standing next to him. It was Sarat Roy. Manik quickly got up as Sarat slowly leaned against his walking stick and eased himself into the chair across from him.

"Manik, isn't it?"

"Yes, sir. Would you like me to order some tea for you?"

"No. I really shouldn't. But thank you. I hear that you have been with us for a year and half now."

"Yes, sir."

"Where are you from, Manik? Are you from Calcutta?"

"No, sir. I am from Bolpur."

"Ah, near Shanti Niketan?"

"Yes, sir."

"Lovely place."

"Yes, sir."

Sarat hadn't said a single word during the entire meeting earlier and had let his son do most of the talking. As Manik got a closer look at him, he could see that he was old and tired. He also had a pleasing disposition.

"Tell me, Manik. What do you think about the article? Never mind what transpired after that. I want to ask you your opinion. I realize that my son never asked you that. But I want to know from you what you think. You can be honest with me. This conversation stays between us."

"Sir, I think it was a good article."

"What else?"

"That some of it is probably true. That's why it rubbed people the wrong way."

"Hmm. And you think publishing it was the right thing to do?"

"Yes, sir. It is the job of a newspaper to question things in addition to reporting events. The readers can then judge for themselves."

"An idealist, I see." Sarat smiled.

"I am sorry how it all turned out, but I still think it was a good article and that publishing it was the right thing to do, sir."

"I appreciate your candor, Manik. Do you understand, though, why we need to do what we need to do now?"

"Yes, sir."

Sarat slowly got up from his chair. Manik helped him get his walking stick. Once he stood up, he leaned over with his stick beside him, looked at Manik, and smiled.

"It was nice talking to you, Manik. Thank you for taking the time to let me know what you think."

"Thank you, sir."

As he saw Sarat Roy walking away, he realized the other people in the cafeteria were looking at them. And as Sarat slowly walked past them, he smiled, nodded, and acknowledged their greetings. They didn't see much of him in this building. But they all knew who he was. Manik waited a bit longer at the table, wondering why Sarat was so interested in getting his opinion and why he hadn't brought this up during the meeting earlier in the day. He was still sad and disappointed about the events of that morning.

He finished his tea and started making his way upstairs to Swaroop's office. On his way, he bumped into Avik, who told him that they would be leaving work around 7:00 p.m.

Manik then found himself outside Swaroop's office. He greeted his secretary, Rajan, who asked him to wait. He could see through the large glass windows of Swaroop's office that there was a meeting going on inside the room. While he was waiting, he recalled his interview with Swaroop when he was joining the *New Eastern Herald*. He had been impressed with Swaroop's vision for the newspaper. During his time at the *Herald*, Manik had always seen him in a positive light. He was well aware of the pressure that Swaroop was under from the Roys following the publication of the article. At the same time, he expected Swaroop to stand his ground and back his employees. He had seen some of that earlier during the meeting with the Roys, but not enough. Then again, he wasn't aware of what had happened in the other meetings.

While he was contemplating this, he saw the people filing out of Swaroop's office. He recognized some of them. They were from the printing press. He was relieved that it wasn't yet another meeting on the article.

Once Manik got inside, Swaroop asked him to take a seat on one of the chairs across from his desk. He was finishing up a phone call. Manik sat down and looked around. This was a room he was familiar with. He had come to plenty of meetings here. Swaroop liked to have meetings in his big room. Unlike the Roys' offices, Swaroop's office was an absolute mess. He had a huge desk on one side of the room, but every inch of that desk was filled with piles of papers, files, and stacks of journals that looked like they could fall over at any time. At the other end of the room was a large conference table with ten chairs for meetings. Again, another absolute mess, with papers and accessories everywhere. There were two other small tables with typewriters and a big bookshelf filled with books, family pictures, awards, and trophies. It was a huge room, but all the clutter made it look small. Manik often wondered how Swaroop could work in an office like this. To make matters worse, Swaroop loved to smoke, and the entire room had a stench of tobacco. When Swaroop finished his call, he made some quick notes on a writing pad and then addressed Manik.

"Manik, did you get a chance to speak to Harish after the meeting?"

"Yes, sir."

"Before we get to your new assignment, do you have any questions on what happened in the meeting with the Roys earlier today?"

"Not really."

"It's all right. You can tell me what you are thinking even though I may not want to hear it."

"It's just that it seems unfair that we have to write an apology and a retraction for an article that was actually an opinion piece, didn't target anyone specifically, and was well researched."

"I understand, Manik. I am not happy about that either. But you have to understand that this is a business, and sometimes we have to pick our battles, and there are other times when we have to compromise."

"This doesn't seem like a compromise, sir. More like an apology, even though we haven't wronged anyone."

"I get it, and I do appreciate that you are being frank with me. However, my hands are tied, and it's a business decision that we have to abide by."

"I get that, sir."

"Good. Now to your new assignment. I am going to pair you up with Kedar Bagchi. Do you know who he is?"

"I have never spoken to him. But I know who he is."

Manik knew that Kedar was sort of a jack-of-all-trades reporter. He didn't write any editorials or opinion pieces. Initially he was working at the sports desk, but then he got assigned to other desks as well. He was also a senior journalist but didn't command the same respect that Harish and some of the other senior staff did. Kedar seemed more laid back, and from what Manik had heard from Avik and Subodh, he was coasting along until his retirement. He lacked the drive and ambition associated with a good reporter. Yet he was a good investigator. He had been at the *New Eastern Herald* for almost five years and had been assigned to different desks dealing with crime, politics, sports, and entertainment. *Truly a jack of all trades*, Manik thought.

"Kedar is not in the office today. He is over at the racetracks following up on a story on gambling. But he will be here tomorrow. I'd suggest you meet him first thing tomorrow morning."

"Yes, sir."

"Any other questions?"

"Does he know I am being assigned to him?"

"Not yet. But he will be calling me tonight, and I will let him know."

"Right, sir."

"Well, if there isn't anything else, I suggest you go over to Kedar's desk and ask his secretary to share some of the files on the stories he is working on. Her name is Anjali, and I have told her that you will be coming by."

"Thank you, sir," Manik said as he got up.

"Manik, I need you to move on from this mess and look to your next story. Trust me when I say that this will blow over, and soon you will be working on other stories."

"Yes, sir."

Manik left the room, walked back to his desk, and sat down. The familiar sight of the open office with reporters at their desks typing their stories on their typewriters made him feel a bit better. As he settled into his chair, he realized that he was mentally drained after the eventful morning. He looked over at the far side of the room, where the desks of the senior journalists were. He could see a number of them huddled around Harish's desk. They were probably asking him about what had happened with Swaroop and the Roys earlier in the day. He couldn't see Harish's expression, but knowing him, Manik was fairly certain that he probably wanted to be left alone. He started looking through all the papers at his desk. The ones related to the article had already been submitted to the lawyers. The rest of the papers were mostly writing pads, some other journals, and notes on some stories that Harish and Manik had talked about potentially looking at in the coming weeks.

He got up and decided to walk over to Kedar's desk to meet his secretary and see if he could start reading up on some of the things that he would be working on. Although Kedar was a senior reporter, his desk was on the other side of the hall, across from where the rest of his colleagues sat. He had ended up in an area with the folks from other departments, like accounting and HR. Manik wondered why that was but was too preoccupied with the events of the day to think about it. As he approached Kedar's desk, he saw Anjali looking through and arranging some papers on his desk. He knew who she was but had never spoken to her. He had heard Avik and Subodh talk about her, her looks, how smart she was, and that she never really gave them an opportunity to have much of a conversation with her. They were right about her disposition. She was smartly dressed and looked confident. And although her glasses probably made her look older than she actually was, they did give her an air of seniority while still looking young.

"Hi." Manik almost startled her.

She turned around. "Yes?"

"I am Manik Bose. Swaroop asked me to pass by to pick up some papers."

"Oh, yes, I remember now. You are the one who worked on that article that got the paper into trouble, aren't you?" Anjali asked.

Manik couldn't gauge whether she was toying with him or she was serious. Either way, he felt deflated and sighed before replying. "Yes."

"Ok. Then you can come to my desk, and I will share some papers and notes on what Kedar is working on at the moment."

"Thank you."

When they reached her desk, she reached out to a bookshelf on the side, took out a stack of papers and files, and gave it to him.

"Please make a photocopy of all these and then return them to me."

"Sure."

"Do you know how the copier works?" Anjali asked.

"Yes."

"Because most newbies don't. That's why I am asking."

"I am not a newbie. I have been here for more than a year and a half," Manik replied, sounding a bit offended.

"Well, lucky you then."

"I will return them as soon as I am done."

"Thanks. If I am not here, just leave them on my desk or on the bookshelf."

Manik nodded and made his way back to his desk. He decided to have something to eat first and then work on copying the documents. He looked around to see whether Subodh or Avik were available. They weren't. He went down to the cafeteria. There were a lot of folks there. It was around lunchtime. He suddenly felt a bit hungry. He was not in a mood to sit down and have lunch with his colleagues. That would mean rehashing and analyzing what had happened. He simply wasn't up for that. After a quick smoke, he bought a sandwich and walked back to his desk.

He took the folder that Anjali had given him and headed over to one of the new copy machines that had recently been installed. He carefully copied all the pages, then neatly stacked all the originals and copies in separate files. He left the originals back at Anjali's desk. She wasn't there, and once he was back at his desk, he devoured his sandwich in a few minutes. Then he started reading the files. It seemed that true to the office gossip, Kedar was assigned to multiple stories across different desks. He was following up on a story on illegal betting at the racecourse. That seemed interesting. There was another one on an impending strike by the labor union in the movie industry. A third one on a suspicious fire in a warehouse. Finally, there was one that he was aware of because he had read about it in the papers and had discussed it with Avik and Subodh. It was about a theft at a well-known jewelry store. None of these stories seemed to include any depth of research or notes compared to what he had worked on with Harish. But he knew he had to make a conscious effort not to compare stories—or, for that matter, even Harish and Kedar.

As the afternoon dragged on, Manik's reading became slower and slower, and by the time it was 5:00 p.m., it was time to take a break. As he headed down to get a tea, he bumped into Anjali. He thanked her again for the papers and inquired what time Kedar usually showed up to work.

"Around ten thirty," she said.

"Does he have any meetings in the morning?"

"Not that I know of."

"Thank you."

"I will see you tomorrow, Manik. Bye."

"Bye."

After a quick tea break and smoke, he headed back to his desk. There was a note at his desk from Harish. When he went over to see him, he found out that Harish had already left for the day. He spent the next couple of hours cleaning the papers at his desk and then continued reading the files from Kedar. At 7:00 p.m. sharp, Avik and Subodh showed up.

"Time to pack up and head home."

"Yes." Manik was happy to see them.

They quickly descended the stairs and started walking back home.

3

New Beginnings

As they walked home, Manik shared with Avik and Subodh everything that had happened on the eventful day. He felt good after talking to them. The three of them had become good friends over the course of the year. Working in the same office and living in the same apartment building meant they could count on one another and share stories. They were all from out of town. That made them even closer. Avik and Subodh could not be more different in terms of personalities. Subodh was quiet and reserved. He was a studious fellow who liked to read, listen to music, and run. He was courting a colleague from work, Roshni. They had met at the *Herald*. Subodh and Roshni were working for the same senior reporter, and that helped move things along in their courtship. Avik, on the other hand, was an extrovert. He liked singing loudly, to the point where his neighbors had lodged several complaints. He enjoyed watching movies and was constantly trying to impress members of the opposite sex. He also loved to gossip, and he knew the ins and outs of every rumor, who did what with whom, who was going out with whom, and so on.

Once they reached their building, they went their separate ways. Although Avik and Subodh wanted to press Manik further on what had happened with the article, they could sense that he was tired and didn't want to talk about it. So they decided to meet up at the canteen across their apartment building for breakfast the next morning to continue their conversation and then walk to the office together. The walk and the conversation with his friends had lifted Manik's spirits somewhat. He decided to have an early supper and then go to bed.

The next morning Subodh was the first one to arrive for breakfast at the canteen across the building. It was a daily ritual not only for them but also for a lot of people who stayed in the building. The apartments were small—with either one or two bedrooms. Most of the tenants were single men and women from out of town who were working in Calcutta. Being in the outskirts of the city meant that rent was cheap. But for those who worked in the city, it was quite a commute. Manik showed up a few minutes after Subodh, and they quickly ordered their breakfasts. As always Avik was the last one to arrive. He sat down and immediately addressed Manik. Manik had sensed that Avik had wanted to talk to him about something the day before but had held back, sensing that he was a bit tired and sad following the day's events.

"Manik, so what's the deal with Anjali?"

"What do you mean?" Manik asked, amused by the question. He wasn't surprised that Avik had brought it up.

"I saw you talking to her at her desk and also downstairs when she was leaving."

"So?"

"What do you mean 'so? I think she is pretty. I mean, let's admit the obvious. She is beautiful. I wish I could work with her. It would give her the opportunity to see what a great guy I am," Avik said and lifted his collar.

Both Manik and Subodh started laughing.

"Well, she is my new boss's secretary. So I will be seeing her regularly. If you want, I can put in a good word for you and let her know what a great catch you are," Manik said with a smile.

"Why do you want to do that to the poor girl?" Subodh said with a mischievous smile.

"You guys realize that we have the perfect opportunity to find our partners?" Avik stated, ignoring Subodh's remark.

"How so?" Manik asked. He was always interested in listening to Avik's theories. At the very least, they were entertaining.

"Think about it. None of us are from Calcutta. We work at an office where there are single women. We live in a building where there are single women. Granted, some of them are a bit weird. But it's our best chance to find our life partner and elope."

"I like the way you think, but how has it worked out for you so far?" Manik asked with a smile on his face, knowing full well that Avik wasn't getting anywhere.

"I am trying. My point is, if we don't do this, then our parents will find us girls back home and get us married in our hometowns. Then we have to bring them over and hear them complain and whine about how much they miss their hometowns and their parents. Life will become miserable."

"It seems you have really thought this through," Manik said.

"Yes. Look at Subodh. He is quiet but the smartest one of all. He has already roped in Roshni, and now it's just a matter of time before he settles down," Avik said, sounding a bit more serious.

"I am not exactly unsettled," Manik said.

Subodh finally decided to join the conversation. "First of all, I didn't rope anyone in. Secondly, most importantly, I don't know if Roshni's parents will agree to the wedding. We have different backgrounds and speak different languages at home, and I think they want her to marry someone that they have already selected."

Avik and Manik both looked surprised.

"So Roshni has not told her parents about you?" Avik asked.

"No," Subodh replied.

"You are completely screwed, my friend," Avik said.

"Why not?" Manik asked, ignoring Avik's comment.

"I think she is scared of how her family will react," Subodh said in a serious tone.

"You are definitely screwed," Avik said again, nodding his head.

"I can't believe that you guys have been going out for almost a year and she hasn't been able to tell her parents. Is she serious about this relationship?" Manik asked.

"Yes. But as I said, she is scared of what the reaction will be at home," Subodh replied.

"Your only hope is to elope, have a kid, and then tell your parents. Once grandkids are in the picture, everything changes," Avik said.

Both Subodh and Manik sighed.

"Well, I think it's time for us to head to work. We won't solve this over breakfast," Subodh said.

"Right," Manik said and got up to pay for the meal.

As they were walking to work, Manik turned to Avik and asked him about Kedar.

"You have worked with Kedar before. How is he to work with?"

"Yeah, I was on a story with him for three weeks. He is definitely weird and somewhat unpredictable."

"How so?" Manik was curious.

"Well, for one, he is constantly juggling multiple stories. He has a hard time focusing on one thing, and that is quite frustrating."

"What else?"

"He doesn't get along with the other senior reporters. I am not sure why, but there is some history there," Avik said.

"Wow. Look at that. There is some gossip that even Avik is not privy to. Imagine that!" Manik said.

They all started laughing while picking up their pace to get to work before 9:30 a.m.

"Then there's the thing about his language. Usually he is very polite. But when he gets angry, he has been known to use very colorful language, if you know what I mean. I didn't see that during my short stint with him, but I did overhear him and Swaroop arguing loudly late at night a few months ago. Again, there may be a history there that I am not aware of. That's all I know, Manik. I never had issues working with him," Avik said as they turned toward the gates of the majestic *New Eastern Herald* campus.

"Thank you, Avik. So, is there anything you want me to ask Anjali about? Maybe put in a good word for you?"

"No. I am pursuing another interest at the moment," Avik said, sounding a little guarded.

It wasn't surprising. He was always trying to please some girl. What was surprising was that he hadn't mentioned who it was to Subodh or Manik.

"Are you going to tell us about it?" Subodh asked.

"Not just yet. It's a bit tricky. Maybe in a few days, and then you will understand why."

They reached the entrance to the building, and after some quick nods, they headed to their respective desks. Once Manik had reached his desk, he strained his neck to glance toward Kedar's office. He wasn't there, and neither was Anjali. Manik decided to head over to Harish to ask him about the note that he had left for him the day before. Harish was already there. Usually, he was one of the first ones to arrive at work.

"Good morning, sir. You left me a note yesterday."

"Yes. How are you, Manik?"

"I'm fine."

"I wanted to ask you if you would like to come over to our house for dinner this weekend. My wife is organizing something for my sixtieth birthday, and she has left it up to me to invite my favorite people at work. You are definitely one of them."

"Thank you, sir. Certainly. I'd be happy to come."

"Splendid. You have already come to our place, so you know where it is. It's next Saturday evening. Be there around six thirty."

"Sure, sir. Thank you."

"So, you have been assigned to Kedar, from what I hear?"

"Yes, sir."

"Have you spoken to him yet?"

"Not yet, sir."

"Hmm."

Manik couldn't make out from the expression on Harish's face whether he liked Kedar or not. He remembered the comment that Avik had made earlier about other senior reporters not getting along with Kedar. He wasn't sure if Harish was one of them. He didn't press the matter any further. It almost seemed like Harish wanted to tell him something about Kedar, but he held back.

"Good luck, then. I hope you get an exciting story and it takes your mind off what happened yesterday," Harish said with a smile.

"Thank you, sir. Do you need any help with the new article?"

"No. Forget about that. I need you to move on for both our sakes."

Manik nodded, turned, and headed back to his desk. It was close to ten, still half an hour before Kedar normally showed up. He could see that Anjali was already there. She saw him and asked him to come over. He picked up his writing pad and notebook and headed over to her desk. When he arrived, she gave him an envelope.

"What's this?"

"It's something Kedar gives all new assignees. You can open it and take a look."

Manik looked inside. There was a new notebook, a few pens, a writing pad, and a small book on meditation. He had no idea what this was all about.

"Thank you for this," Manik said.

"You can thank Kedar. One more thing: he wants people working with him to have a good typewriter. I know you have one. Is it good? Are you happy with it? If not, we will get you a new one."

"I am fine with the one I have. Thank you."

"Fine with what?"

Manik turned around; it was Kedar, a few steps behind him, walking toward his desk.

"My typewriter, sir."

"Ah, yes. Tools of our trade. We shouldn't mess with those," Kedar said with a smile.

"Good morning, sir, and thank you for this," Manik said as he held up the envelope that Anjali had given him.

"You are most welcome. I see that you have already met Anjali. That's good. Now, Mr. Manik Bose, let's head over to a conference room for a quick chat. Shall we?"

"Sure, sir."

"You can leave the envelope and all your other things on my desk for now."

"Thank you, sir."

Manik followed Kedar into one of the many small conference rooms at the end of the hallway. They picked one that was empty and walked in. As they sat down, Manik saw Kedar up close for the first time. He knew that he was close in age to the other senior reporters and close to retirement. He was probably approaching sixty. But he was in good shape, dressed smartly, and looked more like an executive in a bank than a reporter. He could sense that Kedar was physically active. He wasn't overweight like most of his peers and had a spring in his step.

"So, tell me, Manik Bose, where are you from? When did you join the paper, and what have you worked on so far?"

Manik then went on to tell Kedar about his background, when he started, and all the projects that he had worked on since he joined the newspaper. Kedar did not interrupt him, and Manik could see that he was listening attentively. When Manik finished, Kedar looked at him and spoke with a more serious tone.

"I know you were assigned to Harish and both of you worked on the land article. It is unfortunate how things worked out. I am sorry that you had to endure such an experience so early in your career. Harish is a good journalist. I know it must be hurting him a lot, and I am sure it's on your mind as well."

"Yes, sir."

"Well, the only way to get over it is to work on something exciting that will take your mind off what happened."

"Yes, sir."

"Some ground rules when you are working with me."

"Sir?"

"First, always get a good night's sleep. If that means showing up to work at or after ten, I am fine with that. Second, please dress properly. Clean clothes are a reflection of a mind ready for fresh ideas. You must look smart—not to impress others but yourself. I like people who dress well because they want to look good for themselves. Finally, and this is the most important one, don't take any criticism to heart from anyone, including me. You will see that we will be meeting folks who are not always happy or don't want to talk to us or get irritated and brush us off. Whatever maybe the case, when you leave work, you leave work at work. Understood?"

"Yes, sir."

"You have a book on meditation in your envelope. Do you meditate?"

"No, sir."

"Well, it's never too late to start. Read the book and start tonight."

"Yes, sir."

"That's all there's to it, really. You have already seen the stories we are working on. I am guessing you have already read up on the file that Anjali gave you?"

"Yes, sir."

"Good. Now let's get back to our desks, and we can talk about all that, and I can fill you in on where things stand on each of them. Before we leave, do you have any questions for me?"

"Yes, sir. Just one. I see that you are working on multiple stories at the same time. Is there something you want me to focus on first?"

"Yes. I am glad you brought that up. One thing that is a bit different with me is that during the course of the day, we will be dividing our time and working on different things. That may change only if there is something that is deemed critical or high priority, which might happen, of course. But mostly we will be working on various stories across different areas. Does that make sense?"

"Yes, sir."

"Good. Now let's see what the universe has in store for us today," Kedar said as they both got up and started walking to their desks. They were met midway by Anjali. She quickly walked up to them with something written on her writing pad.

"There's a gentleman here to see you regarding a theft at the state archives."

"To see me?" Kedar was surprised.

"No, sir. I meant Manik," Anjali replied.

It was now Manik's turn to be surprised.

"I don't know anyone in the state archives. It must be a mistake."

"His name is Prafulla Kumar. He said that he was your professor in college," Anjali said.

"Yes. I know Professor Kumar. I didn't know he was now working at the state archives."

"Well, I am not sure of all the details. But he is downstairs and wants to meet you."

Kedar turned to Anjali and asked, "You mentioned something about a theft?"

"Yes. Apparently that's why he is here. He feels it has been underreported or not reported properly in the papers."

Kedar turned to Manik. "Well, bring the good professor up to one of our conference rooms, and let's see what he has to say."

"Yes, sir" Manik replied. He turned to head down the stairs to meet the professor. He knew the professor well. Prafulla Kumar Ganguly was, by far, his favorite professor in college and was popular among the students. He taught history and was a great storyteller. He was gracious with his time and often invited students to come to his house close to campus if they needed help and during festivals. He was considered an authority on Indian history during the British rule and postindependence. He had written several articles that had been published in magazines and newspapers.

There was another reason, of course, that Manik liked visiting the professor during his college years—his daughter Sucheta. She had gone to the same college, and they were close during their college years. The professor retired when Manik got to his second year. But he would occasionally show up on campus for events and seminars. He was well liked, and unlike most of the other professors, he had a good sense of humor and seemed to get along with his students. When Manik started working at the paper, he told him about it, and the professor was extremely happy. He offered to put

Manik up at his home in Calcutta till he could find a place. It didn't come to that, and Manik had made it a point to visit the professor twice since he joined the *New Eastern Herald*. Sucheta had moved to Bombay after graduation, and he had lost touch with her.

Manik was pleasantly surprised to see the professor show up at his office. On seeing him, he immediately gave him a big hug. There was a big smile on his face, and Manik could see that he was getting old and was looking a bit frail. His glasses were thicker, and his bald head made him look older. As the professor got up, Manik could see that he was now walking with a slight hunch that made him look shorter than he actually was. After they exchanged pleasantries, the professor got down to business.

"I am actually here to see if you can help me with something." He had come with a folder with a big stack of papers inside it.

"Before we continue, do you want to go upstairs, sir? My boss would like to meet you, and maybe you can tell both of us at the same time why you are here. It will save you the trouble of repeating the same thing twice."

"Are you sure he wouldn't mind?"

"No. It was actually his idea."

"Oh. How long have you worked for him?"

"I started with him today." Manik didn't want to go into all the details, in particular the fact that an article written by him had caused all sorts of problems.

Anjali had booked a conference room for them. She offered them tea, and once they were all settled in, Kedar turned and addressed the professor.

"My name is Kedar Bagchi. This is Anjali Ghosh. She practically runs everything that we work on and keeps us on our toes. You of course know Manik better than all of us. So, tell us, Professor, what can we help you with today?"

"I am a retired history professor. As you may have guessed, Manik was one of my students in college. Since retiring I have been keeping busy writing articles for journals that are willing to publish them. The one that I am working on is about princely estates and their relationship with British India. My visit today has little to do with any of this."

The professor paused to catch his breath.

"Would you like some water?" Kedar asked.

"I am fine; thank you."

"Please continue."

"One of the places that I visit for my research is the Bengal State Archives. They have an excellent collection of records, deeds, covenants, and a wonderful library. I usually go there twice a week to spend a few hours doing some reading and making notes. A couple of weeks ago, during one of my visits, I saw the police there. Since I am one of the regulars, I asked the librarian about it, and he told me that there had been a theft from the collection of materials from princely estates. Apparently, a box of papers has disappeared. That's the reason why I am here."

"Professor Kumar, I think this looks more like a police case than something that a newspaper can help you with," Kedar said.

"I have been to police twice since the incident happened. They have the report but aren't doing anything about it. It seems they are always busy with other things."

Kedar, Manik, and Anjali easily guessed why this was not a priority. In a city where they had to maintain law and order and solve murders, armed robberies, and the like, the theft of a box of papers from the archives that didn't involve injury was not that important.

"Why do you think that our newspaper should look into this?" Kedar asked.

"Because the theft makes no sense," the professor replied.

"How so?"

"The box was taken from a room full of artifacts, some jewelry, and other much more expensive items. None of that was touched. The thieves came and took only this particular box and left."

"Hmm. That does sound weird," Kedar said thoughtfully.

"The archives are well guarded, of course. But there are no cameras in all the rooms. It seems the thieves knew how to get in and out without raising any sort of alarm."

"Sounds like someone from the inside may have helped them," Kedar said.

"Yes, that is a possibility."

"Tell us, Professor, do you have any idea what may have been inside the box, its contents?"

"That's the bit I don't know. But whatever it was, it was more important than all the other things in that room."

"Do we know anything else that might help?" Kedar asked.

"Yes. The box was part of the collection sent to the archives from the estate of the Maharaja of Surinampur."

"I am sorry, Professor, but you have lost me there," Kedar said.

"You are aware, of course, that the privy purse has now been abolished."

"Yes," Kedar replied.

"Manik, Anjali, do you know the details surrounding the privy purse?" the professor asked.

"Somewhat, professor, but perhaps you can give us a summary," Anjali said.

"Absolutely. When India became independent, it was a collection of more than five hundred princely states. The rulers called themselves rajas and maharajas, or other titles. But in reality most of them were just landlords with estates of varying sizes. Postindependence, the privy purse gave some of these rulers an allowance and allowed them to retain their titles. Most of these rulers presided over small estates and used most of this allowance for sustenance. Not every princely state is Jaipur or Gwalior, which could maintain some of their past glory. In fact, they are the exception. Over time, most of the estates sold their land, and what remained was mainly the titles and probably an ancestral home. Surinampur falls into this category. As you are aware, in 1971 the privy purse was abolished by parliament. The estates lost their allowance, and the so-called rajas and maharajas lost their titles. Last year the last surviving member of the royal family of Surinampur passed away, leaving most of his possessions to a trust that has now started disbursing the items in accordance with his will." Prafulla paused for a moment to let this sink in and also to catch his breath.

"The box that went missing belonged to the ruler of Surinampur?" Kedar asked.

"Yes, exactly. A couple of weeks ago, in accordance with the ruler's will, his collection of artifacts, some papers, and gifts that he had received from other rulers were sent to the state archives. The missing box was part of that collection."

Manik, who had been quiet all this time, addressed the professor. "Sir, have the police done any sort of investigation? Have they questioned the employees at the archives?"

"Well, they have taken their statements. From what I understand, they have visited the scene a couple of times, but that really hasn't amounted to much. I don't think they are taking this seriously."

They could sense the disappointment in the professor's voice. Kedar turned to the professor.

"I will tell you what, Professor—how about we pay a visit to the archives later this week. If we think there is something that should be in the newspaper, either in terms of this theft or the investigation or lack thereof by the police, we can decide whether to publish anything on it," Kedar said.

"Thank you. That's all I was expecting. All I am asking for is for you take a look and then decide for yourself."

"We will," Kedar replied.

"I will be going to the archives tomorrow afternoon. Would you like to join me?"

"Yes. That would be a good idea. You can introduce us to the folks you know."

"Certainly. Well, I have taken up a lot of your time. I really appreciate this. I can meet you at the archives. What time do you want to meet? The building and the library close at four. So we can't meet too late, assuming we want to spend at least an hour or so there."

"Let's say two o'clock." Kedar replied. "Manik and I will be there."

"Thank you. I will leave this folder with you. It has some articles on Surinampur, its history, its rulers, etcetera, that might be of interest to you."

"Thank you, Professor. We will make a copy and return your file to you when we meet tomorrow."

"Thank you," the professor replied as they all got up.

"I will show you out, sir," Manik said as he opened the door. Once they reached the gates of the campus, the professor turned to Manik and gave him another affectionate embrace.

"It was so nice to see you. Please do drop by sometime, Manik. Since Sucheta left for Bombay, I have had a hard time keeping myself busy. Retirement and old age are not always kind. Thankfully, all this has kept me busy."

"I will surely make it a point to come by regularly. Please give my regards to Sucheta when you speak to her next."

"I will. I am proud of you, Manik. Working in a place like this—that's wonderful."

If only he knew what transpired as a result of the article, Manik thought.

They nodded, and as the professor started to walk away, Manik felt bad for him. The professor had dedicated his life to the college and his students. He had brought up his daughter entirely on his own. His wife had passed away when Sucheta was very young. Now she had graduated and left the city for work. Most of his students were probably busy with their work and families. He was glad that the professor had found something to keep him busy.

As Manik slowly made his way back to his desk, he wondered what Kedar and Anjali would think about this. Just as he was about to sit down, he saw Kedar, seated at his desk, looking at him and waving him over. He was pointing to the conference room.

When they sat down, it was Anjali who spoke first.

"The professor really likes you."

"Yes. He was one of the best ones I had in school or college," Manik replied.

Kedar looked at him as he was going through the folder that the professor had left them. He then handed it to Manik.

"Well, you have your homework for the day. I want you to go through all this and give me and Anjali a summary tomorrow morning. Also, I want you to head to the library upstairs. They have quite a few publications and articles on the privy purse. Maybe there's something there on Surinampur as well. The legislation to abolish the privy purse passed in 1971, but it took a few attempts to get it through successfully. That's what I recall. Read up on it, and then you can tell us all about it," Kedar said with a smile.

"What about the other stories?" Manik asked.

"Yes. We will tackle them as well. For now I want you to start with this; we will see after the visit to the archives how important this is."

As they left the room, Anjali turned and asked Manik, "I am heading downstairs for a tea. Do you want to join me?"

"Sure."

"Sir, do you want to join us or need anything from the tearoom?" Anjali asked Kedar.

"No, thank you. Please carry on. I need to make a few calls."

They found an empty table in the cafeteria, which was getting a little busy, mainly with folks from the printing press on the ground floor taking a break. As they sat down, Manik looked at the far end of the room. He could see Subodh and Avik. They looked at him and Anjali and smiled. Anjali turned to see whom Manik was looking at. She waved back at them.

"Your friends?" Anjali asked with a smile on her face.

"Yes." Manik sighed, knowing that Avik would probably be on his case after work to know what, if anything, was going on with him and Anjali.

"Manik, what do you think of Kedar?"

"He seems different from his colleagues."

"He is."

"How long have you worked with him?"

"Since I joined the paper around three years ago. He doesn't treat me like a secretary. He gets me involved in what he is working on and values my opinion, and I like that. I have seen how the other reporters treat their secretaries, and I am happy to be assigned to him."

Manik knew that she was probably right. The other reporters that he had worked with, including Harish, had never asked their secretaries to sit in on meetings or solicited their opinions on what they were working on. He knew that many of the secretaries wanted to be reporters as well and had degrees but couldn't find jobs. They were biding their time till a position opened up and they could then apply. A disproportionate number of them were women. Although there were quite a few women reporters and some of them had started as secretaries, they were a minority. Most of them were assigned to desks that were considered "light," such as entertainment, lifestyle, and health. Things were changing, and he had heard that many of them were keen to join the more sought-after desks dealing with politics, law and order, and the like.

"Do you think he is taking this story seriously?" Manik asked.

"Yes, for now. Otherwise he wouldn't ask you to do research and agree to go to the state archives with you tomorrow."

Manik seemed pleased. They talked a bit more about what else was on Kedar's plate. Anjali filled him in on the upcoming state elections. He had heard about that. The paper was diverting additional resources from all departments to cover the story. The upcoming elections were important ones, and in a country and state where politics was the favorite topic of conversation and arguments, the senior management at the paper was determined to carry multiple stories every day that would include interviews with politicians of all stripes. It was seen as an opportunity to increase circulation of the paper and rope in a new generation of readers. That meant that in a few weeks, Manik, along with most of the other junior reporters, would be working on the election desk.

"Time to do your homework—and for me to get back to my desk," Anjali said as they got up.

"Yes."

Manik took the folder that the professor had given them and headed to the library. He always liked spending time there. It wasn't busy when he got there. He started going through the cards catalogue to look for articles and publications on the privy purse. There were many. He then shifted his focus to Surinampur. There weren't any on that topic. So, for that he would have to rely solely on what the professor had given them. He decided to sit at one of the large desks in the library, and once he had collected all the material, he made a neat pile and started reading. The professor had summarized the impact of the abolition of the privy purse really well. He could see that many princely estates were in trouble. They were trying to sell off their remaining land to sustain themselves. Many of them were planning to convert their ancestral homes and palaces into hotels. There were others that had simply not been able to stay afloat. Eventually the government seized their properties and auctioned off whatever they could to salvage some value out of them. He spent nearly three hours looking over all the documents, with a few stretch breaks in between. He took notes on what he considered relevant.

He turned his attention to the folder the professor had given them. It seemed that Surinampur had fallen on hard times as well. What had complicated matters was that there were several ongoing cases between the princely estate and other parties, including the government, on land acquisitions, property disputes, and workers' wages at the estate. When the last owner passed away, many of his officials were accused of stealing funds dedicated to the upkeep of the estate and artifacts belonging to the family. From what he could make out, it seemed like a total mess. The last ruler had had no remaining family. He had left all his assets in a trust, which was responsible for selling all the remaining land and the ancestral home and disbursing the proceeds to all the workers after all remaining liabilities had been paid. From the look of it, that wouldn't amount to much. The will also included a provision indicating that all artifacts and valuables in the family's possession should be donated to the museum in Calcutta and the Bengal State Archives. All this seemed straightforward enough, except the records of the land in Surinampur and some holdings in Calcutta were sketchy. Some of them were now mired in the courts, and resolution of these cases normally took years.

Manik figured that he had read enough. He returned all the material to the librarian, except for the professor's folder. Just as he was leaving, he saw a new announcement on the library notice board. The library had now started cataloging published articles by journalist. He knew that many users had been asking for that for a while. It gave him an idea. He went back to the librarian and asked him if he could go through all the published articles of Kedar Bagchi. Once he collected those, he sat down again in a corner, making sure no one was at his table, and started going through them. It was a thick folder. That wasn't surprising, since Kedar was probably close to retirement and had been working as a reporter for nearly thirty years. He had worked in different newspapers all over India. That bit was surprising. Usually the career of a journalist or reporter spanned thirty to thirty-five years across two or three newspapers. The *New Eastern Herald* was Kedar's eighth employer. The other bit that was unconventional was that he had worked in magazines, in addition to national newspapers, all over India. He had joined the *Herald* a little less than five years ago and was the most recent addition to the senior team. Manik wondered if that was the reason that the rest of his colleagues weren't that close to him. Harish and most of the other senior members had been there since the beginning of the paper.

As he read through all the pieces, he realized that unlike other reporters, who specialized in one or two domains, Kedar had worked in almost everything—current events, politics, entertainment, business, even sports. He was a journalist more than a reporter in the strictest sense, having worked as an editor, writer, columnist, and reporter. He had even been the local correspondent for a foreign news magazine for a few years. Then there was the bit about awards. He had actually received two national awards for investigative journalism, and during his stint as the Indian correspondent for the foreign magazine, he had received a prestigious award from a European news consortium. It made Manik even more curious as to why Kedar didn't stick around in a single job for too long.

As he read one article after another, he became more impressed with his new boss's past professional experience. The one article that surprised him was from a little more than a decade ago, when Kedar had been working for a national daily. It was not the article itself that caught his eye, but rather the authors. It was written by Kedar and Harish. *So, they knew each other and worked together*, Manik thought. But when he spoke to them, they never mentioned each other. The only passing comment that he had heard from Kedar was that Harish was a good journalist. In the better part of the year or so that Manik had worked with Harish, Harish hadn't mentioned anything. As he started looking through the articles, he realized that Kedar and Harish had collaborated on six articles over their three years working for a previous employer. There was nothing after that. Kedar had moved on to another job. They hadn't worked on anything together at the *Herald*. That in itself was surprising, since they had been at the paper together for nearly five years. He had never seen them in a meeting or at the cafeteria together. Now that he thought about it, it almost seemed that they avoided one another. Maybe there was a reason why Kedar's desk was far from where the rest of the senior staff sat. Or maybe it was just that he was the newest addition and they didn't have any additional room at the time of his hiring. Unlikely, Manik concluded.

He went back to the librarian to get the folder containing all the articles written by Harish. There was a lot of material there. The *New Eastern Herald* was his second and presumably last job before retiring. Manik had read through some of Harish's articles before. They were all related to either politics or corruption. He had received several state and national awards for his editorials. While Kedar had worked in different areas of journalism, Harish had focused on being a reporter and an editorial writer. Harish's stint at the *Herald* had been impressive. It was clear from the list of internal company awards he had received that he was well liked and respected by senior management and his peers.

As he returned the folders containing the published material for Harish and Kedar, he wondered whether he should ask around to find out more. He knew that Avik and Subodh wouldn't be able to help him. They had all started at the same time. Neither could Anjali—she was fairly new as well and perhaps didn't know what had happened in the past. Moreover, he was not comfortable asking her. He didn't know if she would tell Kedar about it, and he certainly did not want his new boss to know that he was trying to find out about his past, especially the time that Kedar worked together with Harish. The only other folks who would know would be the other senior staff. But he did not know anyone well enough.

After he went back to his desk, he decided to focus on going through his notes and reading the contents of the folder that the professor had left them one more time. He spent the rest of the day doing just that. He wanted to call it a day. He looked around. Most of the folks had already left. Avik and Subodh had already told him that they would be late. So he walked back home on his own. As was the case during this time of the year in Calcutta, the evenings were foggy.

As he stepped out of the gates, he looked at the wonderful mist ahead of him, as well as the beautiful illuminated street lamps. The scene seemed like something out of a movie. Although it was a bit damp,

Manik enjoyed his walk back. It had been a much better day. Kedar was a bit different but seemed nice. He had a new story to work on that seemed exciting, and he had been happy to see his professor. He was looking forward to meeting him the next day.

4

The Archives

When Subodh, Avik, and Manik met for breakfast the following day, the conversation was all about Anjali. Manik had anticipated that the other two wanted to talk to him about her, but his mind was elsewhere. He was thinking about what he had discovered in the files in the library on Harish and Kedar. He was also looking forward to his visit to the archives and meeting with his professor.

"You are not with us today, Manik. What's going on?" Avik asked.

"Have you guys noticed that Kedar is usually not with the senior reporters? He hardly ever talks to them unless there is a meeting, which is rare because he never seems to collaborate on a story with any of them. I have never seen him in the cafeteria with any of them either. Don't you think that's rather odd?" Manik asked.

"Well, he is a bit strange. I told you yesterday, he is kind of weird. He wants us to dress properly, and I am sure he gave you a book on meditation," Avik said.

"Maybe because he joined later than the rest of them. He is sort of new compared to the others. Or maybe he is just hard to get along with or likes to keep to himself," Subodh said.

"Hmm. Maybe," Manik replied, but he wasn't convinced.

"Can we catch a movie this evening? I am not sure what's playing at the Globe. But if we all finish early, we can head over there directly after work," Avik said, hoping that the rest would agree.

"I'm not sure if I can make it. I have to head over to the state archives. I don't know how long that will take."

"What's with that?" Subodh asked.

Manik proceeded to tell them about the professor's visit, the theft at the archives, and his research on Surinampur and the privy purse. He left out the part about Harish and Kedar. He did not want to risk Avik or Subodh asking around and trying to find more details and dragging his name into it. He was still reeling from the aftermath of the land article, and although he had turned the page, he knew that until the retraction was printed and the paper was sure about avoiding any litigation, he would still be under the scanner.

Once he reached work, he quickly made copies of documents the professor had given them. Then he waited for Kedar to arrive to brief him on his research on Surinampur and the abolition of the privy purse. When Anjali showed up, she informed him that Swaroop had called a meeting before lunch of all the junior and senior reporters in the large hall downstairs. It was regarding allocation of assignments for the upcoming elections. He wondered whom he would be paired up with. He was not looking forward to it. Usually these assignments meant lots of interviews with candidates of different parties, and in a country like India, there were many. There was a lot of waiting, traveling, and sometimes seeking out constituents who would like to be interviewed. That was tiring. But he was not alone. Everyone else was in the same boat.

Kedar finally arrived around 10:30 a.m. and asked Manik and Anjali to look for a conference room where they could all talk. Once they settled in, it was Kedar who asked the first question, and it wasn't related to the theft at the archives.

"Manik, did you read the book on meditation?"

"No, sir. I was tired and went off to sleep."

"No harm done. As I said, sleep is important for people like us who are chasing stories. So, tell me, what have you found that may be relevant to our visit this afternoon?"

Manik opened his notebook and the folder containing the papers from the professor and slowly laid out everything that he had researched. He knew that he had done quite a thorough job. Both Kedar and Anjali listened to him without interrupting. Finally, when Manik finished, Kedar pointed to the folder the professor had given them. Kedar handed it to him, and he started leafing through the pages slowly.

"What's your gut feeling about this? Is this something worth our time?" Kedar asked.

"To be honest, I don't know, sir. With everything else that's going on in the city and the upcoming elections, I don't know how much time we will have to look into this."

"Hmm. Yes, that's true."

"What about you, sir? What do you think?" Anjali asked.

"There's only one thing that irks me about this, and the professor touched on it yesterday. It has nothing to do with the privy purse or the will of the last ruler."

"What is it, then?" Anjali was curious.

"It's the fact that the thieves who broke in stole only that box and left with nothing else. That's definitely strange, don't you think? That's why I think there may be something here," Kedar said as he got up.

"I do have a question for you, sir," Manik said.

"Go on."

"Shouldn't we check with the police as well about where they are with the investigation?"

"Yes, we should. I will be making some calls before we leave to see if I can find out who is in charge of this case. Most likely it's being handled by the Chowringee police station. That's the one closest to the archives. I know someone at the station, and if he is there, we will see if we can drop by there as well."

"Thank you, sir."

"Well done, Manik. Many young reporters don't like to do this sort of stuff. They find reading and research to be boring. I am glad to see that you are not one of them. All right, then, let's be ready to leave at one thirty."

"Sure, sir."

Once they were back at their desks, it was time to head downstairs for the meeting with Swaroop. Manik could see people getting up from their desks and slowly making their way to the stairs. After a few minutes, the entire floor seemed silent. The clickety-clack of the typewriters had stopped, and as he made his way toward the stairs, he looked back. Without the people and all the noise, the floor with all the desks, papers, typewriters, and bookshelves looked really big. It was a giant hall with lots of desks. There were no cubicles or offices. He often wondered if reporters needed this sort of big, noisy, and chaotic environment to thrive.

Once he reached the auditorium on the ground floor, he found out that it was already packed. All the seats were taken, and the only room he could find was a place to stand near the door. Swaroop was already onstage and trying to adjust the microphone. As he stood near the door, he could sense that there was some general excitement in the air.

Swaroop's lecture was predictable. He wished everyone a happy new year and conveyed his gratitude for another stellar year for the paper in terms of growing circulation and revenues. He went on to say that more resources would be added for the election period. He reminded the folks in the room that election "fever" in India lasted weeks, if not months. The elections were a few months away. He also went into a monologue on how newspapers were the most important source of information and opinions and that they had a responsibility to report things accurately.

Manik knew he was right. There were hardly any television sets in Indian households. Although people listened to radios, it was mostly for music, cricket, and news snippets. The government owned and controlled all the programming and content of the channels. The print media was the only mechanism that offered the general public contrasting views and differing opinions. There was no mention, of course, of the article that Harish and Manik had written that was causing all sorts of problems for the paper. Most of the people in the room were already aware of it, and it was understandable that Swaroop could not talk about it due to the threat of litigation.

While Manik was listening intently to the lecture, he realized that Anjali had showed up and was standing next to him. There was no way for her to move forward. The place was packed. Manik moved aside to give her space so that they could stand side by side. She nodded and strained her neck to see if she could see Swaroop while listening to the rest of the lecture.

The interesting bit was toward the end. Swaroop mentioned that some of the interns and secretaries who were aspiring to be journalists would also be given assignments. If indeed they performed well and the paper was able to increase its circulation, some of them would get promoted to junior reporters. Manik looked at Anjali when Swaroop announced this, and he could make out from her expression that she was pleased.

Swaroop had also announced all the pairings of the senior and junior reporters assigned to different political parties and candidates would be on the notice board by the end of the day, a fact that was of interest to Manik. Bengal had four main parties contesting the election and around ten other smaller, regional parties. In a densely populated state, there were also many independent candidates and celebrities who would be running for election, especially in the constituencies in and around Calcutta. Then there were four other states in eastern India where elections were happening at the same time. The *New Eastern Herald* had a presence in those states, and they would be going all out to cover the elections there as well, in a bid to increase circulation.

Manik wondered whom he would be paired up with. The speech ended with the usual call to support one another and a request to work longer hours if needed, at least until the elections were over. As the crowd started dispersing, Anjali and Manik were the first to leave, being nearest to the door. They headed to the cafeteria for an early lunch. The café wasn't very busy. Some people had come from the meeting. As they sat down to eat, Anjali broke the news.

"You don't have to wait until the end of the day to know who you are assigned to."

"How do you know?" Manik asked.

"It's Kedar. We both have been assigned to Kedar, and your friend Subodh as well."

Manik wasn't surprised. They were already working together, and he figured it made sense for Swaroop to assign Anjali and Manik to Kedar. He would have expected another senior reporter as well. Usually there were four to eight reporters in each group. Subodh being in their group of four meant that they were probably not going to be assigned one of the main parties. They were either going to be allocated one of the smaller regional parties or some independent candidates. He didn't mind that. But he tried to press Anjali as to why no other senior reporter was on their team.

"Our group will only have one senior reporter?" Manik asked.

"Yes."

"Do you know why?"

"No. Well, as you may have noticed, Kedar rarely works with other senior reporters. At least I haven't seen him working with another one, and I have been around almost since he started here."

"Do you know why that's the case?"

"I am not sure. I think it's probably because of the stories he gets assigned. He ends up getting stuff that no one else wants to work on or things that come directly from Swaroop."

"These are outside the weeklies?"

"Yes. Kedar never goes to those anyway."

Manik wasn't sure whether other news outlets used the term "weeklies," but at the *New Eastern Herald*, weeklies were Monday-morning meetings of the most senior reporters with Swaroop to discuss who would be assigned which stories. If the stories required more resources, there could be more than one senior reporter assigned to it, along with junior reporters, of course. Manik was surprised to hear that Kedar wasn't part of the Monday-morning weeklies with Swaroop and the senior staff. He was senior enough. As he was playing this out in his head, Anjali knew what he was thinking.

"You are trying to figure out why Kedar is a bit different and is treated differently."

"Yes," Manik said.

"When I first started working for him, it seemed a bit odd to me too. It's not that he keeps to himself. But he seems to socialize with everyone except the senior staff. I mean, the senior reporters are a tight bunch and have been around much longer than Kedar. As you may have noticed, unlike Kedar, they don't socialize with folks from other departments."

"Hmm." Manik was disappointed that he couldn't get Anjali to give him more details.

"All I can say is that I have enjoyed working with Kedar from the beginning. He always treats me with respect and values my opinion on things. I'd much rather be assigned to him than anyone else."

"Right."

"The rest of the dynamics between him and the other seniors—I don't really care."

"Do you know which party or candidates we will be assigned to?"

"No. I don't know everything. Just more than you," Anjali said with a smile as they finished their meals.

Once they were heading back to their desks, it was almost time for Kedar and Manik to go to the archives. He made sure he had the professor's folder and notebooks, and a camera. He could see that Kedar was on the phone and waited for him to finish his conversation. Since theirs was an open office, it wasn't hard for him to figure out that Kedar was talking to someone at the Chowringee police station. Once Kedar had finished, he walked over to Manik.

"Ready to leave?"

"Yes, sir."

"That was someone at the Chowringee police station, someone I know who has agreed to meet us. Let's go."

"Sure, sir."

Once they reached the gates, he expected Kedar to hail a taxi or use one of the many cars belonging to the paper with PRESS imprinted on them. The paper had procured a number of secondhand vehicles. They were mostly Jeeps and Ambassadors. They were shared by all the reporters, and there was a booking system that the secretaries of the senior reporters maintained. It wasn't easy to get one of these cars. Calcutta was going through a period of labor unrest and strikes, and some areas had started reporting scuffles between various groups of people. The city was also recovering from politically motivated communal riots that had left people injured. The police were also investigating killings in the outskirts of the city. They weren't sure whether the murders were related to the riots. All that meant the police were busy, and so were the reporters in the crime desk following up on the events and investigations.

"The best way to get there is to walk to the end of the street, cross the park, and get on a tram," Kedar said.

Manik was a bit surprised, but he did not complain. He liked taking the trams. They were such a beautiful sight as they went through this part of town. Although the *Herald* building was in the outskirts, it was not far from the tram lines. If they cut across the park, the nearest tram stop was a good twenty-minute walk. Once they were on the tram, it was easy. The state archives was next to a tram station. The ride, barring any traffic jams, would take around thirty minutes. But it was a city prone to jams and processions. It was always good to leave early. As they started walking, Manik realized that they would be walking past the apartment building where he lived. He started telling Kedar more about the professor and how he knew him.

"That's where I live, sir." Manik pointed to the building as they were walking past it.

"You are from Bolpur, right?"

"Yes, sir."

"I had family there once."

"So, you have been there, sir?"

"Yes, quite a few times. Lots of fond memories."

"Most people visit Shanti Niketan. It has become quite a tourist destination. My parents live a few miles from there."

"You moved to Calcutta for work?"

"I moved here to go to college. I applied for jobs all over India, but this was the first good one that I found."

"Yes. The whole world moves to places where jobs are. Calcutta must have been quite a change for you."

"Initially, yes. But then I started enjoying it. It was my first time away from home. I had a good group of friends in college."

"That's nice."

"How about you, sir?"

"Well, I have been all over, really. I am a Bengali, but from Bombay. Of course, as most Bengalis do, I have family here. I visited them regularly, and as you can imagine, lots of ties here. I love this city. There is a vibe to it that I don't find anywhere else. But if there's one city I'd call home, it would have to be Bombay. I grew up there and hopefully will settle there after retirement."

Manik didn't want to press further on all the other places that he had seen Kedar had worked from his file in the library. Soon they were near the park and started making their way across it. It was a beautiful morning, and there were lots of people in the park. Most of them were either taking a stroll or having a laugh with their friends. Everyone seemed relaxed. Once they had crossed the park, they made their way to the tram stop a few yards away and decided to sit on the benches to wait for the next tram.

"Have you been to other places in India, Manik?"

"Not many, sir. I have been to Delhi and Bombay a couple of times with my friends. We have some extended family in Lucknow and Kanpur. I have been there for some weddings. With my family I have gone on vacations to Kashmir and Goa. I have never been to the south or the northeast. I love to travel. It is one of the things I want to do but haven't been able to."

"Well, you are in the right profession for it. You have just started out. Hopefully, you will land yourself a story or a desk that makes you travel."

"Yes, sir."

They could now hear the rattling sound of the tram on the track. It was a few hundred yards away. They got up once it stopped and got on board. There weren't too many people in it. It was easy to find seats, and once they settled in, they continued their conversation.

"Have you been to the state archives before, Manik?"

"No, sir, I haven't."

"Hmm. Well, it will be the first time for both of us then."

"The professor always told us to go visit, but we never got around to it."

"College students are not interested in going to visit archives filled with artifacts of the past. I am sure they have other interests," Kedar said with a smile.

That put a smile on Manik's face as well. They started looking out the window, and as the slow-moving tram snaked its way past the sights and sounds of Calcutta, they marveled at the expanse of the city and its inhabitants. They could see a sea of people on the sidewalks going about their daily lives. As always, the roads were full of cars, but thankfully no jam. As the tram slowly turned a corner toward the avenue leading up to the state archives building, it came to a screeching halt. Manik and Kedar looked out of the window to see what had caused the tram to stop so abruptly. A huge procession was crossing the avenue. These had become a regular occurrence.

The labor unions had been organizing flash strikes as a bargaining chip to get as much leverage as possible for the upcoming elections. They were mostly peaceful. This one consisted of a large group of people who were slowing down traffic and taking their time to get across the intersection.

"Let's just walk the rest of the way," Kedar said.

"Sure."

They could see the archives building far ahead, a few hundred yards away. Once they made their way to the sidewalk, they were able to cut across the procession. The professor was waiting at the entrance to the library as they approached. He waved at them, and they immediately went over to meet him. The professor told them that they had to wait a few minutes before entering. One of the librarians and his assistant, who were his main contacts in the building, had told him to wait and that they would come and get him at a designated time. They were early.

"You will meet one of the librarians, Asutosh, and his assistant, Vinod. I have known Asutosh for a long time, since I was a college professor. Vinod is new and was hired only a few months ago. They have been rather generous with me with their time, on occasion listening to my monologues on the history behind the collections in this building," the professor said with a smile.

"Tell me, professor—if you don't mind my asking—what exactly is your area of interest here?" Kedar asked.

"I was wondering when you would ask that. For the past year or so, I have been interested in colonial and postcolonial records relating to land acquisition. This place has an excellent repository. Of late the building has been acting as a central depot for papers, deeds, documents, and artifacts from the princely estates that have either been donated or auctioned off due to financial troubles. There is some talk of moving these objects to another building. Of course, most of the artifacts and jewelry will end up in the museum. They are just being shipped here and held temporarily."

"Why the interest in Surinampur?"

"Oh, that's a bit personal. I used to have family there. I had heard lots of stories about the ruler and his lavish lifestyle," the professor replied.

"Did you ever meet him?"

"Who?"

"This Maharaja of Surinampur?"

"Oh, no."

Manik had waited patiently up until this point and was listening to the conversation. Both Kedar and the professor had paused for a bit, and he decided to ask the professor something that he had read in the file that he had left with them.

"Professor, I read that the maharaja claimed that he had land in Calcutta too. In an interview he said that one of his uncles had shown him records of property purchased here as well."

"Yes, Manik, that is correct. I am happy to see that you did your research. The executors of the estate were able to find some papers associated with that. The recent maharaja's grandfather had purchased land in the outskirts of Calcutta. I am guessing now it will be auctioned off and the proceeds will be used to pay of all the liabilities, and if anything remains, it will, or should, go to the employees of the ancestral home."

While they were engaged in this conversation, they could see two gentlemen coming toward them. Asutosh was elderly but well built. He was the professor's friend, and although he might have been in his late fifties or early sixties, he looked a good five years younger. Vinod looked as if he was in his twenties, but his glasses made him look a bit older. They immediately went over to the professor and shook hands with him. It was obvious from their gestures that they knew and respected the professor. Manik and Kedar introduced themselves, and then they slowly walked up the stairs through the doors and into a big hall. The archives were actually two separate buildings connected by a short, wide corridor. The building that housed the library was impressive but looked old from the outside. The inside, on the other hand, looked better. Although it had been completely renovated, it still retained some of the antiquated look. There was a large reception and waiting area on the ground floor. The library was on the upper level of the two-story building. The high ceilings on each floor made it look massive. They climbed up the stairs, and once they were on the second floor, they could see the library through the glass doors on one side of the staircase. On the other side, there were massive doors that led to a big hall that had lots of desks with plenty of storage boxes on them.

"We are using that hall as the storage area for all the material we are collecting from the princely estates," Vinod said, looking at Manik and Kedar and pointing to the hall.

"The box in question was stolen from that storage room?" Kedar asked.

"Yes," Vinod replied.

"What else is in that room? I see that some boxes have been opened—I see artifacts, statues, jewelry boxes," Kedar said, pointing to some vertically oriented crates.

"Oh. Those are marble statues that the maharaja had in his ancestral home. The movers left them here, and we haven't been able to move them because they are so heavy. Eventually everything except for documents and papers will most likely move to the museum," Vinod said.

As they started walking into the room, Asutosh gestured for them to stop.

"Please try to understand, gentlemen, that there has been a theft, and the police are investigating. You are welcome to look at these things from a distance, but please don't touch or move anything."

"Can I take some pictures?" Manik asked.

"No," Asutosh said, pointing to the wall behind them, which bore a sign clearly stating there was no photography allowed.

"All these cannot be from Surinampur. There are over a hundred boxes here," Kedar said.

"Oh, no. These are from six different princely states. They have been arriving for almost two years now," Vinod replied.

"If you want, we can move to the library. There is an office there that we can use to chat," Asutosh said.

"Sure, that's a good idea," the professor replied.

Manik could see Kedar was looking up and down the hall, the corridor leading up to the library, and then the doors on the other side, which were closed.

"Where do those lead to?" Kedar asked.

"Those go to the other building. You must have seen the entrance. That's actually the main building; it houses all material that has been identified, marked, and cataloged. The hall that you were in is mostly used as a temporary storage and holding area," Vinod replied.

As they entered the library, they could see a few readers occupying the desks. The library was huge, with a vast array of books lining wall-to-wall shelves in every direction. They headed to an office near the entrance, through a set of glass doors, and sat down.

"Would you like to have some tea?" Vinod asked.

"Sure," Kedar replied.

Once Vinod left the room, Asutosh asked everyone to take a seat around the table. Once seated, Kedar looked at the professor and Asutosh.

"First of all, I want thank you for allowing us to visit. I haven't been here before. I have marveled at the architecture of the building from outside whenever I have gone past it. But I have never been inside. It really is impressive."

"Thank you," Asutosh replied.

"Tell me, Asutosh, do we know anything at all about the contents of the box that was stolen?"

"No. We never had a chance to go through it and catalog it."

Just as he was about to ask the next question, Vinod entered the room with a tray with cups of tea for everyone. They paused for a bit to get their tea before Kedar continued.

"When did you realize the box was missing?" Kedar asked.

"The next day, when I arrived, and I told Asutosh, sir, right away when he came in. I was the first to arrive," Vinod said.

"We have discussed all this with the police. I am not sure what else we can add," Asutosh said, getting visibly annoyed with this line of questioning.

"I simply want to ascertain the facts to see what we can tell our readers," Kedar replied with a smile.

"Well, your readers haven't been interested in the state archives for a while. We don't get many visitors. Our visitors are mostly academics and students who are studying history, and tourists from out of town," Asutosh said.

The conversation then switched to the history of the building, how it was founded, the rich collection that they had managed to assemble since India's independence, and the sudden surge of material coming to them following the abolishment of the privy purse. The professor held court as he went into great detail explaining how the institution had changed over time.

"With so many princely states in trouble, we have had a hard time keeping up with all the new things that are arriving," said Asutosh.

"I read somewhere that there are plans to move?" asked Manik.

"Yes, eventually we will have to," replied Asutosh.

They finished their tea. It had already been over an hour since they had arrived at the building.

"I think we have taken a lot of your time. I want to show Manik and Kedar the other side of the state archives quickly before we leave," said the professor.

"Sure," said Asutosh, and they all got up and slowly walked out of the room and then the library.

"The best thing would be to take the corridor on the ground floor linking the two buildings. Vinod will take you downstairs and show you," said Asutosh.

Before the professor could reply, Kedar said, "That would be great. Thank you for your time. I am sure we can write up something that will get our readers interested in coming to the archives. I hope the police are able to find the box and return it to you," Kedar said as he gestured to Vinod to lead the way.

Vinod led them down the stairs with Kedar next to him, the professor and Manik following a few steps behind. Once they reached the ground floor, they walked toward the corridor linking the two buildings. Just as he was about to enter the corridor, Kedar turned to Vinod to ask the same question that he had asked Asutosh upstairs when Vinod was not in the room, having left to fetch the tea.

"Vinod, one last question: Was anyone aware of the contents of the box that went missing?"

"No. That's the strange bit. It arrived that morning. We were expecting it. The good professor here had told us that something was coming from Surinampur. Asutosh had spoken to someone in Surinampur. From what I understand, they didn't know much either. We just counted the boxes and then left for the day. The plan was to start opening them up and cataloging them the next day. Then this happened," Vinod said thoughtfully.

"Do you usually wait between the arrival of the boxes and checking its contents?" Kedar asked.

"Yes, we have been doing that for a while. Sometimes, there are too many things arriving at the same time, and we simply don't have the manpower to always process everything the same day it arrives. That day we did leave a bit early. We were both tired. Asutosh was able to persuade our head librarian to give us an early break."

"Both of you work in the library and not the other department that deals with collections. So why are you and Asutosh involved in this?" Kedar asked.

"Oh, that's because of the volume of the items coming in. The director has assigned different people for each collection. So Asutosh and I drew the straws for Surinampur, I guess. I am not sure of all the details. But we didn't mind. The professor had already gotten us interested."

"Thank you, Vinod. You have been most helpful," Kedar said as he shook hands with him.

Once Vinod left, they started making their way to the other building through the glass corridor. Manik and the professor were leading the way while Kedar was walking behind them, very slowly. Manik could sense that Kedar was thinking about something, but he didn't want to ask him. Once they reached the end of the corridor, they came across another large reception area. This was the main building, which had all the exhibits for the public. They made their way into the various rooms and halls.

It was an impressive collection, mostly of records. Manik regretted not coming here earlier. He could see Kedar stopping and checking out some of the exhibits in great detail. Each object was joined by a description, details of where it came from, and a short historical context. The lighting in some of the rooms left much to be desired, but overall the contents were in good shape. It looked more like a museum than an archive. Manik thought that it would have probably been better if some things had been sent to the museum. Museums were usually well guarded and had some sort of an alarm system. From what they could see, there was nothing of the sort in this building—two guards, certainly no alarm system, and an employee working at the reception area doing rounds to check whether everything was in order. The only room that was well guarded was the one with jewelry. It wasn't a big room, and there wasn't much there. The professor informed them that most of the jewelry and high-value items were sent right away for safekeeping to the museum vault.

This building mainly housed records, land deeds, some pictures, some odd paintings and artifacts that were deemed not valuable or important enough to make it to a museum. While they made their way around the section that had exhibits on display for the public, the professor was giving his own narrative on the historical context of most of them. Once they had seen enough, they made their way to the main exit and onto the pathway leading up to the main road. They could see the gardens on either side. The employees had done their best to keep everything neat and clean. They also noticed that there was a side entrance that was not open to the public. A sign above it read that it was for deliveries only, and they could see that it was locked, unlike the gates to the other two entrances. The professor turned to Kedar and Manik.

"What do you think? Is this newsworthy?"

"Well, it's definitely something the police should look into. It would be interesting to our readers if they had some sort of idea as to the contents of the box," Kedar replied.

"I may be able to help you with that next week," the professor said.

"How so?" Kedar asked.

"I am planning on going to Surinampur. I contacted the lawyer who is acting as the executor of the estate. Although he doesn't have copies of all the material that was sent, he did note down what each box contained and has some sort of list that he can give me," the professor replied.

"Did he tell you whether it was important?"

"No, he doesn't know. As you saw, there were over fifty boxes and around fifteen crates. It was impossible for him to keep copies of everything and note down in detail what he was sending us. He was relying on the state archives to do that. It seems the ruler was not exactly organized about these things, and most of the material was in the storage area of the ancestral home. There's a lot of paper, thousands of pages—most if it useless, I'd imagine."

"Well, Professor, they were valuable to someone, or else why would they have been stolen?" Kedar asked.

"Yes, that's where I am hoping you can help me. They have already made a police complaint, but honestly, I don't think there has been a thorough investigation."

"When are you leaving for Surinampur, sir?" Manik asked.

"I will be leaving on Monday. It's a two-and-a-half-hour train ride from Calcutta. I am planning to take the early-morning train, meet with the lawyer, take a look at the ancestral home, and then head back the same night. I should be back by midnight. I can call you first thing Tuesday morning to let you know what happened."

"That would be great, Professor. I will give you a number where you can reach us," Kedar said as he brought out a business card.

"Thank you."

"Most likely Anjali will be picking up the phone. We will let her know to expect your call, and she will come find us. Please do let us know if you find anything interesting."

"Thank you. Manik, please do come visit. Some of my students come by, and you are certainly most welcome."

"Thank you, Professor. I will."

"I will let Sucheta know that I spoke to you. She does ask me about her college friends, especially you."

That made Manik very happy. Kedar smiled and shook hands with the professor, and as they turned to walk back toward the tram stop, they realized that they had spent nearly two hours in the state archives building.

"Next stop, Chowringee police station," said Kedar.

"Yes, sir."

"So, what do you think?"

"I don't know, sir. It doesn't seem that interesting. It would be if we knew what was in the box."

"Yes. That would be interesting indeed. But there's something strange going on here. I just feel that in my gut. I can't put my finger on it yet. Something doesn't seem right."

"About what?"

"The box arriving the same day that it went missing. No one really knowing about its contents. Both Asutosh and Vinod taking off early the day it arrived. I don't know," Kedar said thoughtfully as they walked up to the tram stop.

While they waited, Manik could see that Kedar was lost in thought. He strained his neck down the track to see where the tram was. It was turning the corner into the avenue where the stop was and would be there in a couple of minutes. As he stood there, he considered the professor's comment about Sucheta. He had thought about her often and initially after graduation had written to her a few times after she moved to Bombay. She had written back. But after a few months, they had lost touch. Both of them had become busy in their new jobs.

Once the tram arrived, they got on board and found some seats.

"Who is Sucheta?" Kedar asked.

"The professor's daughter."

"A good friend of yours?"

"She was."

"Was?"

"Well, sir, we lost touch. She is in Bombay now."

"Ah. If only we could figure out a way to see our friends from afar every day."

"Yes, sir," Manik replied in a low voice, looking outside.

"Does the professor know how much you like her?" Kedar asked with a smile.

"He knew we were good friends."

"That's not what I asked. By all accounts, both of you like each other. Never mind the professor; have you told her yet?"

"No, sir."

"What exactly are you waiting for?"

"It's complicated, sir. She is in Bombay. I am in Calcutta. I don't know if she is already with someone. I am not sure what to tell her."

"Yes, it seems the whole world is full of people waiting for someone to tell them how they feel about them," Kedar said and smiled.

It was a short ride to the police station, and once they got off the tram, they headed to a small coffee shop behind the station.

"Aren't we going to the police station, sir?" Manik asked.

"Not really. They don't like reporters coming into the station and hanging around. My contact is meeting me in the coffee shop. He can speak to me more freely outside the station."

"Is he a police officer?"

"Yes. He has been in the force for ten years now. So he is fairly senior but still not among the most senior officers in his station."

"How do you know him, sir?"

"Cards."

"Sorry?"

"I play cards at the same bridge club with his father," Kedar said.

"Oh."

"I have known him since he was a kid. His father and I go back a long way. He is also good at cards and chess. In my experience, that makes him a good police officer."

"Is he assigned to the case?"

"No. But I figured before we start asking the station directly, I will try to find out informally where the investigation stands. If we don't get any answers, then we can approach them formally. In my experience, once we do that, they become defensive and give tailored responses. Let's order something while we wait."

They ordered some tea, and while they waited, Manik and Kedar went through what they had learned from the professor's files and their visit to the state archives. The big missing piece, apart from the box itself, was what it held in terms of content. They were hoping that the professor's visit to Surinampur the following week would give them some answers.

"Sir, would it be possible for us, or me, to go to Surinampur with the professor?"

"I know, Manik. I was thinking about that. The problem is that we won't be able to get it approved by Swaroop," Kedar replied.

Manik knew Kedar was right. Traveling within the city was not an issue and didn't require any approvals. But going out of town required some justification.

There simply wasn't enough here for them to justify a trip and get it approved.

A few minutes later, a gentleman walked in. Kedar got up and met him halfway across the room and brought him over to the table where they were sitting.

"Manik, let me introduce you to officer Rudra Pratap Singh—or RP, as we all call him. He is one of the finest officers in the station and a wily bridge player."

"Good afternoon, sir," Manik said as he shook hands with him, and they all sat down.

"Come, come. We have a senior reporter buttering up a cop. Now I know that you really need something from me." Rudra Pratap smiled.

"Well RP, we are hoping that you can assist us in a small matter."

Kedar ordered some tea. After exchanging a few pleasantries and talking about the upcoming elections and cricket, they switched to the matter at hand. It was Rudra Pratap who broached the subject first.

"Kedar, after our conversation this morning over the phone, I tried to find out where things are with the theft of the box from the state archives."

"Are the police investigating this?"

"Well, no one seems to know what's missing," Rudra Pratap replied.

"But it was stolen from the building," Kedar said.

"Yes, but how valuable are its contents? The officers who went to take the statements looked through some of the other boxes, and they contained records of tax receipts, old books, handwritten letters, and really useless pieces of paper."

"But those were not stolen, and this one was. Whatever it had must have been valuable to the people who took it."

"I understand. But you must understand the police's point of view. This station is still investigating what happened during the riots, as well as unsolved murders and the armed robberies at the two banks three weeks ago. Add to that numerous complaints of break-ins and thefts of valuables and other such crimes. With limited resources, finding a box with unknown contents is hardly a priority. I am sure they will eventually get to it. But as you can imagine, we simply can't prioritize this."

"Can you tell us whom this has been assigned to?"

"Not really. This is all off the record, as I am sure you are aware."

"Absolutely, RP," Kedar replied.

"Why is it important that you find this box?" Rudra Pratap asked.

"I will let Manik give you a bit of history on what we know so far," Kedar said.

Manik then told Rudra Pratap everything, starting from the professor's meeting, the research that he had done, what he had read up on in the professor's files, and what had happened earlier that day in the archives. Rudra Pratap listened to all of it without interrupting. Kedar was impressed with how well Manik had explained everything.

"So, tell me, Manik, what's irking you about this theft?"

"That whoever took the box knew exactly what was in it. There were plenty of other boxes there, and some of them contained valuable artifacts. If this was a robbery, why take only one box of papers? It makes no sense."

"It doesn't." Rudra Pratap agreed.

"What do you think, RP?" Kedar asked.

"Honestly, I don't know. But once you hear back from the professor and he gives you an idea of the contents of the box, it will certainly help. If it's deemed valuable, the police will definitely prioritize the investigation. If not, you reporters will be blaming us for trying to find a missing box with unknown contents while there are killers on the loose in this city," Rudra said.

"Understood, RP. As soon as we have more information, we will let you know. Thank you so much for meeting us."

"Anytime, Kedar, and it seems your visits to the bridge club are not as frequent as before. You will soon lose your touch," Rudra Pratap said with a smile as he got up. He shook hands with both of them, thanked them for the tea, and headed out. Manik was impressed with Rudra Pratap's physical appearance and mannerisms. Unlike other senior officers, who seemed to put on weight with each promotion, Rudra Pratap was surprisingly well built and had an athletic figure for someone his age. He wasn't arrogant and seemed genuinely interested in what had happened. Manik also realized that Rudra Pratap and Kedar had known each other for a long time and really well, much more than Kedar had initially led him to believe.

Manik and Kedar headed back to the office. By the time they got back, they could see some employees leaving for the day. Once he reached his desk, Anjali came over to ask him how things had gone. Kedar was already at his desk making phone calls. Manik quickly told Anjali what had happened at the archives and with Rudra Pratap. When he finished, Anjali handed him a note.

"Harish and Rajan came by to see you. They have left for the day. But you have a meeting with them and Swaroop tomorrow morning upstairs."

"Are the Roys going to be there?" Manik asked with a worried look.

"No."

"Thank you."

"Well, I will be off, then. I will see you tomorrow."

"Bye."

The day had gone off relatively well. Although they didn't have many answers, the events had taken his mind off the meeting with the Roys and Swaroop on the article that had gotten the paper into trouble. Now it came roaring back, and he couldn't get it out of his head.

5

Secrets

When Manik arrived the next morning, he was one of the first ones in the office. He had told Subodh and Avik that he wanted to get an early start and had left without them. He could see that some of the workers in the print shop were leaving after their night shift. He slowly made his way up the stairs to his desk. He looked over to the far side of the room and could see that Harish was there. He walked over to Harish's desk. He was on the phone and waited for him at a distance to give him some privacy. As soon as he was done, he walked up to Harish's desk, and Harish asked him to sit at the chair opposite him.

"The article is ready. I left it with Swaroop yesterday. He was going to head over to the Roys to get their blessing, and it will be printed tomorrow."

"That was fast, sir." Manik was a bit surprised.

"Yes. Tarun Roy and Swaroop were in a hurry to get it out. They really do not want to get entangled legally. Hopefully this will go a long way in addressing that," Harish said with a worried look on his face.

"I hope it all works out," said Manik.

"Look, I really didn't want to involve you in any of this and even tried to keep you out of the meeting today. But Swaroop insisted that you be there. I suspect he wants to tell you to not respond to any questions that might arise as a result of this article. I am not sure why any would. But let's see what he has to say."

"Yes, sir."

Just as Harish was about to continue the conversation, they saw Rajan calling out to them. They headed over in his direction.

"Swaroop wants to meet both of you in his office," Rajan said.

"Ok. Let's go." Harish picked up his notepad and started walking with Rajan. Manik followed them a few steps behind. He knew that Rajan and Harish were good friends. That worked out well for Harish. Whenever he needed anything approved by the Roys or Swaroop, Rajan would put the request on top of the pile and put in a word on his behalf. Rajan made it a point to assert his authority and show his seniority with the junior journalists. He took his time in reviewing their requests for cars, always asked for more details on their expenses, took his time in forwarding their approval requests, and generally was a bit aloof and distant from them. None of them wanted to really get on his bad side or irk him, since he wielded this sort of power, but when they spoke privately among themselves, it was clear that none of the junior employees liked him very much. It was not that he was not nice, but he seemed to be on a power trip. They also saw the senior journalists cozying up to him, since Rajan was trusted by the Roys and Swaroop and had their ear.

Once they reached Swaroop's office, Rajan asked them to wait outside. He knocked on the door and went inside. He came out a few minutes later.

"You can go in now."

"Thank you, Rajan," said Harish as he walked in with Manik following him.

"Good morning. Please take a seat," Swaroop said.

Harish and Manik sat down across from his desk. He was holding two sheets of paper in his hand. Manik assumed that this was the retraction that was going to be published. He was right.

"Yesterday evening I was at the Roys' residence. Tarun went over the article; he had asked the lawyers to be present as well. After reviewing it, they have suggested a few changes. Nothing major—the original tone and intent of the article stays the same. However, the wording needs to be altered a bit. Take a look," Swaroop said as he handed over the article to Harish.

Manik could see that there were a few red marks on each page indicating the changes. He could make out from Harish's face that he was not particularly thrilled with the changes but had now reached a point of resigned acceptance. Although he didn't say anything, once Harish had reviewed all the changes, he sighed and nodded. He handed it to Manik.

Manik quickly read the article. It was well written. That wasn't surprising. Harish was a good writer. But he could see why Harish's face had changed on reading the changes. The updates requested by the Roys and the lawyers made the tone of the article almost apologetic. Manik knew that they were in no position to argue, and Swaroop confirmed that.

"Harish, please make the required changes and send the new draft to me. I will approve it for publication in tomorrow's paper."

"Sure," Harish said in a low voice.

"I wish things had turned out differently. But this is something we have to do, and we don't have much of a choice," Swaroop continued.

"I understand, Swaroop," Harish said.

"The reason I asked both of you to be here is because I don't want you to respond to any questions from anyone about the contents of this retraction and the original article. Is that clear?"

Both Harish and Manik detected the stern tone in Swaroop's voice. "Yes," they said almost in unison.

"We will see soon enough where this gets us, and hopefully if things cool down, we can get back to worrying about our regular jobs," Swaroop said.

"Yes, sir," Manik replied while Harish kept silent.

"Well, that's it, really. Is there something you want to ask from your end?"

Manik and Harish looked at each other and then at Swaroop. It was clear that they wanted to leave the room. As they walked out, they could see Rajan on the phone. He waved at them to wait before they went back downstairs. Once he was off the phone, he looked at them.

"Tarun wants you to be in the office the rest of the week. No outings or travel. He wants both of you to be reachable if they want a meeting regarding the article that will be published tomorrow."

Manik and Harish both nodded. Before they could carry on their conversation, Rajan's phone started ringing. As he talked, Harish and Manik left and made their way down the stairs and back to their desks. Once they reached their floor and were about to go their separate ways, Harish looked at Manik and pointed to the papers that Swaroop had given him with the changes that he wanted.

"Don't worry about this, Manik. I will get this done," Harish said.

"Thank you, sir."

"I know you feel the same way as I do. It seems unfair. But sometimes that's just the way it is," Harish said in a low voice.

It shouldn't have to be, Manik thought, but he didn't say anything.

"How is your new assignment?" Harish asked, changing the subject as they reached their floor.

"It is interesting," Manik said and quickly told him about the missing box in the archives.

"Hmm. Well, I got to get cracking on the changes," Harish said as they were about to go their separate ways.

"Is there any help you need from me, sir?"

"No, that's fine. Stick to your new assignment. Kedar is a good journalist, you know. You can learn a lot from him," Harish said as he turned and walked toward his desk.

This was the first time that Harish had ever talked about Kedar. As was the case with other senior reporters, whenever Kedar's name had come up, Harish had always switched topics to talk about something else. Once Manik was back at his desk, he looked over to see if Anjali and Kedar were in the office. They weren't. He decided to go to the cafeteria to get a tea and head outside for a smoke.

He saw employees slowly filing in through the gates. He wondered what the aftermath of the retraction would be. Manik wanted to put it behind him and focus on the new story. He saw Kedar a few yards away, heading to the entrance. Manik quickly put out the cigarette.

"Good morning, Manik," Kedar said with a smile.

"Good morning, sir."

"I have a job for you today. We will have to look at another story I am working on. The one on illegal gambling at the racetracks."

"Yes, sir."

"Let's talk when we get upstairs. Do you want to get a tea?"

"No, sir, I just finished one."

"All right. I will meet you upstairs in a few minutes. Can you please get the files from Anjali?"

"Yes, sir."

He went back inside and headed over to Anjali's desk. He hadn't seen her come in through the main gates, but there was another entrance on the side that employees liked to use as well. He headed back upstairs, and when he reached his desk, he saw that Anjali was at hers and was settling in.

"Good morning, Anjali."

"Good morning. You must tell me more on how your day went yesterday. I was in a hurry to leave, and I didn't get to hear all the details."

"Sure. I was wondering—do you have the files for the gambling story?"

"Yes," she said, and she opened one of the drawers in her cabinet, picked up one of the many files, took a quick look at it, and handed it over.

"Thank you," Manik said as he started leafing through it.

"Is this what you are going to be working on?" Anjali asked.

"Yes."

"Well, I can fill you in with some more details. There are some things on my writing pad that I haven't put in the file yet."

Kedar arrived with his briefcase in one hand and tea in the other. "All right. Let's head to an empty conference room."

"Yes, sir," Anjali said.

They headed over to one of the conference rooms and settled in. It was Kedar who started speaking. "Before we get to this, is there anything you want to talk about from yesterday?"

"Yes, sir," Manik replied.

"What is it?"

"I would like to see if we can get approval for me to travel with the professor to Surinampur on Monday for the day trip to visit the estate and the estate lawyer," Manik said.

"All right. Let's finish talking about this, and then we will head over to Swaroop's office and ask him. I doubt, given the little we know, he will approve the trip. But there's no harm in trying."

"Thank you, sir."

They started talking about the story on gambling at the races. It was an interesting one. Everyone knew that there was illegal betting at the racetracks and a lot of money changed hands. But it was all done quietly, with no paper transactions or records. It was all word of mouth, and the entire operation was based on trust; it had been going on for some time, and it was remarkably efficient. It had been difficult to pinpoint who the masterminds were. No one had really lodged any serious complaints for the police to investigate. Kedar was convinced that some bad apples from the police force were in on it too.

Kedar and Anjali had been working on it for a few months now and had even employed some actors to place bets with hopes of catching the culprits. All they had identified were some small-time bookies who took the bets and made the payouts and nothing else. The bookies themselves were insulated from the top-level masterminds. So even they did not have the full picture. Kedar and Anjali had also managed to compile a list of folks who were regularly placing bets. The list wasn't surprising. It was mostly people who frequented the racetracks, including those who probably had an addiction. And the list wasn't in the files, but rather on Anjali's writing pad. She handed it over to Manik, and he started looking at the names on the list.

"Are these the regulars?" Manik asked.

"Yes. We don't have much. Nothing close to a story. We want to find out who is in charge of the operation. All we have are names of some small-time bookies and the list that you see, most of whom have a gambling problem. There is some talk among the medical community that this habit is a sort of addiction. Not much to write, really."

"I see Arun's and Rajan's names here. Some of them are businessmen. I have read their names in the paper in other articles."

"Yes. Most of them are rich and successful. There are several others on the list who have suffered financially and are not that well off. Arun and Rajan are the only ones from this floor. There's another name of someone who works in the print shop downstairs too. You may have seen him," Kedar said as he pointed his name out.

"Do they know that we know?"

"No. There's no need to. We are not going to publish names of gambling addicts," Kedar said.

They continued discussing what their next course of action would be. One avenue that Kedar was exploring was to rope in a bookie who was no longer working there and had left under a cloud of suspicion. Kedar and Anjali had just come to know of this recently. They knew it was a long shot. Folks who ran this operation were connected and powerful. People who worked for them were afraid of them. Even though this bookie might not be working with them anymore, he would be afraid of the consequences of offering any details. Then there was of course the matter of how much he actually knew. But in the absence of anything else to go on, they decided that they would give it a shot. Kedar had tracked down where he had been working since leaving the racetracks.

"Let's head over to his new address and see if he is open to talking to us," Kedar said.

"Why would he be? Won't he be afraid?" Anjali asked.

"Yes. But if he left in a hurry, maybe he was thrown out. Maybe he is angry with them and would want to tell his side of the story. Who knows? Let's at least pay him a visit and ask him. Maybe he can give us other names that might help us," Kedar said.

"I can't go this week," Manik said.

Kedar and Anjali were both surprised. They turned to look at him.

"Why not?" Kedar asked.

Manik proceeded to explain what had happened with Harish in Swaroop's office. Swaroop had directed both him and Harish to be in the office should they be needed following the publication of the retraction.

"But the article is coming out tomorrow. Why can't you get out of the office today?" Kedar asked.

"That's what I was told. Something about 'if the lawyers need to get in touch with us right away.' I am sorry, sir."

Kedar looked at him and sighed. He knew it wasn't Manik's fault. They went back to reviewing the files.

"All right, Manik. I will take Anjali with me today, and we will let you know how it goes."

"Yes, sir."

"I think we are done for now. Manik, give me a few minutes, and we will head over to Swaroop's office to talk about the approval for Surinampur. I am not going to be forceful about it, because I am not convinced myself that it's worth going there at this stage. But we will ask."

"Thank you, sir."

They all left the room and headed back to their desks. Manik opened his cabinet and brought out the railway timetable. He wanted to make sure he knew the timings of the train to and from Surinampur on Monday in case Swaroop asked him. Day trips were less expensive and easier to get approvals for than overnight stays. The professor had already told them that he was leaving on Monday morning and coming back the same night. If Manik and Kedar got the approval for the trip, he would recommend that they join him. In any case, he had decided to pay the professor a visit over the weekend. Harish and his wife had invited him and some of his other colleagues on Saturday. Manik figured that he would visit the professor on Sunday. He looked over, and Kedar was still on the phone with someone, presumably working on the illegal betting story. He headed over to Anjali's desk to see if he could use her phone. Phones were usually at the desks of the senior journalists and their secretaries. The paper was trying to get phones on all their desks, but it was taking a while. He saw her reviewing a stack of files, and she brought out a form and handed it over to Manik. It was for travel approval.

"If Swaroop agrees, you need to fill out this approval form and hand it in to Rajan," she said.

"Thank you. Can I please use the phone? I want to call the professor regarding the missing papers from the state archives."

"Sure," Anjali said. She turned the phone in Manik's direction and asked him to take a seat on the chair across from her desk.

Manik nodded, brought out a piece of paper, and started dialing the number. Luckily, the professor was home and was the one who picked up. Manik quickly asked whether he was going to be home on Sunday so he could visit. He also tried to find out if indeed the professor had been able to find out more details on the contents of the box. That might help justify the trip, Manik thought. The professor told him that he did have a conversation with the estate lawyer and was convinced that it had something to do with land records and covenants. Manik thanked the professor, hung up, and turned the phone back toward Anjali. He could see that she was reading the first article that he had written with Harish. She looked at Manik, put away the article, and could sense that he was worried.

"Are you worried about Harish's article tomorrow?"

"Not the article, but the aftermath. Hopefully, we can put this behind us."

"So, you are fine with the retraction?"

"No. It shouldn't have come to this. We are a newspaper, and it's our job to question things," Manik said forcefully.

"Ah, the idealism of youth," Anjali said and smiled.

"Not really. Just principles. Otherwise, why bother writing anything that might be deemed controversial?"

Manik said. He hadn't realized that Kedar had finished his phone call and was standing right behind him.

"I agree completely," Kedar said with a smile, and it startled Manik.

"I am sorry, sir. I didn't realize you were there."

"Don't be. I agree with your stance. You and Harish did the right thing to question the system. It is what papers are supposed to do. It was a good article. I understand that a newspaper is a business too. But I can easily argue that if this sticks with the readers, it might actually increase circulation," Kedar said.

"Yes, sir." Manik was pleased to hear all this from Kedar.

"I think the scandal here is not from a readers' standpoint. It's more that it threatens to expose the dealings of some of the other businesses held by the owners," Kedar said.

"Yes, that's my understanding too, sir."

"Well, nothing much we can do until we see what happens tomorrow and the day after. Do you have the travel approval form?"

"Yes, sir," Manik said.

"All right. Let's head over to Swaroop's and see what he thinks."

Once they reached Swaroop's office, they saw that the door was closed. Through the glass window they could see he was on the phone with someone, and Rajan was in the room with him taking notes. They waited outside. As they waited, they saw some journalists coming out of the library on the other side of the hallway and reception area. Manik recognized Arun and Subodh. He knew that Subodh was assigned to Arun for a story related to the riots that they were following up on. Manik recalled his time working with Arun.

Arun was the first senior reporter he was paired up with before Harish and Kedar. He had a different style of working. He was more of a micromanager and liked to control everything. Manik had to keep him apprised of what he was doing at all times, and he seldom got approval to follow up on a story on his own. He also would take off in the middle of the day without informing anyone. Most people assumed it was probably for lunch breaks. But now, after seeing his name in Kedar's files on the illegal betting in the racetracks, Manik knew better. He wondered if anyone else knew about Arun's gambling habit. He figured Harish would probably know, since they were close. In fact, it was Arun who had recommended that Harish take Manik under his wing once their assignment was completed.

Manik was thankful for that. He was also relieved that he had moved on to Harish, who was much easier to work with and much less controlling. Manik considered the fact that Rajan probably also knew about Arun's addiction since Rajan's name was also in the files. He remembered what Kedar had told him. The story that they were working on was not about addiction but the masterminds behind the whole operation. As he was thinking about this, he saw that Swaroop had finished his call, and Rajan was coming out of his room.

"Rajan, we need to talk to Swaroop," Kedar said.

Rajan saw the travel approval form in Manik's hand.

"Well, if this has to do with travel, I might as well sit in. It will save me the trouble of getting it approved later," Rajan said.

As they entered Swaroop's room, he gestured to the chairs across from his messy desk, inviting them to take a seat.

"What's this about?" Swaroop asked.

"I will let Manik summarize," Kedar said.

Manik went on the explain what this potential story was all about—the missing box from the archives, the police not prioritizing the investigation, and what he had found in the professor's files on the estate. He could sense that Swaroop, Kedar, and Rajan were letting him finish before asking any questions.

"We still don't know what was in the box?" Swaroop asked.

"I just spoke to the professor. He told me that the estate's lawyer thinks that it was mostly old land records and covenants," Manik said.

"Is he sure?" Swaroop asked.

"Sort of, sir. The professor will let us know once he is back from his trip."

"Hmm. But we are not sure?" Swaroop asked.

"No, sir," Manik replied. He could sense that Swaroop was not convinced that they needed to go to Surinampur. Kedar had already warned him that it would be difficult to get approval with such little to go on.

"Well, let's see what the professor comes back with, and then we can decide whether we want to spend more time and resources on this story. I will bring this up in my Monday-morning meeting with the senior team to see if they have any contacts in Surinampur that you can talk to. At this time it doesn't seem like we have much to go on," Swaroop said.

The Monday morning meeting that Kedar doesn't attend, Manik thought. This was Thursday, and the fact that Swaroop was going to wait until Monday to ask around meant that he didn't think this was worth pursuing.

Manik decided to make one last plea before giving up. "I have known the professor for a long time, sir. He wouldn't call us to investigate the missing box or make the trip himself to Surinampur if he did not think it was important," Manik said.

"I understand, Manik, and I commend your initiative. But at this point, there answer's no. Let's revisit this next week, when we know more," Swaroop said with a degree of finality in his voice.

Kedar, Rajan, and Manik all got up, left the room, and headed back to their desks. Manik wasn't happy with the outcome, and Kedar sensed that. Kedar walked over to Manik's desk to let him know that he and Anjali were heading out to talk to the bookie about the betting story.

"Manik, don't worry. Once the professor comes back and gives us more details, we can follow up. I am sure if it's something important, Swaroop will agree to continue with the story," Kedar said.

"Yes, sir," Manik said and wondered if Swaroop's response would have been any different if he had not created such a stir with his earlier story with Harish.

He knew that he had suddenly become popular for all the wrong reasons, and although many of the journalists probably agreed with his stance on the story, they would not openly say it or back him up.

"Well, if you are going to be in the office for the next two days, please take a look at the other files on Anjali's desk. Also, I know it's probably early, but maybe you can start doing some research on the party we have been assigned to for the election cycle. Let's try to dig up any published articles on the candidates, their platform, background—basically anything that we think might be interesting," Kedar said.

"Yes, sir."

As Kedar and Anjali started walking toward the stairway leading downstairs, Manik headed over to Anjali's desk to pick up the files Kedar had mentioned. He took them over to his desk. Just as he started leafing through them, he heard the familiar voice of Avik sneaking up next to him and whispering.

"Not getting anywhere with Anjali, I see. She has left you," Avik said with a mischievous smile.

"Yes. Kedar and Anjali are out following up on a story," Manik replied with a tired voice.

"We are going down for an early lunch. Join us, and you can tell us why you look so glum."

Manik was happy to see his friends and decided to leave the file for after lunch. They headed downstairs, quickly ordered their food, and made their way to a table in the courtyard outside the cafeteria. January afternoons in Calcutta were a delight, provided it was sunny. Usually the mornings were foggy, and a mist descended on the entire city at night to cover it like a blanket. But when the sun came out, the whole city looked bright and shiny. If felt good to sit outside and chat about meaningless things. It took Manik's mind away from what he was working on. Just as they were about to finish, Subodh asked him about Harish's upcoming article.

"Did you read it yet?"

"Yes," Manik replied.

"Is it good?"

"The article's fine. The fact that Harish has to write it is horrible," Manik replied, and both Subodh and Avik could sense the frustration in his voice.

"Listen, my friend, if it saves your job, that's all you should be worried about," Avik said.

"I know."

"Harish is on his way out, from what I heard. He is taking an early retirement. Word is that it's the article that hastened his departure," Avik continued.

"Yeah, he told me," Manik said. He was impressed with Avik's knowledge of what went on in the office among other journalists as well.

"Apparently his wife's condition has deteriorated. The doctors have given up. On her last leg, it seems. She is back home now," Subodh said.

"How do you know?" Manik asked. He knew Harish's wife was not doing well. She had been undergoing treatment for a few months now. He didn't have all the details, but it was an incurable form of cancer. Harish wanted to retire early or take a leave of absence. Swaroop was more than happy to grant him that. But it was Harish's wife who had insisted that he stay on at work rather than stay home and "watch her die," as she had put it.

"Arun told me. He is close to Harish," Subodh said.

"Yes, I know," Manik said.

"How is it going with your election assignment?" Subodh asked.

"We haven't started yet. We have been busy at the archives, and now Kedar and Anjali are following up on another story at the racetracks," Manik said. He didn't want to tell Subodh and Avik about what he had read in the files on Arun and Rajan, about their frequenting the racetracks and their gambling addiction.

"I don't know why the switch happened. But I can't say I am unhappy. Following a party is better than being tagged with an independent candidate," Subodh said.

"What do you mean?" Manik asked. He had no idea what Subodh was talking about. Subodh, for his part, looked rather surprised.

"Do you know who you and Kedar have been assigned to? For the elections?" Subodh asked.

"No," Manik replied.

"Nirjanjan Sen. He is an independent candidate standing for elections from one of the constituencies in Calcutta."

Manik had heard the name. It sounded familiar. Then he recalled who he was. He was a businessman who owned shops in and around central Calcutta. Although Manik had never had to work on a story dealing with him, he had heard that he was very influential and well-liked across the political spectrum. He was also well-known for his philanthropy. He had financed a clinic for the poor and homeless.

"What do you mean by 'the switch'?" Manik asked.

"First, I heard that I was going to be assigned to a regional party with you, Kedar and Anjali. Then Arun and I were assigned to Niranjan, and after that, Swaroop told us that the list had been updated with a few changes, and now you and Kedar are assigned to him while we are dealing with one of leftist parties," Subodh replied.

"Have you guys started working on the election cycle yet? I mean, it's still a few months away," Manik asked, wondering why Kedar hadn't mentioned any of this to him yet.

"Yes," both Avik and Subodh replied almost in unison.

Manik told them about the invitation to Harish's house on Saturday and that he would be visiting the professor on Sunday. When they finished, Manik headed over to his desk to read up on Niranjan. He wondered why Kedar hadn't spoken to him about Niranjan yet. But mostly he was worried about any potential aftermath of Harish's retraction. Although he tried focusing on the files in front of him, he realized that he was stressed and was unable to concentrate. He read as much as he could but kept looking at his watch for the day to end. Harish came by his desk around six in the evening and told him that he could leave. No one would be looking for them.

The next morning Manik decided to come in early. He picked up a paper from the reception, went to his desk, and read the article. The changes that Swaroop had suggested were all there. He looked around. There were only a handful of junior reporters at their desks. No sign of Harish—or for that matter, any of the senior staff. After an agonizing hour, he saw Harish coming in. He quickly went over to his desk. Harish seemed outwardly calm, but Manik knew him well enough to know that he was worried as well.

"The deed's done, Manik," said Harish with a degree of finality in his voice.

"Any news from upstairs?" Manik asked anxiously.

"None. But no news is good news. I will go upstairs in an hour and ask Swaroop."

"Do you want me to come with you?"

"No. I will let you know it goes."

"Thank you, sir."

"When did you get in?"

"About an hour ago."

"Worried?"

"Yes, sir."

"Hmm. Me too, but I think this will end it," Harish said, pointing to the article in the paper.

Manik sighed and nodded. He decided to head to the café for a tea and then outside for a smoke. It was Friday morning, and Manik was already looking forward to the weekend. Although his mind was preoccupied with what Harish would find out from Swaroop regarding the retraction, he wondered what Kedar had in store for him. As he was finishing his cigarette, he saw Anjali walking in through the gates. He went up to her, and they headed toward the door.

"How did it go yesterday?" Manik asked.

"Not that great. The bookie was a no-show at the racetracks. We found someone else who gave us his address. When we went there, he wasn't at home. We waited for almost two hours, and when he showed up, he didn't much to say," Anjali said, sounding disappointed.

"It seems we have hit a wall with this story," Manik said. Anjali nodded in agreement.

They reached Anjali's desk, and she handed over some files to him.

"We will be talking about this today," she said.

"Thanks."

"How did it go with the article? Any news yet?" Anjali asked.

"No, not yet."

"That's good, I guess," Anjali said with a smile.

"Harish will let me know in an hour or so. He's going to talk to Swaroop."

"Kedar will be coming in a bit late today. Let's grab some tea, and we can fill each other in on the archive and betting stories."

"Sure. Sounds good," Manik said.

"Did you read up on the other files yesterday?"

"Sort of."

"Slacking off, I see."

"Not quite, just a lot on my mind."

"I understand. Don't worry; everything will work out fine," Anjali said.

Just as Manik turned to head to the cafeteria with Anjali, he saw Harish waving at him from the far end of the room. Anjali nodded, and Manik quickly walked over. Harish could see the worried look on his face.

"Time to head over to Swaroop's office. Don't worry; everything is fine," Harish said with a smile. Manik was happy to hear that.

"The Roys and the lawyers are happy?" Manik asked.

"It seems that way," Harish replied.

"That's good, sir."

"But Swaroop wants to meet with both of us. He told me that there's nothing to worry about."

They headed over to Swaroop's office and saw the familiar face of Rajan outside. He quickly led them in, and as always, Swaroop was on the phone. They sat down and could see from Swaroop's expression that he was relieved. Once he put down the receiver, he looked at them.

"Good news. It seems we can put all this behind us now. I spoke to Tarun and the lawyers, and it seems that the threat of litigation has subsided," Swaroop said with a smile.

"That's great," Harish said and looked at Manik, who nodded in agreement.

"Just one thing: no more articles on this from either of you—or for that matter, anyone else—for the time being. I will bring this up during the Monday-morning meeting with the senior staff. We dodged a bullet, and I don't want the paper to get dragged into anything connected with this. Any article on land matters, property disputes, developers, builders, etcetera, is off limits. Is that understood?"

"Yes," Harish replied.

"The good thing is that our readers are getting more interested in the upcoming elections. So let's get moving on that."

Manik and Harish could both see that Swaroop was pleased with the way things had turned out. They were relieved as well and now could focus on other things on their plates. Manik wondered if Harish was still considering early retirement or would stay on for a bit longer. Maybe he could ask him during the dinner on Saturday. As they got up to leave, Swaroop turned to Manik.

"Let me know how things go with the professor. When is he expected back? Surinampur, was it?"

"Yes, sir. Monday night, sir. I will contact him on Tuesday morning."

"All right. If there's anything to it, then let's keep on it. If not, let's start focusing on your election assignment."

"Yes, sir."

Manik and Harish headed back to their desks. They could see that their floor was now full with the clickety-clack of the typewriters, smoke emanating from some of the desks of the senior staff, the ringing of telephones, and the general chaos of the news desk. All this made Manik smile, and he knew he had to share what had happened upstairs with Avik and Subodh.

When he reached their desks, he could see they were not that busy. He quickly told them what had happened. They were happy for him and told him that they planned to head to the movies and dinner that evening. Manik agreed to join them and returned to his desk.

He saw that Kedar had just arrived and was talking to Anjali. He waved at him to come over.

"How did it go with Swaroop?" Kedar asked.

"It went well, sir. It seems it's over. Hopefully, I can now focus on other stories without worrying about all that," Manik said. Anjali must have told Kedar about their conversation earlier. He could see that Kedar was happy with the way things had worked out. It made him happy that Kedar cared about him.

"I need to make a few calls this morning. I want you and Anjali to bring each other up to speed on the betting and the state archives stories. After lunch we will start talking about our election assignment," Kedar said, looking at both Anjali and Manik.

They nodded and headed over to an empty conference room with their files and papers. As they settled in, Manik decided to ask her about Niranjan.

"Did you know that we were tagged to a new party for the upcoming election and now the assignment has been switched to some independent candidate?"

"Yes. I didn't know myself. Kedar only mentioned it yesterday evening when we were heading back to work," Anjali replied with a puzzled look on her face.

"Do you know what happened? I mean, why the switch?"

"I am not sure. It seemed that it came from Swaroop, and Kedar was caught unawares as well."

"Not that it makes a difference to us. We still have to work on his profile, learn about his background, do interviews. It's probably less time consuming. He is one candidate. If you were doing a political party, it would have been multiple candidates."

"Yeah. But Niranjan is a well-known candidate. He is popular in the city and is well liked. Most people think he will win his seat fairly easily. Who told you that things had been switched?"

"Subodh. He and Arun were assigned to Niranjan previously."

"Ah, yes. One of the three musketeers," Anjali said with a smile.

They spent the rest of the morning reviewing the files and making notes. As Manik listened to Anjali, he realized that she was actually very good. He wondered whether she would have gotten promoted and made it further up the ranks had she not been assigned to Kedar. Being a woman also didn't help. Although the paper was progressive compared to other dailies, the senior staff was still wary of assigning important stories to women.

During short breaks, she told him about herself. She came from a well-to-do Calcutta family not unlike his. They were conservative and somewhat traditional. That meant that she was expected to marry at a certain age after finishing college. Apparently, a suitor was arranged by the family, but at the last minute, it fell through. Manik could sense that although her family was not too happy about that, she was actually relieved. He didn't press her further for details. Her family was also not too happy with her working long hours. They had told her to focus on finding someone to marry. Work was not only an escape but also a source of sanity and independence for her. A year ago she had decided to move out and take an apartment in an area that was closer to the office. Initially her family had revolted but had come around when they realized that she was now financially independent and there wasn't much they could do. From the tone in her voice, Manik sensed that Anjali valued her independence.

"It helps, of course, that my flatmate is a woman; otherwise, my parents would have another kind of fit," she said with a smile.

"Right, I can only imagine."

"It's easier for men."

"It is," Manik agreed.

"It helps that your parents are not in the same city."

"To some extent, yes."

"They haven't asked you to settle down?" Anjali asked.

"Not yet. I come from a large family. They were happy that I wasn't a financial burden on them. I think they do want me to marry, but, as you said, it's different for girls, I think."

"It is, and some of these traditions are meant to drag you down," Anjali said, suddenly sounding a bit serious.

"Some of them, yes. Strange how people look at you differently when you are financially independent."

"Totally." Anjali agreed with a smile.

"Money seems to trump some of these traditions."

"Yes. They don't have much hold over you."

They looked at the clock in the room.

"Hungry? Lunch?" Manik asked.

"Sure."

"Yes. Should we get Kedar?"

"I think you may have noticed—he doesn't have lunch in the café," Anjali said.

"Why is that?"

"Habit, I think, and some past history," Anjali replied. Manik wanted to know more, but he could sense that Anjali didn't want to talk about it. She gathered all her files, and they headed out of the room to leave the papers at their desks and go to lunch.

When they got back to their desks, Kedar called them over.

"Please go over to the print desk. They need some help from us this afternoon. It seems some of their folks didn't show up, and they are a bit under the gun to get the paper ready for the weekend," Kedar said.

"Yes, sir," Anjali said.

Manik and Anjali went to the print desk. This wasn't surprising. The weekend paper, especially the Saturday edition, had more sections and pages. Quite often the junior staff would be tasked with checking whether all the pages were in order, reviewing the content, and also proofreading all the columns and articles. They didn't mind. They got a chance to read the Saturday edition before anyone else did. It also gave them a chance to read what everyone else was working on. Manik was particularly interested in the movie reviews, and he scanned them to see if anything would be appealing for that evening. They spent the rest of the afternoon at the weekend publication desk, and by the time they got back to their desk, it was already close to 7:00 p.m. Kedar was on his way out.

"I think you can pack it up for the weekend; we will start with Niranjan on Monday. I already spoke to his secretary, and he has agreed to meet us for a short interview on Monday afternoon. Manik, I need you there with me," Kedar said.

"Yes, sir," Manik replied.

Manik could see that Anjali was heading out with some of the other women.

"It's a girls' night," she said with a smile.

"I hope you enjoy it," Manik said.

"Bye."

Before leaving, Manik headed over to Harish's desk. He had left for the day, but Arun was there.

"Harish told me to remind you to be at his place tomorrow evening around seven. He has left for the day," Arun said.

"Thank you, sir. I will be there," Manik replied and headed downstairs to find Avik and Subodh. They had decided to meet at the gates around seven. When he got there, they were having a smoke.

"Movie first, or dinner?" Subodh asked.

"I am famished. Dinner first, and then movie," Manik replied.

"Sounds good," Subodh said, and Avik nodded in agreement. They headed toward the tram stop. Once they got there, they could see the Friday-evening rush. Everyone was heading out for a movie or meal to start the weekend.

"The girls are having a night out," Avik said, sounding serious.

"That must be driving you nuts," Manik replied with a smile, and Subodh laughed.

"It's not right. This is the kind of thing that shouldn't be happening. We should all be going out together," Avik said.

"Well, we sometimes do. But yeah, I can see that it is disappointing when they don't ask you," Manik said.

"Yes, very disappointing. I could be making some headway with someone in a nice restaurant, but now I have to spend the evening with you lot," Avik said.

"Should we dump him now or later?" Subodh asked jokingly.

"He's all right. After a couple of drinks, he'll be fine," Manik said. They enjoyed a good laugh.

They spent the rest of the evening eating, drinking, and sharing stories from work and their childhoods. Subodh and his girlfriend, Roshni, had not made any headway with either of their parents. Avik offered his unsolicited and detailed advice on how they could elope and reconnect with their families once a baby was in the picture. Once they finished, it was already too late even for the late show.

The next evening Manik decided to head to one of the street vendors that sold flowers to buy some for Harish and his wife. On the way to their house, he also picked up a box of sweets, and by the time he arrived at Harish's residence, he could see many of the guests were already there. He could spot Rajan, Arun, Swaroop, and some of the other senior staff. Kedar was not there. *Not surprising*, Manik thought.

In all the time that he had worked with Harish, he had never been inside his apartment. He had seen Harish's wife, Radhika, twice during Diwali celebrations in the office, when family members were invited for a cultural show. When Manik saw her this time, she looked completely different. She looked old, frail, and in ill health. He knew she wasn't doing well. She was sitting in one corner of the room with a few guests around her. Harish rarely talked about his wife. But based on the few conversations they had had, Manik knew that they had met in college. They did not have any children. They had traveled together in India and abroad. He also knew that she worked as a professor at a college for many years until her poor health forced her to take an early retirement.

Harish waved at him to come over to the corner of the room, where he was standing with his other colleagues. After some quick greetings, Manik headed over to Harish's wife and gave her the flowers and box of sweets.

"You must be Manik," Radhika said.

"Yes."

"Harish told me about you. He speaks highly of you. Thank you for these," Radhika said, pointing to the flowers and sweets. She quickly introduced him to the rest of the women who were sitting with her. He recognized most of them from the Diwali celebrations.

"I will take him, Auntie, and get him something to eat," said a familiar voice from the back of the room. It was Anjali. He was surprised to see her there. He would have thought that she wouldn't be invited. He had never seen her and Harish talk much at work. But he was happy to see a familiar face, someone he could talk to.

"Thank you, Anjali. Make sure he eats well. He is all skin and bones," Radhika said with a smile.

"Thank you," Manik said as she followed Anjali to the corner of the room, where there was a rich assortment of all kinds of spicy snacks and food.

"Surprised to see me here?" Anjali asked.

"Yes," Manik replied.

"Harish's wife, Radhika, is my aunt. My mom's older sister."

"Oh. I didn't know that. How is she doing? She looks tired," Manik said.

"She is not doing well at all. The doctors have given up. I think she is just biding her time. It is sad, really. My aunt was quite a lively person and a lot of fun. It is sad to see her like this."

"I am sorry to hear that."

"She likes these get-togethers. It's a break from her daily routine of staying at home and waiting for the inevitable."

"Maybe with Harish taking early retirement, it will help. He can keep her company," Manik said.

"I am not so sure. Auntie is the one who insisted that he stay at work, and things haven't been quite the same between her and Harish," Anjali said in a serious tone.

Manik didn't want to press any further. He picked up a plate and filled it up with some snacks. Anjali asked him to head over to the balcony. Once they reached the balcony, Anjali slowly closed the glass door behind them to give them some privacy. They could still see the rest of the guests but couldn't hear them.

"I guess you must have sensed that our current boss doesn't get along with Harish," Anjali said.

"Yes. Well, it seems Kedar doesn't get along with anyone in the senior staff," Manik replied.

"Well, I am going to tell you a bit of history now. Most of the senior staff knows—or at least the ones at this party are well aware."

"Know what?" Manik asked.

"Kedar, Harish, and Radhika were classmates in college. They were also very good friends. After graduation both Kedar and Harish worked together for some time and collaborated on some articles, which were very good."

"Yes, I know. I read some of them in the library," Manik said.

"Good to see you do your homework on the boss," Anjali said with a smile.

"So, what happened after that?"

"The story goes that Kedar and Radhika wanted to get married, but her parents did not agree. Kedar left and moved to Bombay. As you know, he has moved around quite a bit. Harish and Radhika got married and settled down in Calcutta. It was an obvious choice. They are both from the city and have lots of friends and family here who can make life fun but also complicated. It didn't help that the marriage didn't produce any children. At one point a few years ago, they separated. I am not sure what Kedar has told you about his family."

"Not much—only that he is a widower and has a son who lives abroad."

"Yes. Kedar got married in Bombay and has a son who now lives in England. His wife died many years ago. He moved to Calcutta a few years ago and then reconnected with both Harish and Auntie while they were still separated. It seems Kedar had an affair with Auntie during this time, and Harish came to know of it much later. That's what started the cold war between them. When Auntie got sick, she decided to move into this apartment. This is actually her place. When Harish came to know that she wasn't doing well, he insisted that he move in with her, although she wasn't very keen. Honestly, I think she would prefer it if she was on her own."

Manik absorbed all this and now understood why Kedar kept a distance from the senior journalists at work.

"I didn't know any of this," Manik said, sounding serious.

"Yes. Harish's friends at work know. They mostly blame Kedar. Although I am not sure it's entirely his fault. Auntie has always made her own choices in life. She has taken responsibility for them and likewise paid the price."

"I guess blaming Kedar is easier," Manik said.

"Yes, it is. I must say that in all this time I have worked with Kedar, he has never mentioned any of this," Anjali said.

"Where do things stand between your Auntie and Kedar now?"

"I think they are still good friends. I am not sure how often they talk, but Harish and Kedar are still at odds with each other."

"Somewhat understandable, I guess," Manik said.

"To some extent, yes. But now Auntie's days are numbered, and she should have her say as to whom she wants to meet with and talk to. Harish was not around when she needed him, and now it seems he is back more out of sympathy and pity than love," Anjali said, sounding a bit frustrated.

"You think your opinion might be just a bit biased?" Manik asked with a smile.

"Maybe. But it is what it is, and that's what I think," Anjali replied, sounding a bit relaxed, a smile on her face.

"Life can be complicated," Manik said in a philosophical tone.

"It usually is. Well, now you know what I know. Let's head back in before the old folks finish all the food," Anjali said as she opened the glass door of the balcony and stepped back inside.

Manik mingled with the other folks, exchanging pleasantries, and then, just as he was about to replenish his plate, Swaroop and Arun caught up with him.

"So, what's that wily fox Kedar up to now? What has he got you working on? Some missing box that no one cares about and horses?" Arun said, reeking of alcohol. Manik could see that he was completely drunk. Arun was a big man and bulging in almost all areas. He was having a hard time standing up properly, and Manik took a step back to make sure he wouldn't fall on him. Swaroop stepped in before Arun could embarrass himself further.

"Arun, I think you need to sit down for a bit and get something to eat," Swaroop said with a stern voice, pointing toward the sofa.

"Yes, sir," Arun said mockingly and headed over and slumped into the couch in the corner. They could see that he was almost ready to either throw up or fall asleep.

"Sorry about that, Manik," Swaroop said.

"It's all right, sir," Manik replied.

"He has had one too many. Please don't pay any heed to what he said."

"I won't, sir."

"Keep up the work on the betting story and the missing box," Swaroop said as he smiled and moved on to another part of the room. Manik wondered how much Swaroop knew of Arun's and Rajan's gambling addictions. Maybe he did, and didn't really care.

Finally, Manik was able to catch hold of Harish, who had been busy making sure all the guests were well fed.

"Thank you, sir, for inviting me to the dinner."

"You are most welcome, Manik. I guess you will come to know soon anyway, but I wanted to let you know that once the elections are over, I will be taking my retirement. I am happy that we got this mess of an article behind us. You will do well, Manik. You have a good head on your shoulders, and you write well."

"Thank you, sir."

"Who are you assigned to for the election?" Harish asked.

"Niranjan Sen," Manik replied.

"Hmm. That's strange. I would have figured you would be assigned a political party and not an independent candidate—and not Niranjan."

Just as he was about to continue, Harish got called over from the far side of the room. Some of the guests were leaving. It was Manik's cue to leave as well. He went over to Harish's wife and thanked her. He then walked over to Anjali. She pointed to the door and asked him to wait. As folks started filing out, he could see only Rajan and Arun staying back with their wives. They were probably going to leave a bit later. Anjali walked up to him with her bag, ready to leave.

"Do you mind walking with me to the tram stop, and we can take the tram together? We are heading in the same direction."

"Not at all," Manik replied. Manik knew that Anjali's apartment building was a few blocks away from his. As they headed out, they could see that a fog had descended on the city. The visibility was poor, but the bright lights of the streetlamps and the cars made it look lively. Saturday night meant lots of people on the road. Once they got on the tram, Anjali and Manik headed toward the end of their carriage, where there were still some empty seats. Once they settled in, Manik asked Anjali what she knew about Niranjan.

"Harish was surprised that we have been assigned to Niranjan," Manik said.

"Yes, I know. He spoke to me briefly after you told him."

"Do you know anything about him?"

"Not much more than what's in the file. You read it too," Anjali said.

"Yes." Manik nodded.

"We can ask Kedar on Monday whether he knows anything."

They could now feel the tram hurtling its way through the fog and the sights and sounds of this gray Calcutta evening. There was a gentle breeze, but it was not enough to clear the mist.

"I will walk you to your building, and then it's a short walk from there to where I am," Manik said.

"Chivalry is not dead, I see," Anjali said in a playful tone.

"So it would seem," Manik replied with a smile.

"I guess you learned something new today about Harish and Kedar," Anjali said after they had gotten off the tram.

"Yes," Manik replied.

"Well, this is me," Anjali said, pointing to the gates of her building.

"It was nice bumping into you at Harish's dinner. Otherwise it would have been really boring for me," Manik said with a smile.

"Are you saying I am interesting?"

"Very."

"Well, then we must do this again—maybe a night out without all the boring people?"

"Sure."

"I will see you on Monday, then. Bye."

Manik watched her walk through the gates. Just before entering the building, she looked back and waved at him. He decided to walk the rest of the way home. It was damp, but the breeze made it comfortable. As he walked back home, he went over what he had learned about Harish, his wife, and Kedar. He also wanted to know more about Niranjan. That would have to wait till Monday, he thought. Then there was Anjali, of course. She was close to both Kedar and Harish, and his wife and knew a lot more than she had told him. He was happy that she had felt at ease confiding in him, and it certainly cleared things up for him as to why Kedar and Harish avoided each other.

Anjali, for her part, was happy that Manik was now working with her and Kedar. He seemed different from the rest of the junior staff. As she entered her apartment, her flatmate, Rina, who had seen Manik walk Anjali back to the building from the balcony, asked her if this was going to be her new love interest.

"Oh, stop it, Rina," Anjali said with a smile on her face.

"He is skinny but handsome, from what I could see from here," Rina said.

"He is a just a colleague from work who was walking me home. That's all."

"Well, I have lots of colleagues at work. But they don't walk me home at this time of the night on a weekend," Rina said.

"Enough. I am tired now, and off to bed." Anjali laughed and sped into her room, closing the door firmly behind her.

Anjali was in a happy place. She knew she was good at her job, and if she performed well, there was a chance that she could become a full-fledged reporter handling big stories, which was what she desperately wanted. On the relationship front, since she had moved out of her parents', things were looking up. She was careful not to date people from work. Rina had set her up with one of her cousins, and that courtship lasted for a few weeks, until he told her that he was moving abroad. Both Anjali and Rina were sort of glad that it had ended, for different reasons. Rina had found out that her cousin's parents were arranging his marriage abroad, and she did not know how to tell Anjali. Anjali, for her part, didn't want to tell Rina that her cousin was starting to become possessive and demanding. When he left, they both heaved a sigh of relief.

Rina worked as a teller in a bank. Unlike Anjali, she was not from Calcutta. When she moved into the city, she was desperately looking for someone to share the apartment with, to share the rent and other expenses. She was happy when one of her colleagues at the bank told her about Anjali. They hit it off and moved into this apartment. Each of them had her own room, and there was a common area that served as a living and dining room. There was a small balcony with a decent view, and although the kitchen was small, it was sufficient for their needs. They had furnished their rooms and the common area aesthetically with modest but elegant furniture, paintings, and plants.

Although Anjali had a good feeling about Manik and he was easy to talk to, she was unsure about dating him. He was younger, but that in itself was not that big an issue. The bigger issue was that he was a colleague at work, and if things didn't work out, it could become really awkward.

Manik was extremely tired when he got back after walking Anjali home. His apartment resembled a room in a student hostel. There was hardly any furniture. A small bed, bookcase, desk, and chair were all that he had purchased. There was one walk-in closet in the single-room apartment, and it held all his possessions. He could have done with another bookcase, but once the space there was exhausted, he had decided to start a neat pile in one corner of the room. The kitchen barely had utensils and provisions for tea and quick meals. He mostly ate out during the day and lived on sandwiches at night. As his head hit the pillow, he started thinking about all the things he had learned from Anjali about Kedar and Harish. Then his thoughts shifted to his time with Sucheta during his college days. Then biology took over, and he was fast asleep.

6

Mist

Sunday morning breakfast with Subodh and Avik seemed to last forever. Subodh was in a hurry to meet up with his own love interest for a late lunch and movie, while Avik was more interested in every detail of what had transpired between Manik and Anjali, down to each syllable and expression. He was somewhat disappointed in Manik that things hadn't gone further between the two of them. Manik, for his part, was looking forward to his evening's visit to the professor's home. He wanted to know more about the case. But he also wanted to know more about Sucheta and what she was up to in Bombay.

When he reached the professor's residence, he recalled his many previous visits to this part of town. The professor lived close to the main college campus, and the area was full of students. This area of

Calcutta was known for its colleges, universities, bookstores, tea stalls, canteens, and of course The Coffee House, an iconic landmark for academics, intellectuals, and pseudo-intellectuals alike. There were many, many places to have endless discussions and arguments on world issues and totally meaningless conversations, consisting mostly of unloading sentiments with little hope of any true impact. Manik and his friends loved all of it, and now that they were in the daily grind of working and earning a living, they missed their college days even more. The professor, for his part, had tried to keep himself engaged with the college even after retirement. He gave free tutorials, participated in seminars, and invited himself to lectures even if they were not directly related to his subject. Some of his students kept in touch, but gradually, as time went by, they visited less, wrote less often, and lost touch. Manik tried his best to visit at least once every six months, but with the recent assignments he had been given at work, it had become more and more difficult.

The professor lived in a small three-room apartment on the ground floor of a two-storey house. He had leased the upper floor. The living room was a large, open area with some chairs, a dining table, and a sofa. There was a constant stream of students coming and going. He had converted a bedroom into a study, and that room was an absolute mess. It had bookshelves and boxes full of papers, files, and documents. There was a small area for a desk and a chair. This was where the professor did most of his reading and writing. When Manik arrived, the professor was seeing off some of his students in the living room, and once everyone had left, he asked Manik to come sit across from him on the sofa.

"Would you like to have tea and sweets?"

"No, sir; I am fine."

"What nonsense." The professor called out to someone in the kitchen and asked him for tea, biscuits, and sweets for both of them.

"I really don't need anything," Manik protested.

"Don't worry. Do it for me. I live alone now, and the help that you see is part time. You will stay and chat a bit longer this way," the professor said with a smile.

"I am so sorry, sir. I should come more often."

"Oh. Don't worry about it. I know all of you are busy at work. I saw where you work. I am very impressed, Manik. You did well."

"Thank you, sir."

"Tell me, Manik, are you still writing music?"

"No, sir. I sent some pieces to a few places in Calcutta and Bombay. But there was no response."

"You should keep at it, Manik. Even as a hobby, it's great. You are the only person I know who composes and writes music. Everyone else is just singing someone else's song or playing someone else's tune the best they can. But you are creating something on your own. Good or bad, whether people like it or not, you should keep at it."

"Yes, sir."

Once the tea and snacks arrived, they reminisced about their time in college. The professor inquired about some of Manik's classmates and friends. Manik took this opportunity to ask about Sucheta.

"What about Sucheta, sir? How is she doing in Bombay?"

"Oh, she likes it. I have a cousin who lives there. Initially, after moving, she was living with her, but now she has moved into her own apartment; she is sharing it with some colleagues."

"And her work?"

"You mean the travel agency? It seems like a lot of work. The country is changing, you know, Manik—probably better than I do. As people get more affluent, they want to travel more. I think she is enjoying it, but then again I don't know much about this line of work."

"Is she coming over to visit you anytime soon, sir?"

"Yes. She is coming next month, and you have to come and visit. She will be here for a week; you should come over for dinner when she is here."

"Sure, sir."

They finished their tea and spoke for some time more about their old acquaintances. Manik was happy to see that the professor was keeping himself busy after retirement. Then the conversation shifted to the missing papers from the archives.

"What did you think of Asutosh and Vinod—you know, the gentlemen at the archives?"

"Yes, I remember. To be honest, sir, we didn't find Asutosh to be very forthcoming or talkative. Vinod seemed more helpful."

"Well, you must understand that something's gone missing. So they are wary of prying eyes. But I have known them for a while, and they are fine. Asutosh is quiet and more knowledgeable, but sometimes hard to read. Vinod is just out to please his boss."

"Yes, it seemed that way."

"It's a pity that you can't make the trip with me to Surinampur."

"I tried, sir. But without knowing what's gone missing, my bosses didn't approve my trip."

"That's totally understandable, Manik. I would have probably done the same."

"Are you all set for the trip tomorrow, sir?"

"Oh, yes. My tickets are booked. I am not staying overnight. All I am bringing is that bag over there and that folder, in case I need to bring back any files," the professor said, pointing to the bag and folder on the dining table.

"Well, sir, you have an early start tomorrow. I will let you get a good night's sleep. Thank you so much for having me over and for the tea," Manik said as he got up.

The professor got up, put his arms around Manik, and give him a hug.

"It was so nice to have you over. I will be back after midnight tomorrow. I will call you first thing Tuesday morning to let you know if I have found anything."

"Thank you, sir. I am looking forward to it," Manik said with a smile.

As they walked to the door, the professor turned to Manik and looked him in the eye.

"You know, Manik, I may be an academic, but I also see things. I know you and Sucheta were close in college. I know for a fact that she likes you and often asks about you. Now, I don't know what's going on with her in Bombay. Kids nowadays don't always say everything to their parents. All I am saying is that when she does come over, you can still talk to her and see if things can move forward between the two of you. That's of course if you want that as well, and if she wants it too."

"I don't know, sir, what the future holds. I will definitely see her," Manik said. He was a bit surprised that the professor had brought this up, but part of him was happy that he had.

"Tell her how you feel. I know Sucheta. Once you tell her, she won't be shy in letting you know what she thinks," the professor said.

"I know, sir."

"More on Tuesday, then."

"Have a nice trip, sir."

"Thank you."

Manik slowly started walking to the end of the lane and turned in to College Street. It was Sunday evening. Most of the colleges were closed, but he could still see a steady stream of students walking past the shops and buildings, making their way in and out of tea stalls and cafés that were still open at this hour. As he reached the tram stop and waited for the next tram, he recalled the last conversation he had had with Sucheta before she left for Bombay. Once they graduated, she was the one who found a job first. It was in Bombay, and she had to join within a week. She didn't have much choice but to accept. During the final year of college, Sucheta and Manik had gone out a few times. They liked each other's company and confided in each other. What the professor didn't know was how far their relationship had progressed emotionally and otherwise. They had hoped that after graduation, once they found jobs, they would take things further and see if they had a future together. They had talked about their futures often and had naively assumed that they would end up working in the same city after graduation.

The rush to move to Bombay meant that Sucheta had very little time the week before she left. She had to make sure that everything with her father in Calcutta was settled so that he could continue without her. She had tried to persuade the professor to move with her to Bombay. But he had flatly refused, understandably, since his extended family and friends were all in Calcutta. Manik, for his part, had been busy with interviews and had found little time to visit her during that last week to talk to her or help her with her move. He still hadn't landed a job, and he knew that he would have to move back in with his parents in Bolpur if he did not find anything soon. He didn't want to do that.

These pressing realities of life meant that any thought of a future together would have to wait. When Manik came to see her off at the station, there were a lot of people there. Her friends and family had come to see her off as well. They weren't able to find any time alone. She wrote to him once she settled in. He wrote back. But as time went by, they became busy with their own work and demanding schedules. They still exchanged cards during celebrations and the new year. But they hadn't seen each other for almost two years. Manik applied for a few jobs in Bombay just after Sucheta moved there. But there was no response from anyone. Manik was looking forward to Sucheta's visit. He wanted to see his friend and talk about what had happened since they last spoke. At the same time, he was unsure of how things stood between them and whether there was any chance at all of a future together.

The first order of business on Monday morning was to read up on Niranjan Sen. Manik had read the file, and everything in it was overwhelmingly positive. For someone who had been successful in so many businesses, this seemed suspicious. As always Manik arrived in the office before Anjali and Kedar did, and he took the opportunity to head to the library to see if there were any published articles on Niranjan. There were lots of articles on companies he owned and quite a few on his philanthropic interests. By all accounts he came from what most people regarded as a "good" family. His family was well-off and had all the right connections to make sure that any scandals or questionable dealings could either be hushed up or "managed." What struck Manik as odd was that for someone who had been in the limelight for almost three decades, Niranjan's image was squeaky clean.

Manik made some copies of the articles and headed back downstairs, where he found a note on his desk from Kedar to meet him in one of the conference rooms. When he got there, he saw that Kedar was already reading old newspaper articles about Niranjan's companies.

"Good morning, Manik. How was your weekend?"

"Fine, sir. I met with the professor. He will call us tomorrow with more news from Surinampur."

"That's great. Well, on the menu today is Mr. Niranjan Sen. It seems you have already read up on him. So, tell me about him."

Manik proceeded to tell Kedar everything that he had found out about Niranjan, his companies, charity work, and family.

"He is a well-respected and connected fellow, it seems," Kedar concluded.

"Yes, sir."

"Nothing controversial? No rumors about payoffs to get licenses? Anything?"

"None that I could see in the files or published material," Manik replied.

"I find that hard to believe. Either we haven't looked hard enough, or he has done an unimaginably splendid job of lawfully creating a business empire without paying off or ticking off anyone," Kedar said with a smile.

"I agree, sir. It does seem rather odd."

"Hmm. All right. Let's start with what he owns. Do you have a list?"

"Yes, sir," Manik said as he shuffled through his file and handed Kedar a piece of paper.

"What's the gist of it?"

"He runs four businesses. The two most profitable ones are a textile plant that makes clothes and accessories and a real estate company that builds apartment buildings. The two lesser known and less profitable businesses are a shoe factory and a transportation company that owns trucks with interstate licenses."

"They must be employing a lot of people?"

"In all, around two thousand people."

"Wow. No wonder all the parties wanted his endorsement. Anything else?"

"Yes, sir. It seems the family has a stake in a company that owns a lot of stores in south and central Calcutta. They are not the main stakeholders, and it's hard to say how big or small the holdings are from the material that we have. If I were to hazard a guess, I'd say just the rental income from the all the shops, based on where they are located, would probably be more than their revenues from one of their larger businesses. But it's hard to know how much Niranjan is making."

"When you were doing your research on the article with Harish, didn't his company or name come up?"

"Not really, sir. We were looking at companies that had had complaints or cases filed against them. His didn't come up."

"Right."

"There is one thing though that is a bit odd."

"What is that?" Kedar asked.

"For most of the things that he owns, there seem to be clear records and documents. But on the one that is jointly owned with the family, there seems to be nothing."

"Well, if it's an old family, that's normal. Most of these records are not public knowledge, and they only come out into the open if there is a dispute. What else do we know about the family?"

"The old man, Niranjan's father, has retired. So has his uncle, his father's younger brother. It's mainly Niranjan and his cousin, his uncle's son, who run the businesses."

"Does our paper have any ties with him? Have his businesses advertised with us? Did you check?"

"Yes, sir, I did. A few advertisements here and there and greetings during the new year and festivals. It seems his companies prefer national dailies to our paper for most of his advertisements," Manik replied.

"Wonder why he wants to enter politics. He seems to be doing well."

"Yes, sir."

"And as an independent candidate not associated with any party, no less. Maybe because he thinks it will be a close election and as an independent candidate, he will have a lot to gain by backing the winning horse after the election."

"That's if he wins, sir."

"Well, by all accounts, he has a good reputation and name recognition. He seems to have done the groundwork with his philanthropic activities. Maybe we shouldn't be this cynical. Let's keep an open mind when we meet him later today," Kedar said.

"Yes, sir."

"We will leave in an hour. Let's take the camera with us. Politicians love to have their pictures in the paper and are willing to open up more if we oblige."

"Sure, sir," Manik said as he started arranging all the papers and files.

Kedar picked up the daily paper and started reading it. He quickly glanced at the headlines and moved to the pages in the middle. Manik figured that he would be looking for articles related to Niranjan and his businesses. Kedar wasn't. Halfway through the third page of the newspaper, he could see Kedar's expression suddenly change. Manik leaned over to see what article he was reading. He couldn't make it out, but Kedar handed him the paper to read.

"Your professor left this morning?"

"Yes, sir."

"Did he tell you the name of the lawyer he was meeting in Surinampur?"

"No, sir."

"Hmm. Take a look at the article and tell me what you think," Kedar said.

Manik read the article. It was only a few lines. There was an attempted robbery in a building in central Calcutta. Among the establishments that were broken into was a law firm, Pinaki Sett and Associates. The article seemed to suggest that nothing much was taken from any of the establishments. The thieves left in a hurry, probably because an alarm had been raised and the watchmen were alerted. By the time the guards arrived, the robbers had left. Manik really couldn't see any connection. Kedar pointed to the bottom of the page where the advertisements were published. There was a very small ad for Pinaki Sett and Associates, which listed the places where the firm had offices. Its presence was mostly within the state, and apart from Calcutta, it had offices in Haldia, Siliguri, and Surinampur.

"You think there's any connection?"

"Unlikely, but something's not sitting right with me. Let's get the folks who printed this in the paper in the room quickly and see if they know any more details. I doubt that will be the case, but let's ask them anyway."

"Yes, sir," Manik said as he headed to the door. Usually these articles were written by the local crime desk, which dealt with petty theft, robberies, and break-ins. They got most of the information and details from the police, who would give papers just enough details to alert the public but not create any panic. That seemed to be the case for this one as well. When the two reporters came in, Kedar asked them for more details.

"Do you know anything more about this attempted robbery?"

"No, sir," one of them replied.

"Do you know who is following up on this at the police station? Who this has been assigned to at the station?"

"No, sir" was the reply yet again.

Manik could sense Kedar's frustration. He quickly thanked them and turned to Manik.

"After we are done with Niranjan, let's pass by this law firm. It may be nothing, but let's ask them what happened," Kedar said.

"What's bothering you, sir?"

"Surinampur is a small place, smaller than even Bolpur. How many lawyers and law firms are there?"

"Probably not that many," Manik replied.

"That's right, and most of them are probably individual lawyers and not representatives of firms based in Calcutta," Kedar said with a distant look on his face.

Manik still had no idea what Kedar was thinking about. Just as they were about to continue, they were interrupted by Anjali. There was a phone call for Kedar that he had to take. Manik quickly gathered all the papers and headed over to his desk. He made sure he had a camera, a tape recorder, and writing pads. Kedar finished his phone call and gestured to Manik to meet him at the stairs. On his way he bumped into Anjali.

"Off to Niranjan's office?" she asked.

"Yes," Manik replied hurriedly.

"Good luck, then."

"Thanks," Manik said as he quickened his pace to reach the stairs.

Kedar was already waiting for him. They went downstairs, and once they reached outside the gates, they decided to hail a cab instead of taking the tram. The black-and-yellow Ambassador taxis were a fixture in Calcutta, especially in and around the offices of the *New Eastern Herald*. There were lots of companies in the area, and that meant a constant stream of visitors from different places. Once they had gotten into the taxi and told the driver where to go, Kedar asked Manik to find out more about Niranjan's family history and background. During the ride to Niranjan's office, Manik could sense that Kedar didn't want to talk too much—there was something on his mind.

Manik looked outside and saw the hustle and bustle of this magnificent city bursting at its seams. Luckily, there were no delays due to strikes or processions. As the taxi made its way through the city, he could see some of its familiar landmarks—Victoria Memorial, the race course, Rabindra Sadan. There seemed to be a constant struggle between the sea of humanity trying to tame this metropolis and the city itself trying to hold its own. Manik often wondered whether the city's inhabitants ever took the time to reflect on its storied past and what it had to offer.

Once they reached his office, they were quickly informed that Niranjan had requested that they meet him at his residence, which was only a short walk away. As they started walking, Manik turned to Kedar.

"Wonder why he wants us to meet him at home, sir."

"Probably because he doesn't want folks at work to think that he is now focusing on his campaign rather than running his business," Kedar said with a smile.

"Do you think he will give us an interview today, or will it just be a meet-and-greet sort of thing?"

"I am not sure. I would have said meet-and-greet, but now that we are meeting him at home, I suspect he may want us to stay a bit longer."

Niranjan's residence was an old building that had been well maintained. The façade hadn't lost any of its grandeur. The iron gates were new, and so was the driveway leading up to the house. On either side were well-manicured lawns with flowerpots and plants. They could see a few gardeners working on them. On one side of the house was a big garage with three cars and chauffeurs whiling away their time under a tree at the edge of a boundary wall. The whole property was surrounded by a wall that seemed to keep the noise and people of the city away from it. It seemed like an oasis in an otherwise busy area.

Once they reached the main entrance, they were let in by a gentleman who they presumed was one of the secretaries. While they waited in what seemed like an outer waiting room or lobby, they marveled at the décor of the house. Everything about it looked expensive and imposing. The large room was full of paintings that looked expensive. Each frame was different and exquisite. The furniture looked as if it had been transported from a different era. The handcrafted tables with their marble tabletops and neatly cushioned chairs and sofas were meant to both impress the guests and make them feel comfortable. Nothing in the room seemed out of place.

A few minutes later, Niranjan showed up. They had seen his picture in the papers. He was a known commodity. He introduced himself, greeted them warmly, and offered them tea and snacks, which Kedar and Manik graciously accepted.

"So, both of you have been assigned to me from your paper?"

"Yes, sir," Kedar replied.

"Please, just call me Niranjan. I asked that we meet me here at home and not at the office. I hope you don't mind?"

"Not at all," Kedar said.

"It's easier to talk at home, without any disturbances or interruptions."

"You have a lovely home," Kedar said.

"Thank you."

The tea and snacks had arrived by then. They waited while they were served. Manik tried to get a sense of Niranjan. He seemed amiable and spoke eloquently. He did not have the trappings or arrogance of someone running a two-thousand-employee business. Or so Manik thought.

"Mr. Sen, if you don't mind my asking, what would you prefer that we do today? We can do a short interview on behalf of the paper, and then, time permitting, we can ask you some questions about your business and philanthropic activities," Kedar said.

"Well, I will make your task easier," Niranjan said. He turned around and called out for his secretary. An elderly gentleman entered the room with a file and some papers. He handed them to Niranjan, who quickly glanced at them and then gave them to Kedar. It was a file full of brochures and papers. Kedar leafed through them quickly and handed them over to Manik, who started looking at them.

"Thank you for this," Kedar said.

"I figured it would make it easier for you," Niranjan said in a serious tone.

"What we would like, though, is something that is not in here. I am assuming most of our readers already know about this. All this information is already in the public domain, and we will certainly use it as needed. Can you tell us, maybe, why you want to stand for election?" Kedar asked.

"Sure. I think I have a lot to offer. One thing that is missing in state politics today is members of the business world. In the assembly, across all parties, we have people from different backgrounds, like union leaders, lawyers, judges, doctors, but not that many people who run businesses," Niranjan replied.

"Fair enough. But why now?" Kedar asked.

"Oh, that's personal. It's mostly because I have reached a point where I have done what I needed to do in business, and I figured I can contribute more in the political arena."

"Why as an independent candidate? Why not join one of the political parties?"

"Well, all of them are corrupt. They have all approached me and offered me a place on the ticket, but I feel none of them really have a platform that I can fully support."

"What would be your main focus if you were to get elected?"

"There were a lot of bills that were stalled in the assembly that didn't get anywhere. I'd like to focus on the ones that matter most to my constituents," Niranjan replied.

Manik had finished looking through the file. Kedar looked at him.

"Manik, do you want to ask any questions?"

"Yes, sir, I do," Manik said as he turned to Niranjan. Niranjan looked at him with a smile.

"Manik Bose, you are the one who wrote the article on the land acquisition, right?"

"Yes, sir," Manik replied.

"Well, that certainly did not go off well. I was happy to see the retraction. And I'm happy to see that your paper takes responsibility and apologizes when they make a mistake," Niranjan said with a smile. Both Kedar and Manik realized that Niranjan was trying to put them on the defensive.

It was Kedar who responded. "We had hoped that the article would be viewed differently. It's a pity because something good could have come out of it if folks had dug a bit deeper. It seems to have rubbed some influential people the wrong way," Kedar said.

"It certainly did. I am happy that Tarun Roy realized that he shouldn't be slinging mud at other businesses," Niranjan said, not at all happy with Kedar's point of view. But he did not want to continue discussing this topic. He needed something positive about him in the papers, and ticking off journalists assigned to cover his campaign was not a good start. He was much smarter than that. He immediately turned to Manik.

"So, Manik, what is that you wanted to ask?"

"Coming back to what you were saying earlier, sir, some of the bills that are stalled in the assembly have to do with land acquisition in and around Calcutta. Will you be trying to get those passed?"

"Those and others too. I think businesses, builders, and landlords are viewed with suspicion in this city. They need not be. They have an important role to play and can be part of the solution. It shouldn't be us versus them," Niranjan said.

"What about the one about charitable trusts? It seems that some folks are skeptical of a bill that makes donations to trusts tax-free for donors and another one that allows a business to be converted to a trust for tax purposes. There is some argument to be made that if certain businesses are turned into trusts, then the government will lose a lot of tax revenue, and the trust can then earn income that will be taxed at a much lower rate. Given that most of these trusts are owned and run by the rich and influential, it would almost seem that it benefits only a few," Manik said. He could sense Niranjan's discomfort but admired his calm demeanor and his response.

"It seems you have done your homework, Manik. Yes, that's one side of the story. The other side of the story is that this would mean much more in terms of charitable donations, and that would benefit everyone. We are talking about schools, clinics, hospitals. They will benefit everyone," Niranjan replied.

"But they will be businesses being run under the guise of a trust?" Manik pressed further.

"Well, we can certainly put some boundaries around that to make the bill better," Niranjan said, trying not to sound too defensive.

Before they could continue their conversation any further, Niranjan's secretary entered the room and whispered something in his ear. Niranjan turned to Kedar and Manik.

"I am sorry, gentlemen. It seems I have been summoned to an important meeting. It was really nice talking to both of you, and I am sure that we will speak again in the coming weeks."

"Sure, sir," Manik replied as they all got up.

"Please keep in mind that I am not a politician. My responses may not always be measured, but I assure you that they will always be honest," Niranjan said with a smile.

"I appreciate your time, Mr. Sen," Kedar said.

They all shook hands. Niranjan turned to his secretary and asked him to give Manik and Kedar a copy of his campaign schedule. He politely thanked them again and left the room. Manik and Kedar left as well.

Once they were back on the street, Kedar looked at Manik.

"So, what did you think?"

"He is already a politician."

"Yes. He seems like a wily character. He will fit right in with all the others that we have running this place," Kedar said, and Manik nodded.

"I think he is in it for himself," Manik continued.

"Yes. But so are many others. I liked your questions, by the way. It's good to see that you are not intimidated. He brought up your and Harish's article on purpose. He wanted to put us on the defensive, and when that didn't work, he immediately went back to being his charming self. Politicians and journalists need one another, and he knows that."

"Yes, sir. What do we write about him?"

"Let's talk about that when we are back at the office," Kedar said as they reached the crossing of the main avenue across from Niranjan's house. He looked up and down the street, then brought out a piece of paper and handed it to Manik. It was the address of the law firm that had been broken into.

"Are we heading there, sir?" Manik said, pointing to the address.

"Yes," Kedar replied.

"I think it may be easier to just walk, sir. We can be there in twenty minutes. If we take a taxi or the tram, we will be stuck in traffic."

Kedar knew Manik was right. Every which way they looked, the roads were packed with cars. They decided to walk the distance, and it felt good to do that on a sunny winter afternoon. Once they reached the building, they were somewhat disappointed. It was a nice office building, but there was police tape all around the ground floor. They spoke to the guards in front of the gate leading up to the building and were informed that they could only visit the next day. The police had cordoned off the area for investigation into the attempted robbery, and no one was being allowed in the building until the next morning. Upon questioning the guards, they found out that there were two businesses on the same floor that had been broken into. One was the law office, and the other one was a company that rented out office supplies. The guards weren't sure what had been taken. They didn't want to share any more details. Manik and Kedar realized it was probably because they could get into trouble if their bosses knew they were talking to reporters about an ongoing police investigation.

Manik and Kedar decided to ask some of the street vendors and stall owners if they had seen or heard anything about the robbery. They hadn't. It seemed it had occurred late at night, when all the establishments in and around the building were already closed. Before going back to the office, Kedar and Manik decided to eat something in one of the small restaurants. After they sat down and ordered, Kedar looked at Manik and pointed in the direction of all the surrounding stores.

"Take a look around, Manik. If robbers wanted to hit something, there are so many other targets. We walked past at least three jewelry stores and some fancy apparel stores, all within a few yards of the building and arguably easier to get in and out of."

"Yes, sir."

"Why would they target a building that has nothing of tangible value, not to mention two offices on the third floor of the building, and nothing else?"

"It seems they were looking for something specific," said Manik.

"Absolutely," Kedar replied.

"No ordinary thieves, then?"

"They could be. But they were definitely looking for a specific item. Given that it's a law office, I am guessing some papers, files, or records that may be important to a case."

"That makes sense, sir," Manik said.

The food arrived, and they realized that they were really hungry as they dived right into their sumptuous samosas and sweets.

"Did you always want to do this?"

"What, sir?"

"Be a reporter. Was that your first choice? If you had all the money in the world, is that what you would do?"

"No, sir. I wanted to be a music director."

"You write music?"

"Yes, sir."

"What kind?"

"Background music, some songs."

"You didn't pursue that?"

"Difficult to make money doing that, sir."

"Yes, that's right. But I hope you keep at it. One of these days, you should come over. I have a piano, and we can try out your tunes," Kedar said with a smile.

"You play, sir?"

"Yes. More like a hobby. Did you ever try sending your tunes to anyone?"

"I did, sir. I sent my compositions to many places in Bombay and Calcutta. No one responded."

"*Yet.* No one responded *yet*. Don't lose heart."

"The film and art world works on connections. They don't usually entertain unknown talents unless they are recommended by someone."

"True, but you should pursue this regardless, for yourself. Music is good for the soul. You write music. That's great. Most people just listen to music composed by others and sing other people's songs."

"It's funny you say that, sir. My professor said the exact same thing," Manik said.

"You mean I have a career in teaching?" Kedar joked.

"Maybe," Manik replied with a smile.

Once they finished, they decided to walk back toward Niranjan's house and then take the tram back to the office. They were not in a hurry. On the ride back, Manik started to think about the interview with Niranjan. He was wondering what sort of article they could possibly start off with. The visit to the law office had been a waste of time, Manik thought.

Once they reached the office, Kedar and Manik headed to their desks. Manik decided to go over some of the notes he had taken during the interview and type them up. It was nearly five o'clock. He could hear Anjali's phone ringing and saw her running toward her desk from the far end of the hall to pick it up. He could sense that she could not hear who was on the other end of the line. After a few seconds, she looked straight at Manik from her desk and frantically waved at him to come over. The phone call was for him.

Manik quickly went over, and she handed him the receiver. He picked it up. It was the professor calling from Surinampur.

"Hello, sir; can you hear me?" Manik asked.

"Yes, Manik," the professor replied.

"Is everything all right?"

"Yes, couldn't be better. I am calling from a public pay phone, and the connection is really bad, so it may be hard to talk."

"Yes, sir—your voice is rather soft," Manik said, raising his voice to make sure the professor could hear him properly. He could sense that the professor was also speaking at the top of his voice, and from his tone, he sounded excited.

"Manik, I found out what was in the box that went missing. I met the estate lawyer, and although he didn't have a copy of what had been sent, he gave me a list of the papers that were in there."

"What was in there?"

"It's original land records, deeds, and covenants. It is much bigger than we thought. I have some other papers, too, that are important. We need to get this to the police right away. A lot of people's fortunes are at stake," the professor said.

Manik was still having trouble getting the rest of the details that the professor was reciting. There was a lot of static on the line, along with the background noise that was making it difficult to hear.

"Professor, can you please slow down and repeat what you just said?" Manik asked.

He realized that the professor was hardly able to hear him either. After a few fervent hellos, the professor finally spoke as loud as he could.

"Manik, I can't talk more. There are a lot of people waiting in line at the booth. It is an open booth, and there is a lot of noise."

"Yes, sir, I can hear that."

"I need to catch my train in a few hours. I will call you tomorrow morning and will bring the list to you. We need to inform the archives and the police of what's missing, and then they will start taking this seriously."

"Yes, sir," Manik said.

"Will you be in the office tomorrow?"

"Yes, sir. What is the name of the lawyer that you visited—what is the name of the office?" Manik asked.

Again, he could hardly hear what the professor's response was.

"Office…near the station…Pinaki…Associates" was all that Manik heard from the professor.

So, it was the law firm that we visited earlier in the day, the one that was broken into. Manik couldn't get the professor to confirm.

After a few more failed attempts at continuing their conversation, they finally gave up. When Manik hung up, he realized that the professor must have been excited at finding out something more than he had hoped for, or he wouldn't have called. He could have just waited until the next day. Manik was glad that he had called and could sense that this story was going to be bigger than what he had hoped for. He looked around to see if Kedar was still in the office. His desk was empty, and Anjali told him that he had left for the day. He had come by to see Manik before he left, but he saw that he was on the phone and decided to leave. Anjali was on her way out as well.

"Was that the professor?" Anjali asked.

"Yes," Manik said.

"He sounded excited."

"He was. But I couldn't hear him properly."

"You must tell me all about it tomorrow. I have to leave right away. I am meeting a friend from out of town," Anjali said and waved goodbye.

Manik went back to his desk, but he couldn't concentrate on typing up his notes anymore. He was also tired. He decided to see if Subodh or Avik were around and planned to ask them if they wanted to go back home. He headed over to Subodh's desk. He saw Harish, Arun, and Rajan there talking about the upcoming election. There was some sort of debate going on between them as to which party would be best for Calcutta. It was Arun who saw Manik first and realized that he must be looking for Subodh.

"Hi, Manik. Are you looking for Subodh?"

"Yes, sir."

"I sent him on an errand. It will take him another hour."

"Ok. Thanks. I will leave, then."

Harish and Rajan looked over and pointed toward his desk.

"Were you on the phone with Niranjan? How did it go with him?" Harish asked.

"We met him earlier today. It went well for a first meeting, I would say. That wasn't him on the phone. It was my professor from Surinampur."

"Ah, yes. Swaroop told us about this story—the missing box, right?" Arun asked.

"Yes, sir."

"All good?" Harish asked.

"Yes, sir. We will see him tomorrow. He found out something important, and it seemed big. I couldn't hear him well, but it apparently has to do with some original land records and covenants. He is bringing back the details with him," Manik said.

"Well, I must be off as well," Harish said.

"Me too," Rajan said with a smile and started walking toward the stairs.

"Don't worry, Manik. If Subodh shows up, I will let him know that you have left for the day," Arun said.

"Thank you, sir."

Manik walked back to his desk, put the papers back in his cabinet, removed the page from the typewriter that he had started working on, then picked up his bag and headed toward the stairs. He could see a lot of people were leaving at the same time. The familiar winter mist had descended upon the city. He noticed a lot of pedestrians on the sidewalk with tired faces.

Some were listening to the little transistors that were becoming popular. The box-sized radios were easy to hold, and people would glue them to their ears to hear the news or music at this time of the evening. The walk made him feel better but also tired. He made himself some sandwiches, tried reading a book, and then gave up and turned in for the night.

7

Providence

When Manik arrived the next morning, he decided to continue typing the notes from the interview with Niranjan. He kept glancing at Anjali's desk to see if her phone was going to ring. That was the number that the professor had been given. Every now and then he also looked toward Kedar's desk. He wanted to let him know about the conversation with the professor. It took another hour before both Anjali and Kedar showed up, within minutes of each other. He walked over to them and told them about his conversation with the professor.

"It looks like there may be something to it," Kedar said.

"Yes, sir, it seems like it. He said he would call me and come over today."

"That sounds great. Did he give you a time?"

"No, sir."

"All right, then, let's grab a coffee and start working on the Niranjan interview, and when he calls, we will see what the good professor has to say."

"Don't worry, Manik. I will be at my desk all morning, and I will come get you as soon as he calls," Anjali said.

"Thank you, Anjali" Manik replied.

Manik headed over the Kedar's desk, and they started discussing what to write about their interview with Niranjan. They spent the next two hours going over all the background material they had, as well as the information they had received the day before from Niranjan's secretary.

"It will be our first piece on him. Let's focus on his background and what he told us about why he is standing for election as an independent candidate," Kedar said.

Manik nodded. He handed his notes and the material on his businesses to Kedar.

"Do we talk about the fact that other parties have courted him, sir?"

"Sure. Why not? I think he will be happy we printed that. It shows the readers that he is important," Kedar said with a smile.

"What about his charitable trusts and philanthropic activities?" Manik asked.

"Let's leave that out for now. In any case, most readers are probably aware of them. Plus, we want him coming back to us asking us to print more on his altruism. That way we can ask him even more questions."

"Yes, sir."

Every now and then, Manik would glance over to Anjali's desk to see if she was still there, as he was still wondering whether the professor had called. He saw her on the phone a couple of times, but she didn't come to get him. That gave Kedar and Manik ample time to put together a first draft of what they wanted to publish. It was almost noon. Manik went to his desk to start typing it up. Normally he would type up the first draft, and then a senior journalist, in this case Kedar, would go over it. Usually it took a few iterations before any article could be finalized. Then it would be submitted to Swaroop for his final approval. Usually Swaroop's blessing was a formality, but after what had happened with Harish's article and retraction, he was scrutinizing things a bit more. It took another hour for Manik to type up an error-free first draft. Once he finished, he walked to Kedar's desk. He wasn't there. He left it at his desk and then headed over to Anjali's desk. She was busy working on her own piece.

"No call from the professor yet?" Manik asked.

"No, nothing yet," Anjali replied, looking up.

"Not sure why it's taking him so long. He was excited yesterday to share what he had learned," Manik said thoughtfully.

"Why don't you call him? You have his number, don't you?"

"Yes. Let me get it from my desk," Manik said as he walked over to get his notebook. He then went to Anjali's desk; she had already turned the phone toward him and pointed at the chair across her desk.

"All yours," she said.

"Thank you," Manik said as he sat down and started dialing the number.

The line at the other end went on ringing. No one picked up the phone. *The professor must be out*, Manik thought. He hung up and tried again, with the same outcome.

"No luck?" Anjali asked.

"Nope," Manik replied.

"Well, maybe he is busy or running errands. Let's go for lunch, and we will call him again when we come back. That will give us an hour or so."

"Sure. Sounds good."

They headed downstairs. The cafeteria was full. It was lunchtime, after all. They took their trays and made their way outside and settled into one of the long benches in the courtyard. They could see some familiar faces. Arun, Harish, Rajan, and some of the senior staff were on one side of the courtyard, around a big table. One table over, they saw Avik and Subodh with some other junior reporters. They waved at Manik and Anjali and quickly came over to their table. Both of them were excited to tell Anjali and Manik about their election assignments. Avik was in his element and gave them a detailed account of his experience in the party office he had visited. Apparently, there was an argument between some of the party workers that almost came to blows, and the reporters had to step in to stop things from escalating. It was comical, and Avik's colorful language while describing the events made it sound even funnier. The longer-than-usual lunch lasted almost an hour and a half. Manik, Avik, and Subodh decided to stay back in the courtyard and walked over to the end of the garden to smoke, while Anjali returned to her desk.

After Anjali left, and as they were enjoying their cigarettes, Avik turned to Manik. "So, what's going on with Anjali?"

"Nothing's going on. Now stop it, Avik," Manik said, somewhat annoyed.

"How was the meeting with Niranjan?" Subodh asked.

"It went off fine, I think. We got his itinerary, and it looks quite busy. Now we have to follow him around," Manik said.

"Yeah, that's the same for all of us." Subodh sighed.

Once they finished, Manik went to Kedar's desk to make sure he had seen the first draft of the interview with Niranjan.

"Any news from the professor?" Kedar asked.

"No, sir," Manik replied.

"Strange, isn't it? Given what you said this morning, I'd have thought he would have called by now."

"Yes, sir."

"Call him, and then we will talk about this," Kedar said, pointing to a file that looked like it was related to the article on illegal betting at the racetracks.

Manik got his notebook, then headed over to Anjali's desk and called the professor's number. There was no answer. He hung up, gave it a minute, and tried again. This time, after a few rings that seemed like an eternity, someone picked up. It was not the professor. Manik was surprised.

"Hello, my name is Manik Bose. Is this Professor Prafulla's residence?" Manik asked, wanting to be sure that he had indeed dialed the right number.

"Yes, it is," said a somber voice.

"I am one of his ex-students. Can I talk to the professor, please?"

"The professor's dead. He died in an accident last night while walking home," the gentleman on the other end of the phone said.

Manik could hardly speak; he was in a state of shock. Kedar and Anjali had been looking at him from afar, and based on Manik's reaction, they knew something was wrong. They saw Manik's face turn white as the receiver fell from his hand, and he slumped into the chair across from Anjali's desk. Kedar and Anjali quickly walked over to him.

"Manik, what happened?" Kedar asked.

"It's the professor, sir. He died in an accident last night while he was walking home," Manik said, trying to hold back his tears.

Kedar had meanwhile picked up the phone to see if the gentleman was still on the other end of the line. He had hung up. After putting the receiver back, Kedar turned to Manik.

"I am so sorry, Manik. Let's go over to the professor's house."

"Yes, sir."

When they reached the professor's residence, they found a number of people about. Manik recognized some of them as ex-students from the college. Kedar and Anjali looked around to see if they could find someone to talk to, to get more details on what had happened. They saw an elderly gentleman by the phone. Manik guessed he was the one he had spoken to earlier. They walked up to him and introduced themselves.

"My name is Utpal. I am Prafulla's cousin," he said.

"I am so sorry to hear about the professor," Kedar said.

"It was all so sudden," Utpal responded. There were at least ten people in the room, all looking sullen and in a state of shock—from their appearance and age, it was clear most were either extended family or friends, whereas the people standing outside the house were mostly ex-students.

"Is he still in the hospital?"

"Yes. It seems it was a hit-and-run traffic accident. They will be doing a postmortem and then release his body for the last rites," Utpal said.

"When did it happen?" Manik asked.

"I don't have any more details." He shook his head. "You must be Manik. I am the one who spoke to you earlier. Are you the one that writes music?" Utpal asked.

"Yes."

"Oh. The professor spoke about you a lot. He liked you. This is all very sad. We are expecting Sucheta to be here by tomorrow morning. We informed her as soon as we came to know."

"When will the cremation take place?"

"Tomorrow, once the hospital has finished with the postmortem. The police have assured us that they won't delay things further," Utpal said.

"The police?" Anjali asked.

"It was a hit-and-run. The hospital had to inform the police," Kedar said.

"How did you come to know?" Manik asked Utpal.

"It was the police who called me from the hospital early in the morning. The professor was carrying his phonebook with him. They started calling the numbers one by one. I got the call around four a.m. and rushed to the hospital. I called Sucheta after that," Utpal said; they could see he was tearing up.

"He was a good, caring man. I will miss him a lot," Manik said, tears in his eyes.

Kedar put his arms around Manik's shoulders, and Anjali gave him an affectionate hug. They could see Manik was deeply affected by what had happened. They spoke politely to a few more people. Manik had suddenly become very quiet. They saw some people coming in and out of the house. Manik recognized some of his classmates from college. He spoke to them briefly. After spending another thirty minutes at the professor's house, they decided to leave.

Once they were back on the street, Kedar looked at Manik.

"Manik, if you want to take some time off, I am fine with that. I will make sure it's fine with Swaroop as well."

"No, sir. I want to know what happened," Manik said in a low voice.

"Fair enough. Let's go over to the hospital and see if we can get more details," Kedar said.

Once they reached the hospital, they headed over to the ER reception and asked about the professor. They were immediately met by a resident.

"Are you a member of the family?" the doctor asked.

"No, sir. I am one of his ex-students," Manik said.

"I must ask you to please go over to the waiting area in the main lobby. His nephew is there making arrangements, and you may want to speak with him," the doctor said.

"Sure," Manik said, and they went to convene with the professor's family and friends. They could see a policeman there as well. Kedar walked up to him and introduced himself.

"It looks like a hit-and-run," the officer said.

"Are you in charge of this?" Kedar asked.

"Not really. I am here to collect the report, and then I have to wait for my boss's approval to release the body. It shouldn't take long," the officer replied.

"Which police station will the report be sent to?"

"Chowringee. That's where all the hit-and-runs go. You must contact them directly. I am sorry; I cannot share any more details with you," the officer added.

"Thank you," Kedar said.

They walked over to the professor's nephew, offered their condolences, and spoke to him for a few minutes. He did not have any more details. All he knew was that the professor had returned on the late-night train from Surinampur. He had taken a bus from the station to the crossing, a few blocks away from his residence. As he was walking, a car hit him and fled. It happened late at night. He wasn't sure if there were any witnesses. The family's priority was to perform the last rites. They were waiting for the professor's daughter, Sucheta, to arrive, and arrangements were being made to complete everything the following day. After a few minutes, Kedar made a quick call from the hospital pay phone to Rudra Pratap Singh, his contact at the Chowringee police station, to make sure he was there, and then they left to go meet with him.

Once they reached the station, they waited for a few minutes and then were ushered into Singh's office. It was surprisingly clean compared to the rest of the station. The desks they had walked past were littered with papers and files. By contrast Rudra Pratap's office and desk was clean and tidy. He was expecting them and immediately got up and asked them to take a seat. He offered them some tea, and as they settled in, Rudra Pratap spoke first.

"Is this the same professor we talked about last week, in relation to the missing papers?"

"Yes," Kedar replied.

"First of all, let me say that I am very sorry to hear what happened to the professor. I can't imagine what the family must be going through. Please do offer them my condolences."

"Thank you, RP," Kedar said.

"What is that you want to talk about?" Rudra Pratap asked.

"The professor uncovered something during his trip to Surinampur. He was supposed to let us know about it earlier today. But he didn't. Then we came to know of his passing. It seems rather strange that this happened the day he was supposed to share this information with us. Don't you think?" Kedar asked.

Rudra Pratap's face suddenly became serious. They could see he was lost in thought, and after a few seconds, he looked at Kedar again and asked, "What exactly had he uncovered during his trip?"

"We don't know, RP. The last conversation he had was with Manik, and I will let Manik give you all the details," Kedar said, turning to Manik.

Manik gave him the details of the conversation he had had with the professor. Rudra Pratap listened to it carefully without interrupting; his secretary, sitting behind them, was taking notes.

"He had a list and some papers, you say, that he got from the estate lawyer?" Rudra Pratap asked Manik.

"Yes, sir."

Rudra Pratap turned to his secretary and instructed him to call the hospital right away and let the constables know that the professor's belongings should not be touched or handed over to the family until the police had a chance to look through them.

Once the secretary left to make the call, Kedar looked at Manik.

"Who else knew about the professor's trip to Surinampur?"

"A few folks at our office. Asutosh and Vinod at the state archives. I am not sure if he had spoken to anyone else," Manik said.

"Whom was he meeting there?"

"The estate lawyer for the recently deceased ex-ruler of Surinampur. I don't know the name, sir," Manik replied.

"It shouldn't be too difficult to figure that out. Surinampur is a small place. We will make some inquiries," Rudra Pratap said.

"Thank you, RP," Kedar said.

"Is there anything that you would like to add?" Rudra Pratap asked, looking at all three of them.

"I think the professor's death was not a coincidence. He was killed," Manik said in a low voice.

"We will certainly investigate that, Manik. In any case, now this involves the death of someone, not just a box of missing papers that no one knew anything about," Rudra Pratap said.

"They are connected, sir," Manik said in a pleading voice.

"Yes, they might be, and rest assured we will make some inquiries at the state archives as well. I will also contact my counterpart in Surinampur to follow up there. Don't worry—if there is a connection, we will find it," Rudra Pratap said in an understanding voice.

"There was one other thing, RP," Kedar said. "There was a break-in at one of the law offices, Pinaki Sett and Associates."

"Yes. I am aware of that. Strange case, that one. It seems the robbers were only interested in something on the third floor. They messed up a lot papers and files, but it seems before they could continue, the guards chased them away, and they didn't leave with anything. They have beefed up security in and around the building now," Rudra Pratap said, somewhat surprised that Kedar was asking about this.

"When you make your inquiries about the estate's lawyer—you know, the one with the office near the station—can you please let us know if it's the same law firm that the professor visited in Surinampur?" Kedar asked.

"You think there is a connection?"

"There could be. It's a long shot, but maybe worth looking into," Kedar said.

"Of course. Anything else?"

"Who owns the building that had the office that was broken into?"

"Oh, that we know. No harm in sharing that with you. It's public knowledge. It's owned by NS and Associates. It's a firm owned by Niranjan Sen's family. They own the building and have rented it out to different firms," Rudra Pratap said.

Both Kedar's and Manik's ears perked up on hearing Niranjan's name. It wasn't surprising, though. The family did own a lot of commercial real estate in the area.

"I think we have taken up enough of your time, RP. Thank you for meeting with us," Kedar said.

"No, thank you. You have given us something to go on. I am sorry about the professor," Rudra Pratap said as they all got up.

Before leaving the room, Kedar turned to Rudra Pratap.

"I will be making a trip to Surinampur tomorrow. I will call you later to get the name of the lawyer, RP," Kedar said.

"Sure, but no meddling with the police investigation. Is that understood?"

"Absolutely," Kedar replied with a nod and a smile.

They left the police station and headed back to the *New Eastern Herald*. Kedar was happy that Rudra

Pratap was conducting the investigation. He knew he was thorough and meticulous. On the way back, Kedar again offered Manik a few days off. He refused. Once they were back at their desks, Manik approached Kedar.

"I want to go to Surinampur with you, sir."

"Are you sure? Don't you want to be here for the professor's last rites? I am sure you want to meet with his daughter, Sucheta."

"Yes, I do, and I will. But I also want to get to the bottom of this. I want to know what happened. I can't rest until I do. I feel there's a connection with his death and the missing papers. He must have uncovered something big and someone found out and that cost him his life," Manik said with his voice suddenly becoming angry and sad.

"I understand, Manik, but that can wait, and we have to let the police do their job. I just want to go and find out for myself what the lawyer told the professor and if there's anything more he can add. I can certainly let you know once I am back," Kedar said.

"No, sir. It cannot wait. If you don't take me with you, then I will take a few days off and go there myself tomorrow, on my own. I need to be part of this, and I need to find out," Manik said in a pleading voice.

"All right, Manik. Let's head upstairs and get approval from Swaroop. It should not be a problem now, given what has happened and what we know," Kedar said.

Once they reached Swaroop's office, they picked up the approval forms from Rajan. As they filled them out, they could see through the glass windows that Swaroop was in a meeting with Arun and Harish.

"They are going to be there for a while. If you want to get this approved, you better go in and get him," Rajan told Kedar and Manik.

"Sure, Rajan," Kedar replied, and he walked into Swaroop's office with Manik and Rajan following him.

Swaroop stopped his conversation with Harish and Arun and looked at them.

"I am sorry to interrupt, gentlemen. But, Swaroop, can you please approve this? Manik and I want to go to Surinampur tomorrow morning," Kedar said. He quickly told them what had happened to the professor, about their visit to the hospital and police station. Swaroop immediately agreed, quickly signed the travel approval forms and handed them back to Kedar.

"When are you leaving?" Swaroop asked.

"Tomorrow morning. First train out. We will be back tomorrow evening," Kedar said.

"I am sorry to hear about the professor. Please offer my condolences to his family," Swaroop said.

Swaroop went back to his discussion with Harish and Arun. Kedar and Manik left the approvals with Rajan and headed back to their floor. It was already late in the evening, and the office was practically empty, with only a few people at their desks typing up their reports. Once they reached their desks, Kedar picked up a few things and, on his way out, came by Manik's desk.

"I will pick you up tomorrow morning around six. It's easier that way—we won't have to find each other at the railway station."

"Yes, sir. Thank you."

"I know it will be difficult. But please try to get some rest. We have a long day ahead of us tomorrow. Please eat properly," Kedar said affectionately.

"Yes, sir," Manik replied in a calm voice.

Manik left after a few minutes, walking slowly back to his apartment building through the mist that had engulfed the city. He didn't notice or feel any of it. The events of the day were still playing out in his head, and although he was exhausted, he was having a hard time trying to sleep. He looked around his empty apartment, searching for things to do. But there wasn't much that needed tending. He picked up a book from the pile in the corner and tried to read. He couldn't concentrate. He resisted the urge to smoke and finally decided to go to bed. He couldn't sleep properly.

He had set two alarm clocks just to be absolutely sure. He didn't need either of them. He was already tossing and turning in bed well before the alarms rang. He got ready and headed downstairs to wait at the gates of the building for Kedar to pick him up. There were only a few people on the road at this early hour. He could see the occasional cars and some taxis passing by. A few cars were parked on the street, but other than that, the usually busy street looked empty. At around six, he saw a taxi slowly approaching the gates of the building. Kedar was in the back seat. Manik quickly opened the door and got in beside him.

"Good morning, sir."

"Good morning, Manik."

The taxi ride to Howrah station was a good forty minutes. Even though there was very little traffic this early in the morning, they had to cross a large swath of the city to get to the station. Manik marveled at the sights of the city this early in the morning. The sun was trying to pierce the heavy fog. Visibility was good enough for him to see the city landmarks. As the car made its way in the direction of the station, he could see Howrah Bridge from afar. It was the most recognizable landmark in the city. The sight of the bridge across the Hooghly River was a fixture in his head associated with the many journeys that had started and ended in the city. He had always marveled at its architecture and grandeur. But today his mind was still preoccupied with the events of the previous day.

Kedar was also not in a talkative mood. He stayed mostly quiet till they reached the station. Once he had paid the taxi driver, they made their way to the ticket counter. They could see that the station was slowly becoming crowded. A few trains had already arrived early in the morning. Manik knew that Sucheta would be on one of them arriving from Bombay. There was no chance whatsoever of bumping into her at the station with so many people and trains arriving and leaving from different platforms. He still glanced in every direction to see if he could spot her.

Once they got their tickets, they made their way to the platform. They had to be quick. Their train was leaving in fifteen minutes, and they wanted to make sure that they made it on time. Luckily, the morning trains were usually full of people coming into the city for work and very few who were actually leaving the city.

Once they found their platform and train, they could see that there were still a few empty seats in all the carriages. They made their way into their compartment, and once seated, they looked around for a tea vendor. Just before the train left, they managed to get some tea and biscuits and were on their way to Surinampur.

The ride to Surinampur would take around two and half hours, with two stops in between. It was a slow-moving regional train rather than one of the fast-express ones that ran between cities. But it was still the quickest way to get there. They wouldn't have to contend with traffic on the roads, the horrendously unreliable bus schedules, or any interruptions on the route due to strikes or processions. Usually train journeys were more enjoyable, even if not always punctual.

Manik noticed that Kedar had been somewhat distracted since he had gotten on the train. He was constantly looking for something in his pockets, glancing up and down the carriage.

"Do you want some more tea, sir?"

"No, thank you," Kedar replied with a smile.

"Any news from Mr. Rudra Pratap on the estate lawyer, sir? I have made a list of all the lawyers in Surinampur from the office directory. There are fourteen of them working at six addresses. We can start with the ones closest to the station. That's what the professor told me. Given that it is a small place, we can visit all of them. But I think if we head to the Surinampur ex-ruler's residence first, there could be someone there who could just tell us," Manik said without giving Kedar a chance to speak. He could see that Kedar wanted to stop him, but he just barreled through.

"No need, Manik. I spoke to RP. He gave me the name and address of the estate lawyer. His office is indeed close to the station," Kedar said.

"OK. That will save us some time. Who is it, sir?"

Kedar handed Manik a paper from his file. The lawyer's name was Soumen Mitra, and he worked for Pinaki Sett and Associates. Manik immediately made the connection, and before he could speak, Kedar looked at him and nodded.

"Yes, the same law firm that had the break-in," Kedar said.

"So, you were right, sir. There is a connection, then?"

"I don't believe in that many coincidences. There's another thing, Manik," Kedar said as he leaned over to get closer.

"What is it, sir?"

"You told me that the professor had a list and some papers that he was bringing back, that he wanted to show us. Right?"

"Yes, sir."

"Are you sure?"

"I am certain, sir. I have played out the conversation many times in my head."

"RP told me—off the record, of course—that they didn't find any such list or papers on the professor. They found a phone diary, a notebook, a railway timetable, his glasses, a writing pad, and a newspaper. Nothing else," Kedar said and paused. He could see Manik's expression suddenly change. He looked out the window. The train had picked up speed and was slowly winding its way outside Calcutta. He could see the city fading farther and farther away.

"He was murdered. This was no random accident or hit-and-run," Manik said in a solemn tone.

"Yes. It seems that way, Manik. RP assured me that they will now give this the priority it deserves. It's no longer a missing box from the archives. It is a murder investigation."

"Yes, sir."

They stayed quiet for a few minutes. Kedar could see Manik was lost in thought and somewhat disturbed by what he had just heard.

"Manik, are you all right?"

"Not really, sir."

"I understand all this is disturbing, but we will get to the bottom of this, I assure you."

"You seem to have a lot of confidence in the police," Manik said, sounding less certain.

"Police, no. But Rudra Pratap, yes. I have known him for a long time. We have helped each other in the past, and I have seen him work. I am confident that he will investigate this seriously," Kedar said.

"I wish the professor hadn't gotten involved in this," Manik said, his voice suddenly becoming emotional.

"I understand, Manik. You and the professor were close, and this is a difficult time for you. I hope you do consider my suggestion of taking some time off. Maybe visit your folks in Bolpur."

"No, that's fine, sir," Manik replied, regaining his composure.

Manik sat back and looked out of the window to see the bright sun now glaring on the fields with its full force. Kedar brought out a newspaper and started reading. Manik thought about his last trip to Bolpur to visit his family. He came from a large joint family. As was the case with most large families, things were complicated. There were expectations and, inevitably, disappointments.

During his last visit, he had had a huge argument with his father and elder brother. They had expected him to come home and help with the family business, which wasn't doing well at all. His family ran two small convenience stores, and this was just not enough for the demands of a large and growing family. He did send money back home to support them financially, but he did not want to go back and live with them. He really didn't see himself living there, and staying close to family meant all sorts of unsolicited advice and intrusions. He had had enough of that growing up and certainly didn't want to move back, having stayed in Calcutta on his own for some time. He knew he would find it difficult to adjust, and his family was too steeped in traditions to offer him any chance of freedom or happiness. He had not talked about this with anyone in any great detail. Subodh and Avik had sensed some of it during their many conversations. He had confided in Sucheta. But she wasn't living in Calcutta anymore.

He sensed that the train was slowing down. It was coming to its first scheduled stop. Once it stopped, he could see people on the platform jostling to get in and out of the train. Kedar left momentarily to get some more tea and returned with some sandwiches. He still seemed a bit fidgety and was looking around. Manik wondered why that was but didn't ask him.

"Nice day for a train journey, don't you think, Manik?" Kedar said.

"Yes, sir."

"Traveled a lot?"

"Not as much as I would like."

"None of us have. The more you travel, the more you realize that there's so much more to see."

"Very true, sir."

The train had started making its way to its next destination. They quickly devoured their sandwiches and tea. Kedar went back to his newspaper, and Manik decided to bring out a book that he had purchased from an old record store that sold used books on music. It was a book with sheet music and some history behind each of the pieces. He started reading it. It took his mind off everything else. He looked out of the window briefly when the train stopped again and then went back to his book. Kedar had now rested his head against the back of his seat, with the folded newspaper as a makeshift headrest.

The next stop was Surinampur. Kedar got up just before the train was arriving at the station. Neither Manik nor Kedar had much with them. They were carrying two small saddlebags that they could easily hang on their shoulders. Every reporter had been given one by the paper, and they found them quite convenient. They were light, easy to carry, and spacious enough to hold a few files and books.

Once they got off the train at Surinampur, the contrast with Calcutta was quite stark. The station itself was small. It had only two platforms. The main building was one big hall that contained all functions of the station. They quickly made their way out of the gates and asked a rickshaw driver for directions to the lawyer's address. He told them it was a fifteen-minute walk or a five-minute rickshaw ride. The decided to take the rickshaw.

Surinampur was a small town and looked like one as well. Manik had picked up a map in the office, and from what he could see, the town had three main roads and plenty of narrow lanes crisscrossing them. The town was well spread out. Once they left the station, they could see that the streets and lanes were not that congested. There were many old buildings, and most of them were not well maintained. There was a lot of greenery all around. Although the streets and lanes were small and narrow, they looked big, as there were very few cars or people. The small town had an old-world charm, and as they rode past some of the buildings, they saw that the main doors of many of them were just open, and they actually heard music emanating from some of them. It reminded Manik of his hometown. Surinampur was much older. They saw the remnants of an old run-down government building with a board in front informing readers that it was going to be the site of a new hotel. The people walking on the sidewalks seemed to have all the time in the world. The contrast in pace of life between Calcutta and Surinampur was striking. The rickshaw driver told them that this was the old part of town. The newer part was farther away from the station and had modern buildings, some small hotels, new shops, and a few offices. Once they reached the address, they could see that it was a building with offices on the ground floor and apartments on the other floors.

They saw a rickety board with "Pinaki Sett and Associates, Law Firm" written on it and an arrow pointing to the door. They knocked and went inside. They entered a big hall with a small number of desks and cabinets. There were a few people working on typewriters, and on the far side, they could see two large offices through big glass windows. They figured that those must be the ones for the lawyers, while the other ones belonged to the secretaries and clerks. One of the secretaries asked them to wait. He knocked on one of the rooms, and a gentleman came out to meet them. Kedar and Manik introduced themselves.

"Good morning. My name is Soumen Mitra. I have been expecting you. Please come inside," he said as he led Manik and Kedar into his office. He instructed the secretary to bring some tea, and when the secretary left the room, he closed the door behind him.

Soumen asked them to sit on the sofa, and he sat on a chair across from them; a coffee table was in between.

"Mr. Mitra, I am sure you have heard about professor Prafulla," Kedar said.

"Yes. And oh, please, call me Soumen. I am very sorry to hear about the professor's accident. I got a call this morning from Mr. Rudra Pratap Singh, the police officer in Calcutta investigating the hit-and-run. He wants to rule out any foul play. I am not sure, but I got the impression from my conversation with him that it may have been premeditated or connected to the professor's visit to Surinampur. He told me about your visit."

"We are here because of what the professor told us. He had come to meet you regarding some papers that went missing from the state archives—papers that I believe were sent from this office?"

"Not quite. Some boxes were sent directly from the ruler's mansion. Most of them were sent from this office. I reviewed most of them. The one in question should have been sent to our office in Calcutta. The copies were kept in another box that should have been sent to the archives. Somehow they got switched," Soumen said.

"So the original papers that were supposed to be sent to your Calcutta office ended up in the state archives. That's the box that went missing?" Kedar asked.

"Yes. The box that had the copies ended up in our Calcutta office."

"That's the office where a break-in occurred a couple of nights ago?"

"Yes," Soumen said with surprise.

"Is the box with the copies still with your firm, somewhere?" Kedar asked.

"It's funny you ask. The policeman from Calcutta asked me the same question. Yes, it is with us. Luckily, one of the partners in the firm ended up keeping the papers in another office. My understanding is that the police are taking possession of that box as we speak," Soumen said.

"Police as in RP—I mean, Rudra Pratap—right?"

"Yes," Soumen replied.

Kedar was relieved to hear this. If indeed there was a copy of the papers, they could see what was in it that was so valuable.

"I am curious, Soumen, what was in the box?" Kedar asked.

"Ah, yes. So that's where all the secrets lie. How familiar are you with the ruler of Surinampur and his family?"

"Not very. We read some articles, and we know that he was in some financial trouble after the privy purse from the government was revoked. He had been selling off his land holdings and things in the mansion to stay afloat," Kedar said.

"Yes, that's a good summary. But not everything. You see, their family had amassed a lot a wealth, but they were not so good at keeping records of things they owned. They were thoroughly disorganized. The papers were in complete disarray, and even people working for the ruler didn't know all the details. Over time they assembled real estate holdings not only in

Surinampur but also in Calcutta. The problem is that the land deeds and records associated with all the purchases are all over the place. Successive rulers were more interested in flaunting their wealth and living the good life, as they say, and things went on like this for a long time," Soumen said.

"But then something changed?" Kedar asked.

"Of course, the privy purse was abolished. Then the last ruler, who was only ruler by name, had no choice but to start getting organized and figuring out what he could sell to maintain his decadent lifestyle. He tried the best he could and was able to salvage some records from different law offices, registrars, and even from his extended family. But most of the properties were either jointly owned or disputed. He started selling off the ones that were not disputed—the only undisputed one left is the family mansion in Surinampur. That is now on the market too."

"The papers in the box that went missing were the holdings that were disputed, or joint properties?" Kedar asked.

"Yes, if you could call them that," Soumen replied. "You see, many of the owners who jointly held these properties were not even aware of their existence. Hence no one laid claim to them. Many of them have now been taken over by the government and auctioned off. The sad part is that many of the joint holdings are with families that could really benefit from having these records. Many of those families worked for the royal family of Surinampur, and they left their land records with them for safekeeping."

"I am not sure I understand," Kedar said. He looked at Manik, who was confused as well.

"You see, the father and grandfather of the ruler of Surinampur either sold off or donated a lot of the land to some of their employees here and in Calcutta. Remember, at the time of independence in the late forties, they were an affluent family with businesses here and in rest of Bengal. The family fortune started going downhill in the early 40's. The family then decided to sell off some of their land to their employees whose families had been loyal subjects, if you will, for a few generations. You cannot look at this from the perspective of an urban mindset in the 1970s. In principalities like Surinampur, loyalty mattered, and so did the royal family, for all the employees who worked for them. Over time many of these employees became part landowners of small pieces of land and hoped to pass the land down to future generations. But most of them kept the papers and original land deeds with the royal family.

That was their mistake. But they didn't know any better. As some generations passed, many of them didn't know what they owned, and those who did didn't have any paperwork. Some even tried to file a case against the royal family, but without any proof, they either lost or the cases are dormant."

Kedar and Manik had listened to this with great interest and were taking notes. Soumen paused for a bit. He looked at both Manik and Kedar to see if they had any questions. It was Manik who decided to ask first.

"The box that went missing had some of these original land records and covenants?"

"Yes," Soumen replied.

"If the families came to know about them, then they could make claims based on those records?"

"Yes."

"Even if they were the original records, they would still be potentially disputed, and it would take years for any of the surviving owners or their descendants to make a claim. I can understand that in principle they should get it back and gain from it. But I can't imagine that it is worth a robbery or theft, not to mention someone's life?" Manik said with a raised voice.

Kedar could sense that Manik was starting to get emotional. Kedar immediately tried to tone things down. "What Manik is trying to say, Soumen, is that if everything you say is true, why would anyone want these papers so desperately? And the timing. Why the urgency?"

"Ah, so that's where you are wrong. You see, the box that was stolen contained original records of land owned by families of the employees of the estate in Calcutta. Much of that is prime land. I suspect a good portion of it has been taken over by the government due to lack of accurate records and then auctioned off to the builders. This isn't the only box that went missing. Over the years, anything associated with records for land on which new buildings have been built has never been found in any of the municipal offices or the state archives. Don't you find that strange? The professor knew this but couldn't prove it. When this box went missing, he saw his chance to finally prove it," Soumen said.

It finally started sinking in. What the box contained was perhaps incredibly valuable to the current owners and builders, who had already purchased the land. They didn't want to get dragged into the courts. The government, for its part, didn't want to come across as the party that auctioned off these land holdings without actually checking whom they belonged to. There was definitely a nexus between various parties, and it was much bigger than just one company or one arm of the government. The professor had unknowingly stumbled upon a much bigger scam that, if exposed, would hurt the interests of too many powerful players. More than ever Manik and Kedar were now convinced that the professor had been murdered. They sat there in silence, trying to absorb what they had just heard. It was Kedar who broke the silence.

"The professor told Manik that he received a list from you, and some papers."

"Yes," Soumen replied.

"What were they?" Kedar asked.

"The list was a partial list of some of the documents and covenants that were in the box. The papers were copies of a land deed that we had recently got our hands on. One of the many that had been misplaced over time and ended up with one of the ex-ruler's cousins. It was of personal interest to the professor. Apparently, he had heard about it from his father," Soumen said.

Manik and Kedar were surprised to hear this. The professor had never mentioned anything about it.

"You mean the professor's father?"

"Yes," Soumen replied.

"I am sorry, Soumen. You lost us there." Kedar said.

"The professor's uncle—that is, his father's elder brother—lived in Surinampur and worked for the royal family. By all accounts, he did not hold any senior position in any of the firms. But he saved up enough money to send his younger brother, the professor's father, to Calcutta for higher studies. The professor's uncle never married. He bought a piece of land in Calcutta hoping to eventually give it to his younger brother. He died, and although he may have spoken to the professor's father about the land, he didn't give him any records. When the professor met me, he asked me whether we could find out about his uncle's land, and indeed we did. We weren't able to locate the original. But we found a copy and gave it to him," Soumen said.

Finally, it made sense why the professor had been so excited when he had spoken to Manik on the phone. Manik could only imagine how happy the professor must have been knowing this, and he would have certainly followed up to see if he could leave this family inheritance to Sucheta.

"Do you have a copy of what you gave the professor?" Kedar asked.

"Sadly, no," Soumen replied. "We figured the originals must be in one of the boxes that were sent to Calcutta. There was no need to keep a copy for ourselves. As it is, it is difficult to manage all the paperwork in this office. Our head office in Calcutta has instructed us to keep all records in the main office there."

"I am curious about one thing, Soumen. When your head office got the box of papers, they must have opened it and seen they were not the originals and the boxes had been switched. Didn't they try to find out where the originals were?" Kedar asked.

"Yes, as a matter of fact, they contacted us right away. Once we realized that the boxes had been switched, we contacted the state archives. But it was late in the day, and everyone had left. When we inquired the next morning, we came to know that it had gone missing the day before, the same day the boxes had arrived in both the archives and our head office in Calcutta," Soumen replied.

"But when we contacted the police after meeting the professor at the archives, they told us they weren't aware of the contents of the box. Had someone from your law firm informed them of the contents, they would have taken it seriously," Kedar said.

"Yes, you are right. But I am not sure what happened there. I don't run the Calcutta office. So you would have to asked someone there," Soumen replied.

Kedar and Manik were slowly coming to the realization that someone in the law office in Calcutta was involved in this as well. They could see from Soumen's expression that he suspected that too.

They spoke a bit more about Surinampur. It seemed the town had gone through a sustained period of decay following the closure of some factories. Most of the younger generation had moved to bigger cities in search of opportunities. But things were looking up. Surinampur was surrounded by forests, and a couple of private tour operators had been successful in attracting a steady flow of tourists. That had led to some hotels opening up, and the hospitality industry was thriving. Having a train station and being close to Calcutta also helped. Manik and Kedar found Soumen to be very helpful. He answered all their questions and was generous with his time. They had spent almost two and half hours talking to him.

"Soumen, how much of this have you told Mr. Rudra Pratap?" Kedar asked.

"Most of it. We didn't go into every detail. He was more interested in the professor's hit-and-run.

We spoke for half an hour. I also had a visit from the constable at the police outpost here. Mr. Rudra Pratap wanted a formal statement. I gave it to the constable."

"Well, you have been most generous with us. I think we have taken up enough of your time. Can I please ask you for a favor, though?"

"Sure."

"Is there a public pay phone on your floor that I can use? I need to make two long-distance calls to Calcutta," Kedar said.

"Oh. Please, don't bother. Please use the phone in my office. Don't embarrass us, Kedar. It's the least we can do for our guests from Calcutta. I do feel bad about what happened to the professor. Please feel free to use the phone," Soumen said as he got up.

"I will be right back, Manik. I will make a couple of quick calls, and then we can leave," Kedar said as he got up and followed Soumen out of the room. Manik could see Kedar entering Soumen's room. Soumen left him there to give him some privacy and headed back to Manik.

"Come, Manik, let's go get some more tea. We have a small cafeteria on this floor. We will let Kedar finish his calls. I asked him, and he said he didn't want anything," Soumen said as he opened the door.

"Sure, sir."

Once they had gotten their beverage, they decided to stand around one of the tall tables. Soumen brought out a pack of cigarettes and offered one to Manik, who accepted. As they started smoking and sipping their tea, Soumen looked at Manik and asked him about the professor.

"You liked the professor, didn't you?"

"Yes, sir. I was close to him. He helped me a lot."

"Well, I hope you get to the bottom of this."

"Yes, sir."

Once they had finished with their teas and cigarettes, Soumen and Manik headed back to the office. Kedar had finished his calls. Manik could sense that he was ready to leave.

"Thank you once again for your help, Soumen. We really appreciate it. I have to ask one last favor—I saw some empty boxes in your stationary room when we walked in. Can I please take on of them?"

"Sure. We will be throwing them out anyway," Soumen said.

Manik was puzzled, and from the look on Soumen's face, so was he. They headed to the small, unkempt stationary room beside the entrance to the office. They saw Kedar going inside and taking his time to select an empty box with a firm cover on it. It almost seemed that he was looking for something specific. When he found one he was happy with, he dusted it off and then came outside.

"I will take this one," Kedar said.

"Sure," Soumen replied, still unsure as to what he would be doing with an empty box.

Manik was starting to get worried about this strange behavior from Kedar. It was highly uncharacteristic of him. But he didn't want to say anything in front of Soumen. Kedar and Manik thanked Soumen yet again and slowly made their way out of the building. Once they were outside, Kedar told Manik that they would be going to the mansion to catch a glimpse of where the erstwhile ruler of Surinampur used to live. They started walking back in the direction of the railway station. They had seen a number of taxis there. They didn't have to go far. They got in an empty cab, and Kedar told the driver to drive them to Ratna Mahal, the mansion belonging to the now-deceased ex-ruler. From the map Manik had noticed that it was at the other end of Surinampur. They would have to cross almost the entire town on one of its main avenues to get there.

As the taxi made its way through the town, Manik and Kedar got a feel of the place. It did not have the hustle and bustle of Calcutta. There were no traffic jams, and the general pace of people going about their lives seemed laid back. As they moved away from the station, they could see the newer parts of town. Despite all the new construction, the town had managed to retain its green spaces. There were lots of trees, parks, and wooded areas.

Once they got closer to Ratna Mahal, the ruler's property, they could see that the surroundings were changing. There were a number of old estates and summer houses belonging to rich families. Many of them were run down, and some of them were being renovated. As they reached the end of the avenue, they could see large gates leading into a forested area. The gates were open, and outside was an engraved sign in Bengali and English saying "Ratna Mahal."

Once they entered the gates, there was a winding road leading up to the ruler's palace. On either side of the road were tall trees and, behind them, what seemed like a mango grove. The winding road leading up to the mansion seemed worn down and in need of repair. As they approached the main building, they got a sense of the massive expanse of the mansion. Like the rest of the estate, it was run down. However, they could make out that it had been, at one time, a beautiful building, and it was easy to marvel at the exquisite architecture, even though it had lost much of its grandeur.

Once they got out of the taxi, Kedar asked the driver to wait and keep an eye on the box. They planned to take a quick look around and then would head back to the station. They could see two old gentlemen sitting on one side of the main entrance. Manik and Kedar walked up to the main entrance, and they were greeted by one of them. He introduced himself as one of the caretakers appointed by the estate lawyers. He told them that Soumen had made them aware of their visit.

Manik asked him if they could take a quick look around, and he opened the main door for them. What they saw inside was the empty shell of a grand old mansion. Most of the furniture, paintings, and decorative objects had been removed. As they walked through the mansion, they could see that at one time it must have been an impressive place. Many of the items in it had already been auctioned off and shipped out. A few paintings and chandeliers remained, gathering dust. The second floor housed a library. Most of the bookshelves were empty, but Manik and Kedar were impressed with the size of it, and the caretaker told them that the previous owner had been a collector of old books and an avid reader.

The massive rooms in the empty mansion still showed remnants of its past glory. The walls were lined with exquisite frames and mirrors. They could see that the large doors and windows still had hand-carved handles and panels. The floors, though not polished, were made of marble, and despite all the wear and tear, they still had a glow. It was a house struggling to maintain its glorious identity in the midst of years of neglect.

Kedar inquired about boxes from the mansion that had been shipped to Calcutta. The caretaker did not offer many details. They got the impression that he did not want to talk too much about it. The back of the mansion had a courtyard leading up to what looked like stables and a garage that was accessible by another road in the back. They were empty, of course, and behind the palace was a massive garden, or what was left of it.

"It must have been quite something in its heyday," Manik said, looking at the mansion and pointing to the grounds outside.

"Yes," Kedar replied.

"It's a pity that it had to come to this."

"Some families know how to keep their wealth, and others don't," Kedar said thoughtfully.

"There must have been a lot of people working here to maintain all of this."

"Yes, that's what we heard from Soumen. Generations of families must have been employed here," Kedar said.

"It seems so unfair that those families won't get any of the estate's proceeds or have any knowledge of whether they owned any land purchased from this family," Manik said.

"The problem is that a lot of the deeds and covenants don't have any central records. A lot of these transactions happened at a time when the folks who worked here trusted these families, and the government did not intervene unless there was a problem. Most of the centralized record keeping started after India's independence. Soumen was right. It is going to be difficult for descendants of employees that may have purchased anything from this family to prove anything without any records or paperwork."

"We must get to the bottom of what was in that box, sir."

"We will, Manik."

They spent a few more minutes walking through the grounds of the estate and then headed back through a winding pathway toward the front of the building, where the taxi was parked. They thanked the caretaker and instructed the cab driver to take them back to the railway station. As they left the estate and the taxi made its way back through the main gates, they could see a few more people hanging around outside. Manik figured that they were most likely folks who were employed to maintain the property until it was sold. They could see a few more cars now on the road.

"There's no need to hang around here any longer," Kedar said. "Let's head back to the station and see if there's an earlier train we can catch."

"Yes, sir. What's with the box, sir?" Manik asked, pointing to the box that Kedar had picked up from Soumen's office, which had nothing but some writing pads and maps in it. He was wondering why Kedar was clinging to it on his lap.

"We will talk about what to do with this when we get back to Calcutta," Kedar said, and Manik knew from his tone that he didn't want to talk about it anymore. Manik was puzzled but did not press any further. His mind was preoccupied with what Soumen had told the professor during his visit. He was also thinking about what, if anything, they could do to locate the missing box or find its contents. The thought of the professor getting killed because of what he had found out during his visit to Surinampur made Manik sad and angry.

Once they reached the station, it was already late afternoon. They quickly checked the timetable and saw that the next train to Calcutta was departing in hour. After getting their tickets, they headed to a tea stall on the platform to get something to eat. The station wasn't busy. Manik could sense Kedar's restlessness. Once they got their sandwiches and tea, they decided to head over to one of the long wooden benches in the waiting area. Manik sat down and realized that he was hungry. Kedar sat down beside him with the box between them. It came in handy, with the top acting as a makeshift table for their sandwiches and tea.

"What do you think happened here, Manik?" Kedar asked. He bit into his sandwich.

"You mean with the professor?"

"Yes."

"I think he found out from Soumen what the box contained. He also got the list and a copy of the deed that showed his own family's ownership stake in land in Calcutta. Once he went back, he was killed. I am certain of it, since Mr. Rudra Pratap told you that the police couldn't find those items on him after the accident," Manik said thoughtfully.

"Right. Let's say, for argument's sake, you are correct. What happened when he went back to Calcutta?"

"Someone must have been waiting for him there, sir. He took a bus from the station. He was killed after he got off the bus and was walking home."

"Yes," Kedar said. He finished his sandwich and looked away toward the end of the platform to see if any train was visible.

"Do you think otherwise, sir?"

"No, you are right to some extent. He was murdered, for sure, for what he had with him. Let's talk about it more when we are back in the office."

"Sure, sir," Manik said. He finished off his own sandwich.

"Are you still planning to take time off? Maybe you want to go see Sucheta?"

"I'd like to, sir. But I also want to know what happened to the professor. I feel I owe it to him to find out the truth. I owe that to Sucheta too—at least I feel that way."

Once they had finished their tea, they waited for the train to arrive. They could see more people arriving at the station and on the platform waiting for the train. It was still not that crowded. They could see the train slowly coming into the station, and once it stopped,

Manik and Kedar looked at their tickets and quickly made their way to their allocated compartments and seats. Kedar preferred to keep the box on his lap. He had picked up a local newspaper at the station. He started reading. Manik felt a bit sleepy after the meal. Once the train started moving, the rocking motion and the gentle breeze through the open windows made him doze off.

He got up when the train made its first of two scheduled intermediate stops. He could see Kedar was looking out the window.

"Would you like some tea, Manik?"

"No, sir. If you want, I can get some for you."

"No, thank you. I can wait till we are back in Calcutta."

Once the train started moving, Manik closed his eyes again. This time he couldn't sleep. He was thinking about Sucheta. He would be meeting up with her for the first time since she moved to Bombay. He had often wondered what would have happened if she had stayed in Calcutta or if he had found a job and moved to Bombay. Now he would be seeing her after her father's tragic death, and she would be grieving. With her father gone, she would have even less of a reason to come to Calcutta. While he was thinking about this, he could see that Kedar was still looking up and down the compartment. He gently tapped Manik on his knee and leaned over.

"Once we reach Calcutta, we will take a taxi and head to the office. I want to talk to you about something."

"Yes, sir," Manik replied.

After the next stop, Manik was fully awake. Kedar started asking him about music. He wanted to know what he wrote. He made him hum a few tunes. Manik was surprised to learn that Kedar knew how to read music. Kedar told him that he had taken lessons when he was a child.

Once they reached Calcutta, Kedar got off quickly and asked Manik to follow him. He offered to carry the box, but Kedar refused. He started following Kedar to the taxi stand and had a hard time keeping up. It almost seemed that Kedar was in a hurry. He wondered why that was. It was already late evening, and by the time they reached the office beyond the Calcutta traffic, it would be close to 7:00 p.m. No one would be in the office, except for the people working the night shift in the print shop and maybe Swaroop and some of the senior staff who might be there late to review and approve the paper before the final publication.

Manik was right. By the time they reached the office, it was already late, well past 7:30 p.m. They headed up to their desks.

"Manik, don't leave the building. We need to talk. Please give me some time," Kedar said.

"Sure, sir. I was planning to walk home," Manik replied.

"No," Kedar said firmly in a tone that surprised Manik, as he looked toward the desks belonging to the senior staff. Manik sensed that he was looking for someone.

"Are you looking for someone, sir?"

"Yes. I am looking for Harish. Can you please go to him and ask him to meet me in that conference room," Kedar said, pointing to one of the rooms on the side.

Manik was surprised but didn't ask. He quickly went up to Harish, who was reading something, and he could sense that Harish was not too happy about being summoned by Kedar. But he followed Manik to the room, and once they were there, Kedar asked Harish to take a seat. He then turned to Manik.

"Manik, can you please give us a few minutes. Perhaps you can get something at the café while I talk to Harish about something. But please don't leave the building."

"Yes, sir," Manik said with a puzzled look on his face. He didn't understand what Kedar wanted to talk to Harish about. Why was the box with the writing pads and maps in the conference room? Manik was tired and headed to the café to get a tea. As he walked through the hall, past the silent desks of all the journalists, he could see that the floor was now empty. Everyone had left. There wasn't a single sound, or even a single stroke from any of the typewriters.

Once he got to the café, the only people there were the folks from the print shop having tea before their night shift. He quickly finished his tea and then went back upstairs. Once he reached his floor, all he could hear were the raised voices of Harish and Kedar arguing with each other. There was no one else on the floor, and it was hard to hear what they were saying. As he got closer, he could only catch bits and pieces of what looked like a heated argument. Manik didn't want to make it obvious that he was listening but was curious. He made his way to a tall filing cabinet near the closed door of the conference room and hid behind it. He looked around; the entire floor was empty. He quietly stood there and listened to the conversation between Kedar and Harish.

"I can't believe you dragged the boy into this," Harish said in a loud voice.

"I didn't know, Harish, and I was with him. Do you think I would knowingly put him in any danger?" Kedar asked.

"I think you should keep him out of this," Harish said.

"I will. But he needs to know the truth. He worked with you, and you know that he is inquisitive."

"Yes, I know."

"He is already involved. The professor was close to him. I will make sure that he is safe till this is over. But I do need your help, Harish."

There was a pause in the conversation. Then Harish broke the silence.

"I am not sure whether this is the right approach," Harish said.

"Why not?" Kedar asked.

"Well, for one, we don't know if anyone here's involved," Harish replied.

"We are doing this to find that out. I am going to talk to Rudra Pratap and get him to buy into this."

"What if he doesn't agree?" Harsh asked.

"That's on me. I will try to convince him," Kedar replied.

There was again a moment of silence.

"After this, you keep the boy out of this. I can't believe he ended up with you," Harish said. Manik could sense the frustration in his voice.

"You know that wasn't my doing, Harish," Kedar said in a much calmer tone.

"I wish you had kept me out of this as well," Harish said.

"This has nothing to do with what happened between you and me, Harish. I wouldn't have involved you had I not needed your help. Strange as it may sound, you are the only one I can trust with this," Kedar said softly.

"Fine. But once this is done, we are done. Is that understood, Kedar?" Harish asked in a serious tone.

"Understood," Kedar replied.

Manik realized that their conversation was coming to an end. He quickly tiptoed back to his desk. By the time Kedar and Harish came out of the room, Manik was back at his desk pretending to read a book. Harish walked past him, nodding at him gently.

"Good night, Manik," Harish said as he walked toward the stairs to leave.

"Good night, sir."

"Time to go home, Manik," Kedar called out from his desk.

"Yes, sir. I'm ready."

"I have to make a quick call, and then I will be with you."

"Yes, sir."

He could hear some of the conversation. Kedar spoke to Rudra Pratap and asked him for a meeting. He could also overhear something about security guards but couldn't make out all the details. Once Kedar had finished, he gestured to Manik that he was ready to leave. Kedar took the box he had gotten from Soumen in Surinampur and headed downstairs. He asked the receptionist to call for a taxi. At this time of the night, it was unlikely there would be any taxis in the stand outside. So they had to call one in from one of the stands farther out. As they waited in the reception area just inside the main entrance for the car to arrive, Kedar turned to Manik.

"Manik, I want you to listen to me carefully. I am taking you home with me tonight. I don't want you staying in your apartment. Also, for the next couple of days, I don't want you to walk anywhere outside on your own."

"Why, sir?" Manik was totally confused.

"I am not sure you realized it, but we were followed the entire day today."

"I don't understand, sir."

"We were followed all the way to Surinampur and then all the way back to Calcutta. At all times, there was someone following us," Kedar said.

8

Entrapment

Suddenly Manik felt a chill. He realized why Kedar had been restless throughout the trip and why he always seemed to be looking over his shoulder. That explained Kedar's odd behavior, but not the box. Before he could ask him, the taxi arrived at Kedar's apartment. His building was in a gated compound. Once they got to the compound, they saw that the gates were closed. Seeing the taxi arrive, a couple of guards came out; once they identified Kedar as one of the residents of the building, they let the car in. Kedar and Manik got out in front of the building. There was a gentleman who looked like a constable waiting for them.

"Did Rudra Pratap send you?" Kedar asked.

"Yes, sir."

"Please," Kedar said as he led Manik and the constable up a flight of stairs to his apartment.

Once they were inside, a servant came to meet them. Kedar told him that the constable and Manik would be staying overnight. Kedar asked him to show Manik to the guest room. Manik followed him, and the constable told Kedar that he would be staying overnight in the living room, near the main entrance to the apartment.

The guest room was very different from what he would have imagined. The big apartment, where Kedar lived alone, was mostly empty. When he had walked in, he had noticed that the living room had only a few pieces for furniture. The room that Manik was sleeping in had a single bed, a bookcase filled with books and photographs, a closet, a small desk, and chair. Manik looked at some of the pictures. They were mostly of Kedar's wife, who had passed away, and their son, who was now living in England. There were a few others that looked like family portraits of extended family members and pictures of vacations that they had taken. There was a knock on the door, and Kedar walked in.

"I am sorry you have to go through all this, Manik. But I didn't want to take any chances, with what happened to the professor after his visit to Surinampur. This should be over soon, and you should be able to get back to your normal routine, hopefully in a couple of days."

"Are you worried that someone might try to harm us in any way?" Manik asked.

"Not quite, but let's talk tomorrow. As you may have guessed, there is more to it than meets the eye. RP will be coming over tomorrow morning. The best thing now is to get a good night's sleep. In the closet you will find some fresh clothes, pajamas, and shirts that will fit you. They belong to my son. He usually uses this room when he comes to visit. Please feel free to change and leave your clothes in the basket. Laxman will take them tomorrow morning and get them cleaned."

"I don't want to be a bother, sir."

"Nonsense, and don't worry about this. Now please freshen up, get changed, and come to the living room for a quick dinner. That door leads to the bathroom," Kedar said, pointing to the door beside the desk.

Once Kedar had left, Manik took a quick shower and changed. He found some clothes in the closet. They were a bit large, but he did fit into them quite nicely. When he went back into the living room, he saw the constable and Kedar sitting around the dining table. Kedar asked Manik to join them. As he walked over, Manik could see the rest of the big apartment. Across from the dining table was a piano, a sitting area with some sofas and chairs. There were bookshelves filled with what looked like souvenirs, mementos, and some pictures. The walls had paintings and Indian handicrafts hanging on them. He could also see some large photographs of landscapes.

"Manik, this is Vijay. He works for Rudra Pratap. You have already met Laxman," Kedar said, pointing to the man who had shown Manik to his room. Laxman brought a tray filled with food and placed it on the table. He had neatly arranged all the plates and cutlery, and Kedar motioned to Vijay and Manik to help themselves.

"Thank you for this, sir," Vijay said.

"We should be thanking you. I know RP sent you for our protection. I am sure you would much rather be in your own home and in your own bed," Kedar said.

"Oh, don't worry sir. I am used to this sort of duty," Vijay replied, helping himself to a generous portion of rice and dal.

"Laxman practically runs the house," Kedar said, looking at him with a smile. "I'd be totally lost without him."

"Thank you, Laxman," Manik said, turning to the old gentleman. Manik could sense that Laxman had probably been with Kedar and his family for a long time.

Once they finished their meal, Manik got up and started to head back to the guest room. He could sense Kedar was tired, and he saw him go to his room on the other side of the apartment. The living room opened onto a large balcony. He could see constable Vijay had made himself comfortable in one of the armchairs on the balcony with a cup of tea on the side table and was enjoying a smoke. Back in his room, Manik looked around to see if he could find a book to help him fall asleep. There were plenty to choose from. As soon as he started reading, he fell into a deep slumber. He did not notice when Laxman came into the room, took the book away from him, put a blanket over him, and turned off the lights before leaving.

By the time he got up the next morning, he realized that it was already late. It was a bright day, with the sun glaring through the windows. The light curtains were trying unsuccessfully to keep the light out. He could hear voices from the living room. He quickly glanced at his wristwatch. It was nearly 9:00 a.m. He had overslept. He didn't recall the last time he had gotten up this late even on a weekend. He didn't notice the blanket over him as he got up but did notice that someone had come into the room and left some clean clothes on the desk for him to wear. He quickly freshened up, and once he was ready, he headed out to join the others in the living room.

He was surprised to see Harish and Rudra Pratap there. Vijay had left. They were sitting around the dining table. As soon as they saw Manik, they asked him to come over to join them. He quickly sat down in one of the empty chairs and could see that Laxman had prepared a sumptuous breakfast of eggs, fruits, bread, and juices and placed it on the table. As soon as he sat down, Laxman brought him an empty plate.

"Did you have a good night's sleep, Manik?" Kedar asked.

"Yes, sir," Manik replied.

"That's good. Now let's eat up. We have a long day and night ahead of us," Kedar said.

"I am sorry for getting up this late."

"Don't worry about that. We need your help with something today, and that might help us in nabbing the professor's killer or killers," Kedar said.

"So, we know who did it?" Manik asked while serving himself some fruit from a basket in the center of the table.

"Not quite," Kedar replied, "but I will let Rudra Pratap explain what he wants from us."

Rudra Pratap had a file filled with papers in front of him, and Manik could see that he was looking at them and making some notes. When he finished, he got up and moved to the head of the table so that he could face Harish, Manik, and Kedar, who were now sitting around the dining table.

"This case has been bothering me because of two things. One, of course, is the untimely death of the professor, and from what we have determined so far, it is more than likely that it was not a random hit-and-run. He was targeted upon his return from Surinampur. If that is the case, then the killer is most likely someone who knew why he was going there and what he was coming back with. The second thing is the missing papers from the archives. There definitely is a connection, as we know now. Luckily, we have the copies from the law firm. My take is that whoever broke into the law firm wanted to get the box, but it was just pure luck that the box containing the copies was not there and had been shipped to a different office. It is also possible that someone in the law office in Calcutta is involved in this, and we are looking into that. But that still leaves the question of the location of the box with the original papers, the one sent to the state archives," Rudra Pratap stated and then paused.

"Do you think the professor was followed like we were to Surinampur and back?" Kedar asked.

"Possibly, but we don't know for sure," Rudra Pratap replied.

"It could be the same people," Harish said, sipping his tea.

"That is what we need to determine to break open this case. From my perspective, solving the murder is a higher priority. But something tells me that if we do that, it may also point to the missing box and its contents," Rudra Pratap said.

Manik was relieved to hear that the police were taking this seriously.

"Why are we meeting here and not in our office?" Harish asked.

"Good question, Harish. Kedar and I spoke about this yesterday, and we came to the same conclusion. That is why we need your and Manik's help, as I am sure Kedar may have mentioned yesterday evening," Rudra Pratap said.

"Yes. He told me he needed our help. I am not sure if Manik knows. Kedar also told us that you will be telling us what you want us to do," Harish said.

"Right, so let's break this down a bit in terms of the sequence of events. Let's say, for the sake of argument, everything is connected—the box disappearing from the state archives, the attempted theft at the law firm, the professor's death, and Kedar and Manik's trip to Surinampur, where you were followed. Now, we haven't been able to establish a connection between all of them in terms of people. But let's look at the last two things first. Many people knew that the professor was going to Surinampur. He told Asutosh and Vinod at the archives. He may have mentioned it to his friends. We don't know. He told Manik and Kedar. Then my understanding is that a few of the senior staff in your paper knew about his trip too." Rudra Pratap paused.

"That's right, sir" Manik said. "We went to ask for approval for the trip and were denied. I think Mr. Swaroop mentioned that he would ask the senior staff if anyone had any contacts in Surinampur that could help."

"Right. Now tell me, Manik, how many people knew that you and Kedar were going to Surinampur?" Rudra Pratap asked.

Suddenly Manik realized what he was getting at.

"Only a few people at work," Manik said softly and thoughtfully.

"Who?" Rudra Pratap asked.

Manik turned to Kedar and Harish. They nodded their heads for Manik to respond.

"When we asked for approval for the trip, apart from Harish and Kedar, there was Arun, Rajan, and of course Swaroop, sir," Manik replied in a calm voice.

"Right, Manik. It is possible, of course, that they spoke to some other colleagues. The timing is important here. You asked for approval in the evening for a trip that you and Kedar were going to take the following morning. My point is that it is more than likely that someone from the paper had you followed to and from Surinampur. Kedar could not recognize the people following you. So they must have employed some professional thieves or miscreants to do that. There's no shortage of those in this city," Rudra Pratap said.

They all paused for a bit. It was slowly sinking in that someone in the *Herald* was involved, at the very least, in what Kedar and Manik were going to discover in Surinampur and perhaps what the professor had learned as well.

"What does this mean, sir? Are you saying that someone from our office was involved in the professor's death too?" Manik asked in a strained voice.

Kedar could sense the emotion in Manik's voice and tried to calm him. "We don't know that yet, Manik. But what we can do is first find out who had us followed. When I realized that we were being followed, I made a call to RP from the lawyer's office in Surinampur. Do you recall?"

"Yes, of course," Manik said in a calmer voice.

"RP and I came up with a plan. That's where the box that I brought back from Surinampur comes in, and where we need your help," Kedar said, and then he turned to Rudra Pratap to continue.

Rudra Pratap sat down on the chair at the head of the table. He turned to Harish and Manik. It was evident that Kedar had already discussed some sort of a plan with him, and they now needed to set it in motion. He poured himself a glass of water and then continued.

"When Kedar called me from Surinampur yesterday to let me know that he was being followed, I asked him to pick up a box from the lawyer's office. This was basically a ploy to make it seem you had received documents of some relevance during the visit. Kedar picked up this box," Rudra Pratap said, pointing to the box that he had been carrying around with Manik the day before.

"The box is similar to the ones we saw at the state archives, if you recall, Manik," Kedar said. Manik nodded in agreement.

"Of course, the contents of the box are useless," Rudra Pratap said, "but the point is that whoever was following you must have got the impression that you picked up something from the lawyer's office that could be important, along the same lines as what the professor picked up."

"So they think that the box has some valuable papers, and they want to steal it from us?" Manik asked.

"Yes. The professor called you from Surinampur from a public pay phone. From the telephone exchange, we traced the pay phone with which the call was made from Surinampur to your office. My counterpart there told me that it is an open booth. So if the professor was being followed during his trip there, anyone close to him could have overheard the conversation he had with you, Manik," Rudra Pratap said.

"Right. They could have overheard that he was bringing back something really important and valuable related to the missing box and its contents?" Manik asked.

"Yes. Do you recall your entire conversation, Manik? I think he also told you that he had a list of what the missing box contained, and some other papers. I think Soumen told you what they were," Rudra Pratap said.

"Yes, sir."

"Let's come back to this box now, Manik. If you were and are still being followed, of which I am certain, the people who followed you and Kedar know that the box is still in your possession and in this apartment. You took a taxi from the station to the office yesterday and then came here via another cab. You did not give them much of an opportunity to get the box away from both of you. They also saw a police presence here, with a police jeep outside, and must have noticed Constable Vijay staying overnight. They did not want to risk breaking into a well-guarded apartment building with multiple occupants and a police presence inside and outside," Rudra Pratap said.

"But if they are still following us and are outside the building, you must have seen who they are," Manik said.

"Yes. We have noticed them but don't want to raise an alarm just yet, which would alert them that we are aware of their presence. It looks as if they are a gang of multiple people, some of whom are known to the police and have been involved in attempted break-ins and petty thefts," Rudra Pratap replied.

"And responsible for the professor's murder," Manik exclaimed.

"Yes, Manik. But we want to know who employed them. Who is the mastermind behind all this? Don't you want to know? If we pick them up now, we won't get the entire truth. They might tell us some names, but we still have no way to link them to the professor's hit-and-run. Remember, these are professional criminals, and they won't squeal, as they are afraid of the consequences of ratting each other out," Rudra Pratap said.

"So how do we catch the people responsible?" Manik asked.

"Entrapment," Rudra Pratap replied.

"I'm sorry?" Manik asked.

"We set a trap for them" came the reply from Rudra Pratap.

"How do we do that?" Manik was curious.

"We know that there are multiple people involved in this. I suspect it's a large, closely guarded nexus involving influential people in the real estate business who have a vested interest in these papers and ensuring their contents are never made public. They want to destroy any presence, mention, or evidence of it. If these were ever to come out, it would cause a massive scandal not only for these businesses but also for the government, who has been auctioning off these lands at throwaway prices to the builders. Now, from what you know in terms of what was in that box, you can imagine what would happen if some of the descendants of these families who are the rightful owners of these lands came to know of its existence," Rudra Pratap said.

"There would be literally hundreds of court cases and demands for compensation," Harish said. He had been silent until now.

"Correct," Rudra Pratap said, "and it would also mean that the government was complicit in this. It is a scandal any way you look at it. Either they knew about this and it's like organized crime at the highest level, or they didn't know—which I doubt—and it's incompetence bordering on corruption. Either way it looks bad, and can you imagine what would happen if this were to come out right before the election?"

"So how do we trap them?" Manik asked.

"We cannot get them all at once. Let's get the ones we can first. We know that someone at the *Herald* is definitely involved. They had you and Kedar followed and have seen both of you come back with a box from the lawyer's office at Surinampur. They don't know the contents, but they probably suspect that it is something important. What we will do is confirm their suspicion," Rudra Pratap said.

"I'm not sure I understand," Manik said.

"If they knew that the box contains important papers regarding land deeds and covenants, or even just copies of them, what do you think they would do?" Rudra Pratap asked.

"They would try to steal them," Manik replied.

"Correct," Rudra Pratap replied with a smile. "Let's give them the opportunity to do just that and then nab them in the act."

"That's where we need your and Harish's help, Manik," Kedar said from the other end of the table.

"How?" Manik asked.

"We will all go to work today like we usually do. Harish will call for a meeting in Swaroop's office with the senior staff. With the elections coming up, he will come up with some excuse to get them all together. I won't be joining, of course. As you may have noticed, I am never invited to these meetings, and if I call for one, it will raise suspicion." Kedar paused.

"The junior staff are not invited to meetings in Swaroop's room. How could I be present?" Manik asked.

"You won't be. What we need you to do is take the box into Swaroop's room while the meeting is in progress and leave it there. You will interrupt the meeting only for a few minutes to enter the room and let him know quickly that the box contains papers pertaining to land records that you and I picked up from the lawyer's office in Surinampur. During your conversation, you have to make it clear that he must keep them safely in his office, as they are important and could be connected to other things that you and I are investigating. Make sure that you speak in a normal voice, not too loud but clear enough that everyone in the room hears what you are saying. Then, you leave." Kedar paused to catch his breath.

"What happens then?"

"Nothing much till the day is over, I suspect," Kedar said.

"Swaroop usually works till late and rarely leaves his office," Manik said.

"Yes, and Harish here will make sure that he stays there with him after the meeting using one pretext or the other," Kedar said as he got up and poured himself some juice from the table. Rudra Pratap walked over to the other side of the room and then opened the door to the balcony. Before heading out for a smoke, he turned to Harish and Manik.

"My understanding is that Swaroop is usually the last one to leave. Once he leaves, I suspect someone will come to steal the box. It won't be any of the gang members who have been following you. They won't be able to get past the reception and the guards in the main entrance without getting noticed. The senior staff all have access to Swaroop's office, and the floor where all of you work is just below the one his office is on. The best opportunity for them to remove the box is when it is in Swaroop's office. If it is indeed any of them, we will catch them in the act. I will be there in the building and on Swaroop's floor all night, along with my constable, Vijay, whom you have already met. There will be plainclothes policemen outside the building and in the plant on the ground floor where the printing presses are, disguised as lorry drivers. Once we nab the person trying to steal the box, we will get the gang that has been following you as well," Rudra Pratap said, and he stepped out onto the balcony for a smoke. He kept the door to the balcony open so that he could continue the conversation. Manik, Harish, and Kedar could see him lighting up a cigarette. Meanwhile, in the living room, Kedar turned to Manik.

"Are you clear on what needs to be done, Manik?"

"Yes, sir. But the people who have been following us—and are probably still following us—have seen you and Harish come here. Wouldn't they suspect that something's wrong?" Manik asked.

"They could," Rudra Pratap said. "They have seen me come in, but not Harish. Kedar warned him yesterday. He came through the back entrance with Laxman. We have already checked. No one from the gang is keeping any eye on that entrance. Harish will leave the way he came in, and we will make sure he isn't noticed."

"Any other questions?" Kedar asked.

"I want to be there when they nab the culprit. This person was probably also responsible for the professor's death," Manik said with a shaky voice.

"Absolutely not," Harish said.

"I have to agree with Harish" Kedar said. "We have already put you in some danger in getting you involved and using your actions as bait. I don't think we want to take it any further."

"If you want me to do this, sir, I want to be there. I want to see it all as it happens. I am already involved."

Harish and Kedar could see that Manik was dead serious and was in no mood for any further arguments on the matter. When Rudra Pratap came back into the room, they went over the details of their plan one more time without leaving anything out. As they were finishing their conversation, Kedar sensed that Manik wanted to ask something; he knew what it was.

"Go ahead, Manik. Ask away," Kedar said.

"The people who knew about our trip—" Manik said and suddenly stopped.

"Yes?" Kedar asked.

"Well…" Manik stopped again.

"Harish was among them, and yet he is here. Is that what you want to ask, Manik?" Kedar asked softly and turned to Harish, who had a smile on his face. He looked at Manik and responded.

"Kedar and I go back a long way," Harish said.

"That's right, Manik" Kedar added. "We have had our differences. But I know Harish well enough to know that he would never get involved in this sort of thing. I needed help in flushing out who was responsible. As you know, my reputation among the senior staff is not that great, and they all keep a distance. Harish, on the other hand, is well liked, and I trust him more than anyone else on the senior team. So I asked him for help, and he agreed. To be honest, we did not want to get you involved in any of this. I wanted to take the box to Swaroop's room myself, but that would have looked suspicious. I normally don't go into meetings with the other senior staff. Swaroop certainly would ask them to leave if I had to speak to him. You, on the hand, would not cause much alarm, except perhaps for the person or persons in the room who are interested in its contents."

Manik realized what the argument between Harish and Kedar the night before had been about. They were arguing about him and how to keep him safe. He suddenly felt good that both of them actually cared deeply about him, and although he hadn't been with them for long, he felt that the events of the past few days had made them closer. He could now see Rudra Pratap and Harish getting ready to leave.

Before leaving, Rudra Pratap turned to the rest of them. "It is very important that you go about your day like you would normally do. Kedar, Manik, there will be a taxi that will enter the gates around eleven. Please let the guards at the gate of the building know that you have called for a taxi, and then they will let the car into the compound. Once you are in the taxi, it will take you straight to the *Herald* building. The driver is a plainclothes policeman. While you are in the car, please resist the temptation to look back to see if anyone's following you. Remember, the success of this plan hinges on not raising any alarm from now until the box is handed over to Swaroop. Is that understood?"

Manik, Kedar, and Harish nodded. They saw Rudra Pratap leave. After a few minutes, Harish left with Laxman through the back entrance. Manik looked at his watch. They had half an hour before the taxi arrived. He could hear Kedar making a call to the guards at the front gate to let them know that a taxi had been called and instructing them to let it in when it arrived. Manik headed to the balcony. He could see the apartment buildings in the complex properly now. There were four buildings in the gated compound. Each building had anywhere between eight and ten floors. The ground floor of each of the buildings was a big parking lot for cars belonging to the residents. There was a huge yard and garden just within the main gates. He could see some kids playing there and a few people enjoying the sun on the benches in the garden. The gates were closed, and he could see the private guards manning the entrance were letting cars in only after checking whether their occupants were residents of the compound. The buildings were new, and he could see from the cars and attire of the people leaving for work that it was an affluent residential neighborhood.

"Let's have another tea before we leave," Kedar said as Manik turned around to see that he had already placed the box on the dining table. Manik left the balcony and went back inside the living room. Laxman had left another pot of tea on the dining table. Kedar had already poured him a cup.

"Thank you, sir," Manik said.

"Ready for what needs to be done today?" Kedar asked.

"Yes, sir."

"Good."

"If indeed it is someone from the newspaper involved in this, then maybe if the professor hadn't come to us, he'd still be alive," Manik said in a low, solemn voice.

"Let's not get ahead of ourselves, Manik," Kedar said in a more serious tone. He could see Manik was lost in thought.

"What about the box from the state archives with original papers, deeds, and covenants?" Manik asked.

"Oh, I think those are long gone. Either they have been put away or destroyed—I don't expect them to be found. The only saving grace is that RP was able to get a hold of the copies that were sent to the law office in

Calcutta. Luckily, they were sent to the office that was not broken into. They are with the police now."

"You think we can take a look at the contents, sir?"

"Sure. I don't see why not."

"Rudra Pratap mentioned that there were other people involved in removing the box from the archives."

"Yes, Manik. I think you may have guessed by now that the removal of the box from the state archives was only possible because someone on the inside was involved. RP has set another trap for them. But one thing at a time. Let's find out what happens tonight first," Kedar said.

Manik sensed that Kedar didn't want to share all the details of what was happening in the archives just yet. He didn't press him any further. It was close to 11:00 a.m. Manik went to the balcony. He saw a taxi outside the gates, and the guards were letting it in. Kedar took the box from the dining table and started walking to the door. Laxman opened it for them. Manik thanked Laxman, and then they headed to the stairs at the end of the corridor. Once they got downstairs, they got into the taxi and headed to the office. Manik had to make a conscious effort during the ride to not give into his overwhelming impulse to see if anyone was following them.

The drive to the *New Eastern Herald* building was quick. Once they entered the gates, the cab came to a halt near the main doors. The plainclothes policeman driving the car told them that they had been followed and reiterated Kedar's instructions earlier in the day to go about their work as they would normally do. Kedar carried the box with him up the stairs, and they headed to their desks.

They could see Anjali on the phone; she greeted them with a smile. Kedar put the box in a large cabinet beside his desk and locked it. He went over to Anjali, and Manik could see that after a quick conversation, she was heading toward the stairs. Kedar waved at Manik to come over to his desk.

"I see that most of the senior staff is not here. They must be in Swaroop's office. I have asked Anjali to go check. She will pretend to go to the library and can see through the glass windows whether indeed the meeting is underway. She will be back in a few minutes," Kedar said.

"Right, sir," Manik said.

"Remember, Anjali doesn't know about any of this either," Kedar said. Manik nodded.

They looked around. Everyone was busy at their desks. The clickety-clack of the typewriters was drowning out the loud voices of reporters talking on the phones. They started reading papers on their desks and looking at some of the files. Manik was excited and worried at the same time. He could see that Kedar was calm but sensed that his mind must be racing as well. After about twenty minutes, they could see Anjali heading back.

"They are in a meeting, sir," Anjali said, looking at Kedar.

"All right. Manik, please go and leave the box with Swaroop," Kedar said as he brought out the box from his cabinet and handed it over to Manik.

"Yes, sir."

As Manik took the box and headed up the stairs, he could feel that Kedar must have added a few more files and papers to it. It felt heavier. He could also see that the lid was firmly closed, and there was tape around it. As soon as he arrived at Swaroop's floor, he noticed Rajan at his desk on the phone. He saw Manik and asked him to come over to one of the chairs and told him to wait. When he finished his call, he turned to Manik.

"How can I help you, Manik?"

"I need to take this to Swaroop," Manik said, pointing to the box he was holding.

"There's a meeting going on. You can leave it with me, and I will give it to him once they are done."

"I am sorry, but the contents are important, and I have been asked to hand the box only to him. I can come back later," Manik said as he got up to head back downstairs.

"Wait, let me ask him," Rajan said as he went inside the room. Manik could see him talking to Swaroop through the glass windows. They waved him to come inside.

"What's all this?" Swaroop asked, pointing to the box.

"Some papers, sir, from the law office in Surinampur that Kedar and I brought back. They are rather important, and we want to leave them with you for safekeeping, for now," Manik said. The meeting had momentarily stopped, and the others in the room were either looking at Swaroop and Manik or looking over their own files on the table. The request to keep papers at Swaroop's office was not unique. Swaroop's office was out of bounds for most of the employees in the building, and he had a big office with cabinets. It was normal for important papers to be kept there.

"All right, Manik. Let's leave them here for now," Swaroop said as he walked over to a cabinet at the end of the room and asked Manik to place the box in there.

Manik turned to leave.

"How was your trip?" Swaroop asked.

"Good, sir."

"Did you find anything useful?"

Manik was careful in answering the question.

"I think so, sir," Manik said, pointing to the box he had just handed over.

"Let's talk about this tomorrow. I will call you and Kedar tomorrow afternoon, and we can go over the details," Swaroop said.

"Sure, sir."

Manik slowly exited the room and headed to the stairway at the end of the floor. He looked back and saw that the rest of the people had resumed their meeting, and Rajan was back at his desk working away on the phone, barking orders at someone in the cafeteria to bring lunch for the folks in Swaroop's office. Manik realized that Harish must have persuaded them to continue the meeting and have a working lunch.

Once he was back at his desk, he saw that both Anjali and Kedar were on the phone. It was hard for him to concentrate on any work. He could not focus on any of the files on his desk. Anjali came over after she had finished her phone call.

"Are you all right? You seem a bit restless," she said.

"No. Just tired after the trip to Surinampur," Manik said in a calm voice.

"When's the professor's cremation?"

"It may be later today, unless it happened yesterday. I haven't had a chance to call his residence yet," Manik replied. He knew that he was probably not going to be able to attend the ceremony.

"You must go. I am sure Kedar would be fine with giving you some time off," Anjali said in an understanding tone.

"I am sure he would."

"How was Surinampur?"

"Good as can be, I guess," Manik replied, trying not to sound too excited.

"What's with the box that you took upstairs?"

"Oh. Those are some papers we got from the estate lawyer there. Kedar wanted me to leave them upstairs in Swaroop's office."

"They must be important for them to be kept upstairs. Well, I am heading downstairs for an early lunch. Do you want to join me?"

"Sure."

They looked over in the direction of Kedar's office. He was still on the phone. They decided to head to lunch. Manik didn't want to talk about the trip much with Anjali. Once they got their food, they headed over to a table where Subodh and Avik were sitting along with some other junior reporters. They were talking about the latest Bollywood movies. It was a welcome distraction for Manik, and Anjali joined the conversation.

Although he was tuning in and out of the discussion, his mind was preoccupied with the events of the day before. He was also curious about what Kedar had said just before they left his apartment about Rudra Pratap setting another trap to flush out the folks at the archives responsible for the papers going missing there. He had guessed rightly that it was an inside job but was unclear about the connection between what was planned tonight at the *Herald* to catch the culprits and what was being planned at the state archives. Rudra Pratap had not shared those details with him and Harish. Only Kedar knew.

During the long lunch, Manik nodded every now and then at the various conversations going on so as not to seem too distracted. But Anjali sensed that his mind was elsewhere. Once they started heading back to their desks, Anjali decided to ask him.

"You seem distracted today, Manik. What's going on?"

"It's the professor's passing. I am still sad about that. And I have a favor to ask. Can I please use the phone to call his residence?"

"Absolutely. I am going to head over to get some tea. I will give you some privacy."

"Thanks."

Once she had left, Manik got out his notebook and started dialing the professor's home number. An old gentleman picked up the phone. Manik inquired if Sucheta was there. He told Manik that she was busy with the arrangements for the ceremony in the evening. He asked him to hold while he went to look for her. Manik could hear a large group of people in the background. After a few minutes, he heard Sucheta's voice on the other end of the line.

"Hello."

"Hello, Sucheta; this is Manik."

"Hi, Manik."

"I am so sorry about your father. I am not sure what I can say to make you feel better. You know I liked him very much, and I am really sad that he is gone," Manik said with a heavy voice.

"I know, Manik. This is all so sudden. I haven't been able to even catch my breath to grieve. There are so many things that need to be done," Sucheta said, her voice cracking up.

"I won't keep you, then. I know you are terribly busy…thank you for talking to me. If there's anything I can do to help, please do let me know," Manik said.

"Thankfully, there are lot of people here who are helping. But yes, it would be good if you were here too. I could do with a friendly voice and shoulder. I don't know many of the people here that well. They are distant relatives that I haven't seen in a long time."

"How long will you be here?"

"For the next two weeks. Once the prayer ceremony on the tenth day is done, I will stay another couple of days and then go back to Bombay," she said.

"Right."

"I hope you are able to make it tonight at the cremation at the ghat. We will be there around eight," Sucheta said.

Manik knew he couldn't but didn't want to tell her. "I will try."

"My father really liked you. It would mean a lot if you could make it, Manik. But I need to go now. There are a lot of things that still need to be done," she said.

Manik could hear someone behind her calling out her name. "Bye, Sucheta. Again, I am so sorry for what happened."

"Bye."

He could sense the sadness in her voice and wanted desperately to be with her and console her. He wondered if he could just skip everything else that was supposed to happen tonight and be with his friend. Part of him wanted to. He also knew that Kedar and Harish wouldn't mind as long as he was with other people—he could ask Avik and Subodh to join him. But he realized that more than that, he wanted to find out if there was indeed someone in his office that might have been responsible for the professor's untimely death. The professor was already gone. He was not only sad but also angry about what had happened. That was the part that forced him to stay and find out the truth firsthand. As he was thinking about this, he realized that Anjali had come back to her desk. He quickly got up and made his way to her.

"Did you manage to speak to anyone in the professor's family?" Anjali asked.

"Yes," Manik replied.

But before they could continue their conversation, Kedar asked them to come over to his desk. Manik was relieved. He didn't want to have to explain to Anjali why he wouldn't be able to make it to the professor's cremation ceremony tonight or lie about it.

"We need to get cracking on the betting story and the interview with Niranjan," Kedar said.

"Yes, sir," Anjali said.

Manik nodded in agreement.

"Anjali, I want you to look over all the material that we have collected on the gambling story and start writing the first draft. I want you to focus on the addiction side of it. In the first part, we want our readers to know that there is little or no support for folks that have a gambling addiction. Please reference the psychologist and doctor we interviewed."

"Yes, sir," Anjali said.

Kedar then turned to Manik. "Manik, you need to finish the interview with Niranjan. I have read your first draft, and I have made some changes. We need to expand on some topics that I have marked here," Kedar said, handing him a folder with papers inside.

"Yes, sir. I will get on it right away," Manik replied.

They headed back to their desks, and Manik was left to ponder whether this was just a ploy by Kedar to keep Anjali and Manik separate for the rest of the day so that they wouldn't end up talking about Surinampur. Neither story was that urgent, and both could wait, Manik thought. Either way, Manik found it difficult to concentrate. He started working on what Kedar had given him. However, things were moving very slowly. He glanced at his watch every fifteen minutes. He could see some of the senior staff back at their desks for short periods of time before they headed back upstairs. Harish wasn't there. Probably still in Swaroop's office making sure that someone was always there. The clock struck five, and he could see some people on the floor slowly filing out. He went to the cafeteria to get a tea. As he was coming back upstairs, he ran into Anjali, who was leaving.

"I wonder what's got into Kedar," she said.

"Why?" Manik asked.

"Didn't you see? He was so stern with us earlier today to get working our articles," she said.

"Ah, yes, that. Not sure why," Manik said, looking away.

"Well, I am done for the day. I have left the first draft on his desk. How about you?"

"I am still working away on mine. It will take another couple of hours."

"I will see you tomorrow, then. Bye," Anjali said as she hurried down the stairs.

"Bye."

Back at his desk, the floor was starting to look empty. There were only a few of the junior staff left. Kedar walked over to Manik's desk.

"I am leaving, Manik. I need to let in you-know-who in a couple of hours," he said softly.

"Yes, sir," Manik said.

"You remember the location upstairs, right?"

"In the little storage room at the end of the corridor across from Swaroop's office?"

"Yes."

They had decided the best stakeout point was a little room on the floor where cleaning supplies were kept. It was a room with a door that had a small glass circular hole at the top. From there, one had a clear view of the door to Swaroop's office. A few feet away from the room was the main switchboard for the corridor lights. If necessary, they could quickly turn on all the lights in the hallway and corridors on that floor from one central location. It was a room that no one entered, except for the cleaning crew. Usually they arrived at 7:00 p.m. and were done in an hour. After 8:00 p.m. the room was empty, and so was the rest of the floor, except for Swaroop. The library closed around seven; the secretaries outside Swaroop's office left around six. Swaroop was usually the last to leave, around nine. They had decided to head to the little storage room just before nine and then wait.

Once Kedar left, Manik went back to his article. At around seven o'clock, he saw the senior staff all arrive at the same time at their desks. The meeting in Swaroop's room had ended. They all seemed to be in a hurry to leave. They chatted for a few minutes and then headed home. Arun saw Manik working and came by his desk on his way out.

"Burning the midnight lamp, are we?" Arun asked.

"Almost done, sir. Will be heading out soon," Manik said with a smile.

"Good. Well, good night, then," Arun said, walking toward Harish, who was waiting for him near the stairs.

"Good night, sir."

Once they had left, the floor was eerily quiet. He could see one other junior staff member at the end of the hallway typing away. Usually, at night, all the action in the building shifted to the ground floor, where the printing presses were. If any journalists were required on the shop floor to review anything or make any last-minute changes, they had to be in one of the shared offices on the same floor.

After a few minutes, the last of the employees had left. Most of the lights on the floor were already off. He couldn't see from his end of the room who had left last.

He could see the cleaning crew on his floor was almost done with their work. That meant that they had already completed their shift upstairs. Usually they started on the top floor. There weren't that many people on that floor, so it was easier to clean. Once they had finished on his floor as well, Manik checked his watch. It was around 8:30 p.m. Apart from a few dim lights, the floor was dark and silent. He could hear the general noise and commotion emanating from the ground floor and the print shop. There were getting ready to print the next day's paper.

Manik quietly put away his things, checked up and down the floor and the corridor leading up to the stairs. There was no one there. He slowly made his way up the stairs. It was dark, and he could see only one light at the end of the hallway, in front of Swaroop's room. He was still in his office. There was no way he could see anyone from his room, through the glass window, in the dark. The hard cement floor made it easier to walk without making any noise. Manik slowly headed over to the storage room. He had to be careful. There was very little lighting on the floor at this time. Once he made it to the door of the storage room, he opened it gently and went in. Inside the room a very small flashlight came on, and he could see that Kedar, Harish, and Rudra Pratap were already there. They immediately motioned to him to keep silent by putting their fingers on their lips. They moved over slowly to one side, making room for him to stand toward the back of the room.

Rudra Pratap stayed focused on the small hole in the door to keep an eye on what was happening outside. A small amount of light was visible from the vicinity of Swaroop's office. After about half an hour, they heard footsteps. Rudra Pratap looked through the hole. A few minutes later, the corridor became completely dark. Swaroop had left, and now came the hard part of waiting and watching to see if anyone came to take the box from his office. There was nothing they could do besides wait in the dark.

Kedar and Rudra Pratap took turns looking through the porthole on the door. Nothing was happening, and Manik was starting to get restless. He started thinking about whether anyone had picked up on their plan. He was trying to recall all the events of the last two days and started wondering if anyone in the office had done anything to raise an alarm. It was almost midnight, and Manik could sense that Rudra Pratap and Harish were getting restless too. Only Kedar seemed focused and kept his eyes on the porthole.

Just after midnight, when they were just shifting their weight from one leg to the other, they heard footsteps. They froze. There was someone on the floor. They could see some light, but it was not coming from the fixtures on the walls or in the ceiling. Someone was using a flashlight, and they could see the beam. They maintained their stony silence, and Rudra Pratap now took over from Kedar to see what was going outside.

After a minute he turned around. "Someone's inside Swaroop's office. We will wait for him to come out, and then I will turn on the lights," Rudra Pratap whispered extremely softly. Rudra Pratap kept his gaze on the opening in the door, and suddenly he saw someone coming out of Swaroop's office with a flashlight; he could barely make out that the person was carrying a box. Rudra Pratap ran outside, reached for the switchboard, and turned on all the lights in the hallway and corridors. Kedar, Harish, and Manik quickly followed. Once the lights were on, they had a full view of a person holding the box that Manik had left earlier that day in Swaroop's office. It was Rajan. For a moment he was completely frozen, and then he suddenly realized that he had been caught red-handed. He dropped the box and flashlight and ran toward the stairs. Manik wanted to run after him. Rudra Pratap stopped him.

"Don't worry, Manik; he won't get far."

Rajan didn't. As soon as he started bolting down the stairs, all the lights on the wide staircase came on, and he saw Constable Vijay and few other policemen waiting for him on the steps. There was nowhere else to go. Rudra Pratap slowly made his way down the stairs.

"Mr. Rajan, please come with us to the police station. We have some questions for you. We are arresting you, for now, for attempted theft. But we will be pressing other charges," Rudra Pratap said.

The look on Rajan's face said it all. The once confident, arrogant, and cocky demeanor had now given way to fear, shame, and guilt. He quietly nodded as the policeman placed handcuffs on him and took him away. Kedar, Harish, and Manik quickly caught up with Rudra Pratap, who was now slowly making his way down the stairs.

"Your plan worked, Rudra Pratap," Kedar said with a smile.

"Well, I can't take all the credit. Let's not get ahead of ourselves. Let's see what Rajan has to say first," Rudra Pratap said.

"Yes, of course." Kedar agreed.

"Remember what I said—not a word of this to anyone inside the building or outside. We still have to find the culprits who took the papers at the state archives. Manik, thank you for your help. You will be staying with Kedar again tonight. After one more day, hopefully you can go back to your normal routine," Rudra Pratap said, looking at Manik.

"I don't understand, sir," Manik said.

"Kedar will explain it to you. I must head off to the station to question Rajan," Rudra Pratap said as he turned and started walking to the exit.

"Let's go home, Manik, and we will talk there," Kedar said, looking at him.

"Sure, sir."

Kedar turned to Harish, stretched out his hand, and looked at him. "Thank you, Harish. We couldn't have done this without your help either. I am sorry it was Rajan. I know you were close to him," Kedar said.

Harish shook hands with Kedar. He was still a bit shocked at what had just happened. From the look on his face, it was clear that he had not thought his friend Rajan was involved in this.

"Any time, Kedar. I guess I didn't know Rajan as well as I thought," Harish said.

They all started walking and were just outside the door of the building ready to leave. Rajan had been whisked away very quickly. All the policemen were in plain clothes so as not to arouse any suspicion among the workers on the ground floor. Once they were outside the gates, they got Rajan into an unmarked police jeep and took him to the police station.

"Rudra Pratap has given us the same taxi we took this morning. Harish, we will drop you off on our way back," Kedar said.

"Thank you, Kedar," Harish said.

They got in the car. Harish was sitting in the back seat with Kedar. Manik was sitting next to the driver.

"Don't worry, we can talk freely," Kedar said with a smile. "Our driver here is a policeman."

The driver smiled.

Once they were on their way, it was Harish who broke the silence. "Kedar, you knew that it was Rajan, didn't you?"

"I was not entirely sure, but everything pointed to him," Kedar said.

"How so?" Harish asked. Manik was curious as well and glanced sideways to see Kedar as he started to respond.

"He was the one person who knew all along when the professor was heading to Surinampur and also when Manik and I were heading there. If you recall, the first time around, when Swaroop refused our request, he was there. After the professor died, when we went back to ask for approval again, he was there. Of course, other people knew too. Another thing Manik said that bothered me—you remember that day when the professor called you from Surinampur, Manik?"

"Yes, sir."

"What about it?" Harish asked.

"He only told you, Arun, and Rajan what the professor had told him, what he was bringing back. I had already left for the day," Kedar said.

"Oh, yes, that's right." Harish finally understood what Kedar was getting at.

"I am not sure I understand, sir," Manik said.

"Apart from us, only Harish, Arun, and Rajan knew of the entire Surinampur saga, the professor's trip, what he was bringing back, and our trip. Swaroop did not know what the professor had said to you on the phone until the day after, when we told him about the professor's death and the conversation you had on the phone. Do you understand now, Manik?"

"Yes, sir," Manik said thoughtfully.

"Then there was the gambling addiction, of course. What I found out was that both Arun and Rajan owe vast sums of money to private money lenders. Rajan, however, is the only one with all the connections to other businesses that the Roys own, including links to builders, real estate companies, and the like. What I suspect is that he may have contacted one of them and made a deal with them to hand over the papers for a sum of money so that he could pay back some of his debt. Rudra Pratap confirmed my suspicion when I spoke to him. It is likely that he had us followed to Surinampur. I wouldn't be surprised if the same gang is involved in the professor's murder and the attempted theft at the law office," Kedar said.

The taxi was slowly turning onto the road where Harish's building was located. The familiar mist that had been a fixture during the January nights in Calcutta was no longer there. It was a clear night full of stars. Harish pointed the driver to the building, and just before getting out, he looked at Kedar.

"It could have been Arun or me, as well, or even Swaroop—or, for that matter, anyone in the senior staff?" Harish asked.

"It could have been, yes. That's why we had to set a trap to find out who it was. I needed help from someone in the senior staff. I came to you, Harish," Kedar said.

"Of all the people, you trusted me?" Harish asked.

"Yes. Why wouldn't I?" Kedar said with a smile.

The taxi arrived outside the gates of Harish's building. He looked at Kedar and Manik.

"Good night to you both. It has been an interesting day, to say the least. We will talk again tomorrow."

"Good night, sir," Manik said. Kedar also nodded and waved at Harish as he turned and started walking into his building.

Then the car started heading to Kedar's apartment. Manik was silent rest of the way. His thoughts went back to Sucheta. It was nearly two thirty in the morning. He had missed the professor's cremation ceremony. He would likely have to wait at least another day before he could meet up with Sucheta.

Once they reached the building, they were quickly let in through the gates by the guards. Just as he got out, Kedar asked the driver, "Were we followed?"

"No, sir," he replied.

"That's good," Kedar said.

"We nabbed the ones outside the *New Eastern Herald*, sir," the driver said. "Most likely one of them was following you. But RP, sir, did not want to take any chances. So he has asked me to be with you at least until tomorrow."

"Park the car in one of the empty spots, and come up to my apartment. You will spend the night inside," Kedar said.

"I can sleep in the car, sir," the driver said.

"I will have none of that," Kedar said forcefully.

Once they were all inside, Manik saw that Laxman had prepared a warm meal for all of them. He was hungry and ate without talking much. Kedar was still lost in thought. He didn't seem to have much of an appetite but kept Manik company while he was eating. Once they had finished, Manik suddenly felt tired. Kedar looked at him.

"Let's talk tomorrow, Manik. No need to get up early. Our work is done. Tomorrow we need to see whether the police have done theirs," Kedar said.

"Yes, sir; good night."

"Good night."

Manik saw that old Laxman had washed and pressed his clothes and placed them neatly on the desk beside the bed. He had also put out another set of night clothes for him. He quickly changed and went to sleep.

9

Deception

When Manik woke the next morning, it was already 9:00 a.m. He could hear Kedar on the phone in the living room. Manik quickly got ready and joined him for breakfast at the dining table. Kedar was reading the morning paper, and when he saw Manik, he smiled and gestured with his hands that he should start eating.

"Sleep well, Manik?"

"Yes, sir."

"Well, I was on the phone with RP. Most likely, if all goes well, he will come see us at the office later today."

"Any news on nabbing the culprits from the state archives?" Manik asked while helping himself to the toast that Laxman had just brought in.

"Yes. Well, that's what he wanted me to tell you yesterday. You see, once Rudra Pratap became suspicious that the professor's death and the missing papers might be connected, he started making inquiries at the state archives. The professor told us that he had informed Asutosh and Vinod that he would be going to Surinampur."

"Yes, sir, I recall that as well."

"Right. From our visit to the archives, it was also evident that very few people knew about the contents of the box that arrived and disappeared on the same day. From what we know, the only people who knew were the head librarian, Asutosh, and Vinod. They left early that day, if you recall, and when they returned the next morning, the box was already gone."

"Yes." Manik nodded.

"So it must have been an inside job. But by whom?"

"If it's the same gang that Rajan and company were using, they might tell us. Some of them were nabbed yesterday."

"True, and RP is questioning them, and the name that came up was Asutosh. Unfortunately, there's no evidence against him. The person who was questioned wasn't entirely sure, since he wasn't the one who received the stolen box first time around—it was another, yet-to-be-apprehended gang member, who is still on the run. So RP has hatched another way of catching him."

"How is that, sir?"

"As you may have seen, Rudra Pratap did not want us to put anything in the paper about what happened last night. There's no news today of any gang being apprehended. That said, some of the gang members already know, and the ones who haven't been caught will go into hiding."

"Right."

"Remember Soumen from Surinampur?"

"Yes," Manik replied.

"Well, he is coming with yet another box to be delivered to the archives this morning. A call was placed earlier today from a public booth to the archives. Once the caller got through to Asutosh, he was told to expect another box of important papers and documents related to the Surinampur ruler's estate. It will be delivered later this morning. The caller then told him to bring the box once it arrives to a nondescript tea stall a few blocks from the archives building, on a narrow lane. He will then hand over the box in exchange for the same amount as last time for his services," Kedar said.

"The caller was someone from the police?" Manik asked.

"Yes," Kedar replied with a smile.

"Won't Asutosh suspect something?" Manik asked.

"How? He doesn't know that members of the gang were nabbed yesterday. He doesn't know who is bringing the box. He didn't know the first time around who called him, and the same goes for this time around."

"Did he agree?"

"Well, it seems that he haggled a bit on how much he wanted, and the police obliged him so as not to make him suspicious," Kedar said, still smiling.

"When is this 'exchange' supposed to take place?"

"Shortly," Kedar replied.

"I hope Mr. Soumen is not in any danger."

"None whatsoever. He is traveling by car. He doesn't have anything with him. The gang doesn't know he is coming. They are not aware of any other papers, and most of them have been caught. Once he arrives, RP will meet him at an agreed-upon location. He will give Soumen a sealed box with some bogus papers in them to take to the state archives. Once Soumen delivers them there, RP is expecting Asutosh to find a way to take them to the tea stall and to the welcoming arms of the police."

"Do you think it will work, sir?"

"I don't know, but we will know soon enough," Kedar replied.

As Kedar and Manik were on their way to work, in the outskirts of Calcutta a car was trying to make its way through the morning traffic, heading toward a small coffee shop near the Chowringee police station. The occupants of the car were Soumen Mitra and his driver. They had started early, and they could see the Calcutta skyline. The morning fog had cleared, and the sun was making its presence felt. Soumen was surprised when he received the phone call the day before from Rudra Pratap. He had spoken to him earlier, and Rudra Pratap had told him that he would be asked to come to Calcutta to make another statement and answer some questions relating to the papers. Soumen had agreed. What he did not know was the sense of urgency on Rudra Pratap's part to get it done immediately. Their conversation had made it clear that the police suspected that someone in the state archives was involved with the disappearance of the box. He had been surprised by Rudra Pratap's next request.

Soumen was supposed to meet him at a coffee shop near the police station, where he would be given a box that he would have to hand over to the archives. He had asked the reason for this, but the police had offered very few details apart from the fact that it would help greatly in nabbing the culprit. Soumen was smart enough to figure out that a trap was being set by the police to identify the miscreants. He had agreed. For one, he was upset that the papers had gone missing. The attempted break-in at his firm's offices in Calcutta had made him even more suspicious. He was certain that someone in the Calcutta office was involved as well. And in light of the professor's untimely death, he was convinced that there was a conspiracy, and he wanted to get to the bottom of it.

He liked his trips to Calcutta. He still had a lot of family there. He enjoyed the hustle and bustle of the city for short periods of time before returning to the peace and tranquility of Surinampur. Rudra Pratap had asked Soumen not to mention his visit to Calcutta to anyone till after he delivered the box to the archives. He agreed and kept quiet.

As the car made its way through the busy streets and lanes of Calcutta, Soumen gave instructions to the driver on the exact address of the coffee shop. Once the car turned on to the busy street, he asked the driver to park a few blocks away. He decided to walk the rest of the way. Once he reached the coffee shop,

Rudra Pratap was there, along with two other gentlemen whom he gathered must be police officers. None of them were in uniform. They sat down and ordered some tea, and Rudra Pratap quickly gave Soumen instructions on what he needed to do. He was to go to the state archives, identify himself as the estate lawyer from Surinampur, and then hand over the box in the reception area. The police told him not to engage in any prolonged conversation, and once he handed over the box, leave the building quickly.

"Soumen, we really appreciate your doing this," Rudra Pratap said.

"No problem at all. It all seems simple enough," Soumen said. "Do you want me to come back here?"

"No. You are welcome to do as you please after that. As long as you don't meet anyone from your office here, it should be fine. I doubt anyone else is interested in your whereabouts—plus, no one knows you are here. They are not aware of who is delivering the box," Rudra Pratap said.

"All right. I will drop in to say hello to some of my friends and relatives," Soumen said.

Rudra Pratap nodded. He lifted up a bag that had been under the table. He opened it and brought out a large cardboard box usually used for storing papers, files, and documents. The box was sealed with tape. He placed it on table.

"This is the box," Rudra Pratap said as he got up. "Please take it to your car and then to the archives. One of my men will be following you at a safe distance."

"I understand."

They quickly finished their tea, and Soumen carried the box out of the café and headed to his car. One of the two plainclothes policemen followed him at a safe distance. Soumen got into the car and started making his way to the archives. The policeman followed in another unmarked police car. Once Soumen reached the archives, he headed to the reception area.

Meanwhile, in the archives building, Asutosh was getting restless. He had received a cryptic call that morning telling him that an important box of papers was being delivered. He couldn't remember whether it was the same voice connected to the earlier exchange a few days back. From the conversation, it seemed that the caller knew about the previous box. The caller had given instructions on where to bring the box. He was a bit surprised about the location, but the caller insisted. Asutosh wanted to resist, but the caller threatened to expose him, and he finally relented. He asked for more money, and finally, after some haggling, they agreed on an amount. Still, something didn't seem right. He knew he had no choice. Asutosh needed the money. He also couldn't risk getting exposed. He also knew that the people he was dealing with were dangerous. He wished he hadn't gotten involved in the first place. When the professor had started doing research on the land deeds and covenants, initially Asutosh's interest had been academic. But then, during a conversation with one of his cousins who owned a construction company, he realized how important some of these papers were.

When the Surinampur estate was being folded, his cousin told him to keep an eye out for the land-related documents, as they could be of immense value to private builders and real estate companies. Indeed they were. This period also coincided with his brother's illness and the ever-increasing demands of his wife and children for a better life. Asutosh was always being reminded that he hadn't done well for himself financially. When his cousin offered him the opportunity to make a quick buck, he caved. The first exchange, a few days back, went off without any problems. The money that he received was much needed, and he spent it wisely. However, it bothered him, and he knew it was wrong.

He tried to but failed to get a hold of his cousin after receiving the most recent call, as he wanted to avoid getting further involved. Now there was no time. He had sent Vinod out on an errand to make sure he wouldn't be there when the box arrived. Once it came in, he would be there at the reception to receive it. That wouldn't raise any suspicion. It was part of his job. He would then quickly take the box upstairs to the storage room where all the other papers and boxes were kept. He would find a similar box and label it the same way as the one he was receiving, put some random papers in it, and seal it. There was no shortage of empty boxes or papers. Once that was done, he would take the box that had been delivered through the back entrance and head straight for the tea stall where the exchange was supposed to happen.

He saw an old gentleman arrive at the reception area. The receptionist had seen Asutosh hanging around since morning and called him over. Asutosh took Soumen to a seating area. He quickly took the box and gave him a form to fill out. Once that was done, he kept a copy of the form and gave another one to Soumen. Soumen then told Asutosh that he was late for an appointment and left.

Asutosh headed upstairs with the box. He looked around to make sure that his pesky assistant, Vinod, wasn't there. He quickly reached the storage room.

He found another box and executed the switch. The next step was to put the box in a bag and head to the back entrance. He looked at his watch. With any luck, the lone guard in the back would be off for a tea break and he could quickly leave without being noticed.

Once he reached the back entrance usually reserved for the staff working in the building, he could see the old guard listening to a transistor radio. It was someone he knew really well. The fact that he was carrying a bag could raise some suspicion if he tried to hide it. So he didn't. He went up to the guard and started chatting with him.

"Cricket? Test match?" Asutosh asked, pointing to the transistor radio glued to his ear.

"No, sir, just listening to music," the old guard replied.

"Ah," Asutosh said with a smile.

"Off for some shopping, is it?" the guard said, pointing to the bag.

"Yes. I need to buy some things for the kids. I am going out for an early lunch and then will pick some things up on the way back," Asutosh said with a smile.

"Good luck, then," the guard said, going back to his music.

"Bye," Asutosh said as he slowly exited the gate and walked into the lane behind the building.

He quickened his pace once he turned the corner and saw the tea stall where he was supposed to deliver the box. Once he entered, he saw that it was not as full as he had expected. One of the men at the far end waved at him to come over. The caller that morning had told him what he would be wearing, and he recognized him based on the description. He quickly headed over. He could see that the person who had hailed him had an envelope in his pocket. Asutosh went over to the bench, put the bag on the floor, and brought out the box. As he was ready to hand over the box, he noticed that two people had showed up and were standing behind him. He turned around and saw one of them bringing out a pair of handcuffs. He let out a scream and then gave in and started crying inconsolably.

Meanwhile, at the *New Eastern Herald*, Kedar, Manik, and Anjali had just finished lunch at the cafeteria when they saw a police jeep making its way through the gates. Rudra Pratap came out of the jeep in full uniform, along with his trusted constable, Vijay. Once Kedar saw him, he quickly went up to meet him. The other employees were surprised to the see the police on their premises.

"Good afternoon, RP. How are you?" Kedar asked.

"Hello, Kedar. It's all done. Can we go upstairs and meet Swaroop? I'd like to have Manik and Harish there too," Rudra Pratap said.

Manik and Anjali were watching from afar. They saw Rudra Pratap and Kedar turn to Manik and gesture to him to come over. Anjali was surprised. Manik wasn't.

"You haven't been telling me everything, have you, Manik? I knew it. You were hiding something," Anjali said in a stern but playful voice.

"I promise I will tell you all about it," Manik said, looking at her. Then he quickly walked over to Kedar and Rudra Pratap. He shook hands with the latter.

"Manik, we are heading up to Swaroop's office. Can you please get hold of Harish and meet us there?" Kedar asked.

"Sure, sir," Manik replied, and he headed out to find Harish.

Kedar and Rudra Pratap headed up to Swaroop's office. Unlike the night before, now the halls and corridors were full of lights, with a few people filing in and out of his office. They could also see some people coming in and out of the library. Swaroop meanwhile was talking to someone on the phone while standing near his desk.

There were a few people in his room, and his agitation was visible through the glass windows. Rajan's desk was empty. There was a young man sitting at another desk outside Swaroop's office who was struggling to work the phones and the switchboard. Kedar knocked and entered Swaroop's office. Swaroop was surprised to see him with a police officer. He hung up quickly. He asked the rest of the people in the room to leave.

"Swaroop, this is Officer Rudra Pratap. He would like to have a word with you," Kedar said.

"Please, take a seat," Swaroop said, pointing to the chairs across his desk as he slowly sat down as well.

Harish and Manik knocked and entered the room.

"Good morning," Harish said as he came through.

"Harish, Manik, not now. Can this wait?" Swaroop asked them.

"They need to be here too," Kedar said.

Swaroop was surprised. "I hope this is quick. It has been a total mess today. Rajan decided to take the day off, it seems, without telling anyone. I can't get hold of him. I've got someone new working here for the day, but he is struggling," Swaroop said, raising his arms in the air.

"Rajan's been arrested, Swaroop," Kedar said softly. "I will let Rudra Pratap explain."

Rudra Pratap leaned back and started explaining everything that had happened. Swaroop listened with great interest, and the rest of them could see the surprise on his face when it came to Rajan's involvement. Rudra Pratap also stated that they were closing in on someone at the law office in Calcutta who was involved, and an arrest was imminent. Kedar and Manik were happy to hear that Asutosh had taken the bait earlier that morning and had been taken into custody.

Once he finished, Rudra Pratap turned and looked at all of them one by one. "I need detailed statements from all of you on everything that you know. It is important that you write them yourself, and please include the time line of all the events."

"Does that include me as well?" Swaroop asked.

"Yes. We need to know your whereabouts and whether you mentioned the professor, Kedar, and Manik's visit to Surinampur to anyone outside this office. Please be as detailed and accurate as possible. Once you have the statements ready, please sign them and hand them over to me or Vijay, who is just outside the room. Please write your statements separately. Swaroop, we can leave you to write yours in this room. I see that there are a few conference rooms and a library on this floor. If they are available, I would request the rest of you take one each. We will wait outside Swaroop's office till you are done. We could have done this at the station. But given all the help we have gotten from all of you, it's fine if they are done here," Rudra Pratap said.

They spent the next hour writing their statements separately. Once they were done, they handed them over to Vijay, who had been making his rounds on the floor to make sure that they were doing them. Once he received all of them, he handed them over to Rudra Pratap, who took a quick look at them and nodded. They were standing outside Swaroop's office in the main hallway.

"I think we are done here," Rudra Pratap said, looking at Kedar.

"Thank you, RP. I am guessing a lot of your work starts now—trying to get to the masterminds behind this," Kedar said.

"Oh, I doubt we will get to that. I am happy we have got the people who were responsible for the professor's murder and, of course, solved what happened to the box at the archives. I am confident that some of the gang members will confirm that they were responsible for the attempted robbery in the law office. But beyond that I am not so sure," Rudra Pratap said.

"Why is that?" Manik asked.

"I suspect the real bosses are far removed from the events. The actual bosses and masterminds are rich and powerful. They are intelligent enough to keep themselves away from any of this, and finding a connection will be impossible. Of course, that doesn't mean we won't try. I certainly will. But I have seen what happens in cases like this. Eventually the minions get caught and punished. Their families are well looked after, and the masterminds are somehow never caught," Rudra Pratap said.

"What about the missing box with the original papers?" Kedar asked.

"That's long gone. One of the gang members confessed that it may already have been destroyed—burned, from what I hear," Rudra Pratap replied.

"What about the box with the copies that is in your possession?" Manik asked.

"Yes. I still have that. The police need to hold on to it as evidence," Rudra Pratap responded.

"Can we take a look at that?" Manik asked.

"Maybe after the case is done," Rudra Pratap said as he started walking toward the stairs.

"That might take months, if not years. A good man died trying to uncover what was in them. The least you can do is let us take a look at what's in them, what he died for," Manik pleaded.

"RP, Manik has a point. Even if it is being used for your investigation, you should be able to share the details with us," Kedar said.

Rudra Pratap had stopped just before he was about to go down the stairs. They could see that he was thinking hard about the request. After a moment's silence, he turned to Kedar and Manik. "Come by my office tomorrow, and I will see what I can do."

"Thanks, RP," Kedar said.

"Thank you, sir," Manik added.

"Any other questions or requests before I head out?" Rudra Pratap asked with a smile.

"Can I go back to my apartment and my normal routine now?" Manik asked.

"Yes. Absolutely. I think that should be fine," Rudra Pratap said and headed down the stairs.

Once the police officers left, they all looked at one another in silence. Swaroop was still in a bit of a shock trying to grasp what Rajan had done. He could hear his phone ringing in his room. He slowly made his way back. Kedar, Harish, and Manik headed back downstairs to their floor. Once they were back at their desks, Manik could see Anjali pacing back and forth.

He knew that he would have to tell her what had happened. But there was something else on his mind at the moment, and he needed to speak with Kedar. He could see that Kedar was back on the phone with someone. Anjali came by, and they headed to a conference room. Manik told her everything that had happened. For once, the usually talkative Anjali was completely silent and heard every word without any interruption.

"Wow," she said. The expression on her face said it all.

"Now you know why I was distracted and couldn't tell you everything," Manik said.

"Yes, I understand, Manik. I am not going to hold it against you. It seems you have had quite an adventure."

"Yes. There's something that I need to talk to Kedar about, and then I want to go to the professor's residence," Manik said.

"Yes. You should. I am sure Kedar will be fine with that. Stay in the room. I will see if he is off the phone, and I will ask him to meet you here. I have to take off early today. I will talk to you tomorrow," Anjali said as Manik left to get Kedar.

After a few minutes, Kedar came in and found Manik in a pensive, emotional state.

"Everything all right, Manik? Anjali said you wanted to talk to me?"

"Yes, sir."

"Is it about visiting your friend Sucheta? If so, please go ahead. You can take the rest of the day off—or for that matter, a few days off, if you want. I know the last few days have been mentally draining. If you need some time, don't worry about it."

"Thank you, sir. But there's something else."

"What is it?" Kedar asked.

"From everything that Rudra Pratap told us, it seems Rajan came to know what the professor was bringing back from Surinampur based on the conversation I relayed after speaking to him when he called me. I had told Harish, Arun, and Rajan when the professor was coming back and what he was bringing back. That prompted Rajan to involve the gang, and that's what got him killed," Manik said with tears in his eyes.

"Manik, you don't know that for sure. The people involved here, as you just heard from RP, have long tentacles," Kedar said, trying to calm him down.

"Even before that, I was the one who insisted that we try to get approval from Swaroop to accompany the professor. When we went to get the approval, Rajan was there. He knew just because I was the one who insisted on making the request." Tears were streaming down Manik's face.

"Manik, you are not, in any way, responsible for the professor's death. There is nothing that has happened that should make you feel that way," Kedar said as he came close to Manik and put his arms around his shoulder.

"I know I am. Had I not insisted on making the request for the trip or mentioned what the professor told me when he called from Surinampur, he would still be alive. You know that, sir," Manik said as he tried to compose himself.

"Manik, the good professor came to us to ask us for help. We tried our best to help him as much as we could. You did the best you could, and your intentions were always noble and well meaning. I can't imagine anyone else doing anything more or anything differently knowing what we did at the time," Kedar said as he tried to console Manik.

"I wish the professor had never come to us," Manik said. "He would still be alive."

Kedar gave Manik a handkerchief to wipe his tears. After a moment's silence, he held Manik's arm and looked at him.

"I know you are sad, Manik. From what you have told me, the professor was a good man. You did what you could for him, and later you made sure that his killers were apprehended. Now, I know that it's normal to think about what we could have done differently. But in life we don't get a do-over. There is no rewind button. With time I am sure you will realize that we all did the best we could. I think what you should do now is go see Sucheta and offer your condolences. Spend some time with her, and take some time off," Kedar pleaded.

"I have to tell her all of this too," Manik said with a sad voice.

"Now may not be the right time. She is grieving. You can let her know that her father's killers have been apprehended," Kedar said.

Manik was quiet for a moment. "Thank you, sir. I am not sure what I will say. But she deserves to know the truth. I will be here tomorrow to go with you to the police station to see the contents of the box."

"Sure, Manik. Take your time. I can let RP know that we will visit him in the afternoon. That way, you can come in a bit late."

"Thank you, sir."

Manik decided to call it a day, and for the first time in more than two days, he was able to go back to his apartment. He changed and headed straight to the professor's residence to meet Sucheta. He was still thinking about how to tell her that her father's death was tied to what he was looking into and that what he shared within his organization might have, in part, led to his murder.

It was late afternoon, and by the time the tram snaked its way through the streets of Calcutta to reach the stop nearest to the professor's house, he felt anxious. He got off and slowly started walking. The sidewalk was full of students, and the tea stalls and cafes were starting to fill up. When he finally reached the professor's house, he could see through the gates and the main door, which was wide open, that there were some people there. When he walked in, he was greeted by a lady who introduced herself as one of Sucheta's cousins. There were a few people in the main living room. He didn't recognize any of them. Just before he could ask anything, he heard a familiar voice behind him.

"Manik, is that you?"

He turned around and saw Sucheta walking in behind him.

"Hi, Sucheta."

"Manik, it's good to finally see you," she said as she put her arms around him and gave him a big embrace. The rest of the people suddenly stopped talking and looked at them. Sucheta quickly introduced him. Manik had rightly guessed that most of them were extended family who were visiting from out of town.

"I was just outside seeing off someone at the bus stop. Do you want to go to a café and talk?" Sucheta asked.

"Don't you need to be here? With your guests?"

"Oh, no. They are staying here for the next few days. Don't worry; they have seen enough of me, and I certainly have seen enough of them. I need some familiar faces and friends to talk to for a change."

"Sure," Manik said, and they departed.

Sucheta turned around and quickly informed the rest of the people that she would be out for a while. Once they started walking together, Manik caught a full glimpse of Sucheta. She looked as beautiful as ever. Manik recalled how lively she had been during her college days, her sense of humor and her independent spirit. She had always been confident, and it showed in her mannerisms and the way she conducted herself. He could also see she was sad. She hadn't changed much, yet he could sense that she was very tired. They walked together in silence for a few minutes and turned the street corner. Sucheta pointed to a small café with some empty seats in the back. Manik nodded. They made their way inside, placed their orders, and sat down.

"How have you been, Manik?"

"I have been busy at work…I am really sorry about your father. You know I liked him very much, and he helped me a lot. Both of you did. I apologize for not being here sooner," Manik said.

Sucheta was quiet, and Manik could sense that she had expected him to be there with her earlier. But she didn't show it. "It's all right, Manik. I know we are all busy."

"How did the cremation ceremony go?" Manik asked.

"I am not sure, really. I was in a daze. Sometimes you really wonder about the point of all these ceremonies and traditions. You would expect that people would leave you alone in a time like this. But they don't."

"I think that's the point."

"What do you mean?" Sucheta asked.

"Not to leave you alone. To take your mind off what has happened."

"That's silly."

"Yes, I agree—and quite annoying. I remember when my mother passed away. There were so many relatives who came to visit, and we just had to sit there and pretend to be nice while they tried to console us. Many of them say stupid things like they know what we must be going through or understand what we are feeling. Just plain irritating, if you ask me."

"I know. I haven't seen most of my extended family for a while now. I am not even close to them. I am just keeping up appearances for my father's sake, and once the tenth-day ritual is done, I will be back in Bombay. I hope you make it to that ceremony. It will be at my father's house."

"I will be there," Manik said.

The tea arrived, and they started reminiscing about old times. They recounted how her father had had a knack for telling stories, and they recalled his sense of humor. They talked about their college days, their friends, and the times they had spent together.

"You know my father really liked you, Manik. He never said it, but I am sure he wanted us to be together. He just never got around to saying it," Sucheta said with a smile.

"Yes. I think he sensed we like each other. But did he really know about us? Everything about us?"

"No, of course not. Even though he was a professor and quite liberal, he would have been scandalized if he knew everything. He obviously knew we liked each other, and he did see us going out together. I don't think he suspected how much we were together and how close we had become emotionally and physically," Sucheta said, her voice suddenly becoming sad at the thought of her father.

Manik decided to switch topics to get her mind off her father for a bit. "How is Bombay?"

"It's a great city. People are nice," Sucheta replied, regaining some of her composure.

"Do you like it? Have you settled in?"

"It was difficult at first, not having any friends there. I have an aunt, but I was never close with her. Having her nearby helps. But what I missed was having friends. But now that I am sharing an apartment with some other people, it has helped. I have managed to make some friends at work too."

"That's good," Manik said with a smile, wondering if that meant that she would never consider moving back to Calcutta.

"Is Bombay very different from Calcutta? I have been there only once as a tourist. I am not sure how it is to live there." Manik asked.

"Oh yes, very different. The traffic is worse, if you can even imagine that. But there are no strikes, trains run on time—and the rains, my God, the rains. I mean, it's bad in Calcutta, but Bombay is just like a bathtub and gets flooded like crazy in some areas."

"And the food?"

"Oh, well, that's the good part of being in Bombay. Just like Calcutta, you have people from all over. You would be surprised how many Bengalis live there. Name a cuisine, and there are plenty of restaurants in the city. I haven't quite gotten used to the vada pavs just yet, but I am getting there," Sucheta said, as she finished her tea. They quickly ordered another one and spoke a bit more about the similarities and differences between the two cities.

"There are pros and cons to every place, I guess. We just have to make the most of where we are and find ways to enjoy it" Manik said.

"That's true, Manik. More than the city, I missed my father. I missed my friends and you. It seems our story had just started, and then life took us in different directions," Sucheta said, her voice turning sad.

Manik wanted to reach across the table and give her a big hug. "I don't know if I told you, but I did apply to some positions in Bombay at some magazines that had openings. But I never heard back from them," he said.

"It seems fate has different plans for us."

"I am not sure I believe that."

"You don't believe in destiny, Manik?"

"I am not sure what to believe. I think a lot depends on the choices we make and the actions we take. I think I read it somewhere, this thing about destiny, and it probably sums up what I think."

"What is that?"

"A man does what he can until his destiny is revealed to him," Manik replied thoughtfully.

Another round of tea arrived, and while they were being served, they had some time to pause and collect their thoughts.

"What about you, Manik? Last I heard from my father was that you were working for the *New Eastern Herald*."

"Yes."

"Is that exciting? I know you wanted to be a musician, and journalism was your second choice."

"That's right. I'd have preferred working for a magazine. Some sort of current affairs magazine. I applied to most of the newspapers, magazines, journals. This was the only one that I could find."

"It's a good one, Manik. I am sure you are good," Sucheta said confidently.

"I am not so sure," Manik replied in a low voice.

"What about your music? Are you still writing new music?"

"Not as much as I would like to."

"Did you ever send in your compositions to anyone?"

"Yes, with no luck." Manik sighed.

"Don't worry, Manik. All that means is that the world still has to discover your hidden talents," Sucheta said with smile.

"Or maybe I am not that good, or no one likes it."

"No. I have heard your music, and I like it. My father liked it too. Do you remember when you used to come and play your compositions on the piano for us?"

"Yes," Manik replied. He could see that Sucheta's thoughts had shifted to her father, and her voice had become shaky.

"It was a shock, you know. I know he was getting old. But he wasn't sick. I was hoping he was going to be here for a few more years. To see me get married and have a family of my own," Sucheta said, trying to hold back her tears.

"I know; I am sorry."

"It's how he went too. This hit-and-run. I just feel mad at those horrible, terrible people. I know I shouldn't, but I want bad things to happen to them. I don't care if that makes me a bad person. I just hate them for doing this to my father." Sucheta started crying. The rest of the people in the café started looking at them. An old gentleman inquired if everything was fine, and after Manik told him about what had happened, he offered his condolences. Sucheta regained some of her composure, but her cheeks were still wet. Manik gave her a handkerchief.

"Did the police tell you what happened?" Manik asked.

"Yes," Sucheta replied.

"What did they tell you?"

"There was this police officer who came by before you arrived. He was there only for a few minutes. He told me that they had caught the gang that was responsible for my father's hit-and-run. One of them had confessed, and they were now in police custody. I am glad that they were caught. But it doesn't bring my father back, and I am not sure how I am supposed to feel," Sucheta said.

"This police officer who came—was it Rudra Pratap Singh?"

"Yes, that's right. That's the name. How did you know?" Sucheta asked. He could see the astonishment on her face. She was still in an emotional state, with tears in her eyes. But suddenly she was surprised to hear Rudra Pratap's name from Manik.

"Sucheta, there is something that I need to tell you," Manik said.

Manik then told her everything. How the professor had approached the newspaper regarding the missing box of papers from the state archives, the attempted robbery at the law office in Calcutta, her father's trip to Surinampur, how he had called to let Manik know about what he had unearthed, how Manik had then shared the details with his colleagues, his trip to Surinampur with Kedar, what they had discovered there, how they had been followed, the traps that Rudra Pratap had set to catch the culprits in his office and at the archives. Manik left nothing out, and he could see that Sucheta was grasping every detail and trying to understand everything that had happened. When he finally stopped, there was long pause that seemed to last forever. The expression on Sucheta's face had suddenly changed. It had become serious, and he could sense that she was angry.

"Are you telling me, Manik, that if my father hadn't approached you or told you what he had discovered, and you hadn't blurted out what he said to you to your colleagues, he would still be alive?" Sucheta said in an angry voice.

Manik kept quiet and then reached across the table to take her hand. She quickly moved her hand away.

"Perhaps. I don't know, Sucheta," Manik said in a sad voice.

"You are telling me this now?" she said, raising her voice.

"I am sorry," Manik said in a pleading voice.

"Is that why you haven't come to visit me until now? Somehow you thought that if you showed up after the culprits had been caught, it would be better?"

"No. Not at all." Manik's voice was breaking.

"And you kept quiet all this time. Talking about other things. How do you think that makes me feel? Shame on you, Manik. I don't want to talk to you. I wish I'd never met you. No need to come by anymore. I don't want to see you ever again," Sucheta screamed at him with tears rolling down her cheeks. She got up and stormed out of the café.

Manik wanted her to stay so that he could plead with her, but she was gone. He knew that there was nothing that he could do or say that would make Sucheta feel better. The café was silent. He could sense that all the patrons in the establishment had stopped talking and were listening to what was happening between Sucheta and Manik. Once Sucheta left, Manik got up and paid for their orders.

He slowly walked out of the café and back to the professor's house. The gates and the main door were still open, and he could see from afar that Sucheta was back home surrounded by her extended family. She was talking to an old lady, and then she started crying. The old lady took her into her arms and tried to console her.

Manik turned around and started walking back slowly to the tram stop to make his way back home. It was already evening; the streetlights were on, and a heavy mist had descended on the city. Manik did not notice any of it as he walked. He sat down on a bench near the tram stop. The first tram came and went, and he was still in a daze. When the next one arrived, he took it and went home. Once he was back in his apartment, he saw a note under the door from Avik asking him to join him and Subodh for drinks. He crumpled it up and threw it in the basket. He changed and tried to go to sleep. He couldn't. He tried listening to some music. That didn't help either. Finally, he brought out the notebook that he had kept in his closet, the one that contained all his musical compositions. He started writing.

10

The System

When Manik woke up the next morning, he was surprised to see that he had spent the night sleeping with his head on the desk. He was still sitting in his chair. He had fallen asleep while writing. He wanted to go in to work late. But with how things had gone with Sucheta the day before, he decided to get ready and meet up with Avik and Subodh at the restaurant for breakfast and then head to work. They were already there when he arrived. He hadn't seen them in a while, and by now most of the office knew what had happened with Rajan and Manik's involvement in the case. He was expecting them to ask him lots of questions. But when he arrived, he saw they had sullen expressions on their faces.

"What's with the long faces?" Manik asked.

Avik and Subodh could sense that Manik was not in a good mood either, but they didn't know what had happened with Sucheta the night before.

"Hi, Manik," Subodh said.

"I guess you haven't heard," Avik continued.

"Heard what?" asked Manik as he eased in beside Subodh and gestured at the waiter to bring him his usual breakfast.

"It's Harish's wife," Subodh said. "She passed away last night."

"Oh, no," Manik said. He suddenly lost his appetite.

"Apparently she wasn't doing well. From what I heard, they took her to the hospital yesterday evening, and she died in her sleep," Avik said.

"That's very sad," Manik said. He felt bad for Harish.

They ate their breakfast silently for a while. Avik broke the silence. "Did you go see Sucheta?"

"Yes," Manik replied in tense voice.

"How did that go?" Avik asked.

"Not well at all. I am not in a mood to talk about it now. Let's head to work," Manik said.

Both Avik and Subodh nodded as they quickly finished their meal.

When Manik arrived at his desk, he was surprised to see Kedar already at work. He was on the phone with someone. Anjali was not at her desk. She had probably taken some time off. Harish's wife was her aunt, after all, and it was normal that she wouldn't be in the office. He looked across the hallway toward the desks of the senior staff. He could see Arun, but most of the others still hadn't arrived. Just as he was about to sit down, he saw that Kedar had walked up to his desk and was standing next to him.

"Good morning, Manik. I guess you heard the news about Harish's wife?"

"Yes, sir."

"Well, that's our first stop today. We need to go to see Harish to offer our condolences and then meet with Rudra Pratap. He has called us to talk about the papers. He is going to meet us in the café, not the police station."

"That's a bit strange, isn't it, sir?"

"Yes, it is. Let's get moving. He wants to meet us in a couple of hours," Kedar said. He headed back to his desk to pick up his bag. Manik sensed that Kedar was in a hurry and was worried about something. He figured that he was probably sad at the news of Harish's wife. He remembered what Anjali had told him about Kedar and Harish's wife.

Once they were out of the building, they quickly called for a taxi and headed to Harish's apartment. When they arrived, they saw that it was full of people. Manik recognized many of them. Almost the entire senior staff was there. He also saw Swaroop and Tarun Roy offering their condolences to Harish, who was sitting on a chair in corner of the room. Anjali was sitting beside him. Kedar and Manik slowly walked past the rest of the people in the room, and once Harish was free, they walked up to him.

"I am so sorry, sir," Manik said.

Harish nodded as he looked at him.

"Harish, if there's anything you need, please don't hesitate to ask," Kedar said.

Harish got up. Kedar could see that he had tears in his eyes. "I am all alone now," Harish said.

"I am so sorry, Harish." Kedar put his arms around him, and as they embraced, Harish started to cry.

The rest of the people in the room, especially Harish's colleagues from work, were very surprised to see that. Manik wasn't. From what he had seen in the past few days, he knew that Kedar and Harish were still good friends, and beneath all the bitterness and animosity, they knew that they could count on each other as friends. Kedar slowly helped Harish back into his chair. Other people walked up to offer their condolences. Manik moved aside and started to slowly make his way toward the door. Kedar spoke to Harish for a few more minutes and then joined Manik as they stepped out.

As they exited the building, they saw an old man stepping out of a beautiful antique Morris Minor. The chauffeur had opened the door, and they saw Sarat Roy getting out of the car with his familiar walking stick. When he saw Kedar and Manik, he nodded at them and started making his way to Harish's apartment.

Manik and Kedar got into another taxi and started making their way to meet Rudra Pratap. During the ride both of them were silent. Manik was preoccupied with what had happened with Sucheta the night before. When they reached the restaurant, they quickly walked inside, found a table in the corner, ordered some tea, and waited for Rudra Pratap to arrive.

"Something's not right," Kedar said.

"What do you mean, sir?"

"You were right, Manik. Why would RP want to meet us here and not at the police station?"

"What do you think it is?"

"It has to do with the papers. I am sure it does. Up until now he has not told anyone about their contents, even within his department. Now that the arrests have been made and he has started sharing what's in them, it must have ruffled some feathers with his superiors," Kedar said.

"But they are the police."

"So what? You think the people involved in this who wanted to make these papers disappear don't have contacts in the police? Their reach knows no bounds."

Just as Manik was about to ask his next question, Rudra Pratap arrived with Vijay. They were not in uniform, and they quickly sat down. Kedar could see from the expression on Rudra Pratap's face that he was very serious, and he looked unhappy. After exchanging pleasantries and ordering some tea, Rudra Pratap got right to the point.

"As you may have guessed, Kedar, we are meeting here because some of my superiors are worried about making the contents of the box public," Rudra Pratap said.

"Yes, I figured as much," Kedar said.

"From an investigation standpoint, we need the box as evidence. The good news is that we have now been able to obtain statements and confessions that will help immensely in bringing the professor's killers to justice, and also Asutosh at the state archives. Rajan was certainly involved with the professor's death, and we are still trying to establish if there's any connection between him and Asutosh. But we have got Asutosh for theft, and he isn't going anywhere anytime soon." Rudra Pratap paused.

"Understood, RP. But without knowing the contents of the box, we won't know why all this happened and have no chance whatsoever of catching the masterminds," Kedar pleaded.

"Oh. I don't think it will ever come to that. Trust me when I say that the people involved in this are so well connected and insulated that there will be little evidence to point a finger at them," Rudra Pratap replied, and they could sense the frustration in his voice.

"Can we at least look at the papers?" Kedar pressed Rudra Pratap.

"Officially, no. They are now sealed in the evidence room."

"But you are investigating the case. You can surely share something with us?"

"No. I am off the case," Rudra Pratap replied in a serious tone.

"What do you mean?" Kedar asked.

"As the details of the case and contents of the box emerged, it became clear that if it became public, it could make life uncomfortable for a lot of people, especially now, with the elections coming up. Just think about it, Kedar. Even if there's no direct proof or evidence, just the accusation that there's a nexus between the government and the real estate companies that may have swindled inheritances of a large number of families would cause a huge scandal. Not to mention it would also hurt the bottom line of many of these companies and businessmen. There would be plenty of court cases. That would take years to resolve, and as you well know, land and property disputes can drag on for decades. Add to that the fact that many of these lands have already changed hands, and there would be claims for compensation against the builders and new owners. It would be an utter mess. A total scandal right before the election," Rudra Pratap said.

"So what?" Kedar asked. "It's the right thing to do. We should not shy away from making this public just because it's inconvenient. It will be a scandal, yes. But what about fairness and the rights of the folks who own these lands and never got their fair share?"

"I agree, and that's why we are meeting here," Rudra Pratap said as he turned to Vijay.

Vijay reached into a bag that he had been carrying and brought out three large folders with a thick stack of papers in each of them.

"What's this?" Kedar asked.

"Copies that I was able to make of the papers that are in the evidence room. I couldn't do all of them, but these are most of them," Rudra Pratap said.

"You and Vijay will get into trouble, RP, if your superiors come to know," Kedar said. Manik could sense that there was genuine concern in his voice.

"Well, that's the reason why this meeting never happened, and you did not get the papers from us. I am counting on you not to reveal your sources," Rudra Pratap said.

"Understood," Kedar replied.

"One more thing. If my superiors can be influenced, then so can yours. Please keep that in mind," Rudra Pratap said.

"Agreed." Kedar nodded.

"Well, I must be off now. I am counting on you to take this further. You see, there are times when journalists and police can actually help one another," Rudra Pratap said with a smile as he got up.

"Thank you, RP. Once we get this into the newspaper, things might be different for you too, and maybe your superiors will put you back on the investigation to pursue anything that might come out of this," Kedar said, pointing to the files on the table.

"Oh, I know that won't happen," Rudra Pratap said with a smile.

"Why not?" Kedar asked.

"Both Vijay and I came to know today that we are being transferred. Most likely to Delhi. The transfer order is already in the works."

"Wow. The 'system,' isn't it?" Kedar sighed.

"Yes, the 'system' is fighting back and will take care of its own. What else can I say?" Rudra Pratap got up. They all shook hands.

"We will do our best, RP," Kedar said.

"Fighting the system is never easy. All I can say is good luck, and please do keep in touch. No matter what happens, both you and Manik helped the police immensely in catching the culprits. For that, you have my gratitude." Rudra Pratap turned and left, with Vijay following close behind.

Kedar and Manik sat down and ordered another round of tea and snacks and started going through the papers. The more they read, the more they realized the uproar it would cause. It also convinced them that they had to make it public. And they realized that the originals that had been stolen from the archives were probably destroyed and that any lawsuits by people trying to prove their ownership based on these copies would most likely have to go through the courts and years of expensive litigation. Many of them probably wouldn't be able to afford it. But at the very least, they could seek some compensation. They spent the next three hours going through all the folders. When they finished Kedar turned to Manik.

"We need to come up with a plan," Kedar said.

"Right, sir."

"I am sure we will get some resistance and pushback from Swaroop, but I think we should be able to convince him."

"Yes, sir."

"Well, let's talk it over as we head back to the office and see if we can meet Swaroop."

During the ride back to the office, Kedar and Manik started discussing what to do with the papers, what sort of article they would write, and how they could make the details available in a manner that could benefit the rightful owners who had been denied their inheritance. Once they reached work, they continued their discussion and started with what needed to be done. Kedar called Swaroop's substitute secretary, and he told him that Swaroop was busy in meetings but could meet them at 6:00 p.m. That suited Kedar and Manik just fine. There was a lot that needed to be done.

Manik looked around and saw that most of the folks who had been in Harish's apartment that morning were now back in the office, except for Anjali. Once it started getting closer to six, Manik could see some of his colleagues were starting to leave. Kedar came by with the three folders and the stack of papers that Rudra Pratap had given them, and they made their way up to Swaroop's office. They could see from outside that Swaroop was on the phone. They waited, and when he had finished, they went in. Swaroop asked them to take a seat, and Kedar started recounting his encounter with Rudra Pratap and what they had found in the papers. Swaroop listened without interrupting. Once Kedar had finished, Swaroop was still thinking. Manik and Kedar gave him some time to let it all sink in.

"This is explosive stuff," Swaroop said.

"Yes." Kedar agreed.

"You do realize I need to get this approved by Tarun?" Swaroop said.

"Why?" Kedar asked.

"I think this is important enough that they should know."

"But we will still publish, right? Can we start working on it starting tomorrow?" Kedar asked.

"Yes. I think both of you can start working on it. I am going to the Roy residence tonight for something else, and I can tell them at that time. Can I take the folders with me? Tarun's lawyers will be there too, and I could pass it by them as well, make sure that they are fine with it."

"Sure" Kedar said. "We will leave it with you and pick it up tomorrow morning."

"Good work, both of you," Swaroop said. "Not just on this, but also on helping the police. I still can't believe Rajan's involvement in this. I have known him for years, and I would have never guessed."

"Well, at least that's behind us now," Kedar said as he and Manik got up.

"Come by at eleven tomorrow. Good night."

"Good night, sir," Manik said as he and Kedar left the room.

As they reached their desks, Kedar turned to Manik. "Time to call it a day. We will pick things up again tomorrow."

"Yes, sir."

"Oh. I forgot to ask you. How did to go with Sucheta yesterday?"

"Not good, sir. She was very upset and angry. I think she blames me for what happened to her father," Manik said in a low voice.

"She is grieving, Manik. Give it time. She will realize that it was her father who came to you for help. Eventually she will come around to see that you did your best."

"I am not sure, sir."

"Remember, she is still your friend, and you should try to maintain that friendship. Try talking to her in a few days. If she doesn't talk, write to her. Don't pester her at the moment, but I am sure things will smooth over eventually."

"I hope so, sir. It's just that I don't know what I can say to make her feel better."

"Yes, that's a dilemma for the ages, isn't it? Words are sometimes woefully inadequate in expressing how we feel. But that's all we have. All I can say is don't give up on her. Most importantly, please don't blame yourself. You are in no way responsible for what happened to the good professor."

"Thank you, sir."

"Come, I will walk you out. By the way, I know it wasn't the best of circumstances, but it was nice to have you over at my place. Laxman was happy to have someone besides me in the house."

"Right, sir. Please do thank Laxman for me. I really appreciate what he did, and your hospitality."

"Well, you can thank him yourself. You can come over, you know. I was meaning to ask you. Bring your compositions with you. I have a piano, and I'd love to hear what you have written."

"Sure, sir. Are you heading home?"

"Yes. But first I will pass by Harish's. I want to see if he is ok, and then will head home," Kedar said. They walked together until they reached the gates; they shook hands, and Manik started walking home. He thought about what Kedar had said about Sucheta. He wasn't sure that Sucheta would ever forgive him.

Next morning, when Manik arrived at his desk, he sensed something was wrong. He could see Kedar talking to the rest of the senior staff in the aisle where most of them had their desks. He couldn't recall a single instance when they had actually spoken to him, as a group or individually. From what he could see from his desk, it seemed like Kedar was doing most of the talking, while the rest of them were listening to him, some nodding in agreement. After a few minutes, Kedar walked back to his desk. He saw Manik and pointed toward the stairs, indicating that he should meet him there. Once they both reached the end of the hallway leading up the stairs, Kedar turned to Manik.

"Time to meet Swaroop. From what I hear, the Roys don't want us to publish anything on any of this."

"What?" Manik said in a loud voice.

The rest of the folks on the staircase stopped and looked toward them. Kedar and Manik ignored their glances and continued climbing. Once they were outside Swaroop's office, they saw another gentleman there. Swaroop saw them through the glass window and gestured for them to come inside. Once they were inside, he introduced the gentleman as one of the lawyers who handled cases for businesses owned by the Roys. The fact that there was a lawyer present meant that things weren't going to go smoothly. After some brief introductions, they all sat down around the round table, and it was Swaroop who broke the news first.

"We cannot publish anything related to the papers."

"Why not?" Kedar asked.

"For one, its contents are part of an ongoing police investigation. We don't want to take the risk of jeopardizing their case. Secondly, we can't reveal our source. That in itself will raise lots of questions and expose us to litigation. Finally, these are all copies. There's nothing in here to suggest that they will lead to anything meaningful," Swaroop said.

The lawyer and Manik kept quiet; Kedar and Swaroop were left to argue on the topic.

"Unbelievable," Kedar said. "Since when do we care about what the police think or worry about litigation. Let the readers decide whether it's meaningful or important."

"I am afraid that's not the way we see things," Swaroop said.

"Who is 'we,' Swaroop? You, the Roys, or the lawyers?" Kedar asked.

"If you must know, I have the same opinion," Swaroop replied in a tense voice.

"Are you sure you are running a newspaper? We are supposed to report things, stir things up, not worry about keeping people happy. Your arguments are useless," Kedar answered in a stern tone.

"Careful now, Kedar. They are not my arguments alone. It's a collective decision taken by all of us that we do not go public with any of this. It might do more harm than good."

"Really? What about the families who may yet have a chance to get some compensation and who are getting swindled out of their inheritance by these builders and real estate firms?"

"That is not our concern, Kedar."

"Why not?"

"We are not here, as a paper, to take sides."

"We are not taking sides. We will just report what we found."

"You know it's not that simple, Kedar."

"No. It actually is. I don't know if you have thought this through, Swaroop. If this newspaper is the first one to report this, then imagine how your readers will perceive it. Your readership, which you care so much about, will actually grow."

"Yes, we thought of that. The risk of putting this out outweighs any potential increase in circulation," Swaroop replied.

"You are sitting on a great story. One that has the potential to define this paper. Something that can actually benefit a lot of people. It is also the right thing to do. You are foregoing all that because you don't have the balls to publish," Kedar said angrily.

"Enough, Kedar" Swaroop shouted back. "I have just about had it with this discussion. The decision has been made, and let me remind you that I do have the final say in approving the content. This won't make it."

"Fine. Just out of curiosity, did you, the lawyers, and the Roys even see what's in the papers?"

"Yes, we did," the lawyer said.

Kedar and Manik turned to look at him.

"And?" Kedar asked.

"As Swaroop rightly said, the decision to not publish this is in the best interests and reputation of the paper," the lawyer replied.

"Wow. The reputation of the paper. Interesting. What exactly is the reputation of the paper now?" asked Kedar. He was still angry.

"All right. I am putting a stop to this now," Swaroop said, ignoring Kedar's question. "We are going around in circles."

"Where are the files?" Kedar asked, looking around the room.

"We are going to hold on to them, Kedar," the lawyer replied. "We don't want this to fall into the wrong hands."

"And you and the Roys are the right custodians to hold on to them. Is that right?" Kedar asked with a sarcastic smile.

"There's nothing more to discuss on this," Swaroop said.

"There actually is, sir," Manik said.

"What's that, Manik?" Swaroop asked as they all turned to look at him.

"There was a good man who was killed because of this, murdered in cold blood. Someone who uncovered the truth and paid for it with his life. The least we can do is make sure that people know why he died. Don't you think that's fair?" Manik pleaded.

"I know, Manik," Swaroop replied in an understanding tone. "We are all sad about the professor's tragic death. But from what I understand, his killers have been caught, and the police are doing what is necessary to get justice for him."

"Justice? No" Kedar replied. "Yes, they have got his killers. They found out who actually committed his murder. Justice would be to expose the conspiracy behind all this. That would mean making the contents of the papers public."

"I have to agree, sir," Manik added, turning to Swaroop.

"I am sorry, Manik," Swaroop said in a low voice. "The decision has been made, and it's out of my hands."

"Well, Swaroop, I must say this is extremely disappointing and, honestly, shameful. There's no other word for it. I am speaking for myself. Please convey my thoughts verbatim to the Roys. Better still, I will do it myself," Kedar said as he got up.

"I am not sure that's a good idea," Swaroop said in a pleading voice.

"What I tell the Roys is my decision. Thankfully, I don't need your permission or a lawyer's approval for that," Kedar said in a much calmer voice. He had gotten up and was about to leave when Swaroop spoke again.

"Before you leave, I have one more thing to ask you and Manik. It's not related to the papers—more about the election."

Before Swaroop could continue further, the lawyer got up, shook hands with everyone, and left the room.

"What is it, Swaroop?" asked Kedar.

"It's the election assignment," Swaroop replied.

"What about it?"

"You and Manik had been assigned to Niranjan Sen."

"Yes, we know. We have already met him once."

"Right. Well, do you know about something called 'polling'?"

"Yes, I have read about it," Kedar replied, sounding surprised. "It is common in the West."

"Yes, it is." Swaroop said. "It seems a consortium of newspapers has now employed a domestic polling firm to poll voter intentions. You know, like take a sample and ask them whom they would like to vote for, what they think the main issues are, which party will tackle them better, etcetera."

"It would be hard to get a representative sample in a country like ours. It's too diverse, and what's to say that people won't change their minds between now and when they cast their ballot?" Kedar asked.

"Yes. All valid points, Kedar. There's actually a science behind it. How to get a representative sample, how to formulate the questions, something called the 'margin of error,' and other technical stuff that I am not entirely sure of."

"Right. So, what does this have to do with us?"

"Yes. I am coming to that. I want you and Manik to accompany this polling firm that has been contracted by us and some other regional papers."

"Accompany them where?"

"Basically, go to each location, see how they are doing the polling, make sure they are collecting the data properly and not fudging it before sharing it with us, and maybe help them with the sampling as well. Remember, the polling firms may know the science, but we as journalists know our regions very well and know where to go and can recommend areas and communities that they should be targeting in each state that's holding elections."

"What about Niranjan Sen?" Kedar asked.

"We will assign someone else to him. You and Manik can focus on the polling. It will mean extensive travel as well in the next few weeks, till the end of March—basically up until the election," Swaroop replied.

Manik and Kedar were quiet. Swaroop thought that they would be more enthusiastic about this assignment and the opportunity to travel. But they weren't.

"When do we start?" Kedar asked.

"You will start having meetings with the polling firms right away and then start traveling with them probably in two weeks. Any questions, comments?"

"It's Niranjan Sen, isn't it?" Kedar asked.

"Not sure what you mean, Kedar."

"The papers. Niranjan's companies own or at least partly own a lot of those lands. You don't want us asking him too many questions. We read the documents, Swaroop, so we know he has a lot to gain by the documents not getting published or getting questioned on them," Kedar said.

"I think the polling assignment is a good opportunity for both of you," Swaroop said, ignoring Kedar's comments.

"Just out of curiosity, Swaroop, who was there when you went to talk about the Surinampur papers yesterday at the Roys' residence?"

"Tarun and his lawyers. Sarat joined us later but stayed mostly silent. As you know, Tarun takes all the decisions now," Swaroop replied.

"Yes. So, here's my decision. As per my employment contract, I have to serve two months' notice before leaving. Well, I am giving you my notice now, and I will give you a signed letter later today. I know that the election cycle is busy. So I will stick around until the first week of April, until the elections are over. After that I think I will call it a day. It will also give you enough time to find my replacement," Kedar said.

"I am sorry to hear this, Kedar. I think you should take some time and not do this hastily," Swaroop said.

"I am not, Swaroop. When I joined this paper, I thought it had a different sort of vision. I am getting tired, and old as well. I think this place needs a different kind of reporter. There are plenty of them, and I am sure you will find someone who will fit right in," Kedar said with a smile. The animosity in his voice was completely gone.

"I wish you would give it a bit more thought and reconsider," Swaroop pleaded.

"Oh, no. I think it will be less of a headache for you too, Swaroop."

"Well, we will still have you around for the next few weeks. I am hoping we can change your mind. If not, let's make the most of your presence here. Please do know that I appreciate all the hard work that you, Manik, and the staff put in every day. Things don't always go our way. We shouldn't pack up and leave when they don't."

"Understood, Swaroop," Kedar said as he got up.

Manik got up as well. He was still trying to process what had happened. He understood Kedar's point of view. If he had the option, he would have probably done exactly the same thing. But he needed the job and was not one to take a decision like this on impulse. They got out of Swaroop's office and quietly walked back to their desks. The morning meeting had left them exhausted and deflated.

Kedar was back at his desk and on the phone setting up meetings with the polling firm. Manik couldn't focus on anything. It was as if he had been in a grueling match and had just been defeated. Part of him was also angry. His anger was directed toward the Roys, Swaroop, and the system. "The system" seemed to have prevailed over any sense of justice or fairness.

It had been successful in getting the professor out of the way, stealing the original papers, transferring the police officer who was seeking answers, and silencing the journalists who wanted to make all of it public. It seemed hopeless to even try to fight it.

11

The Visitor

Manik and Kedar spent the next two weeks meeting with the polling firm and trying to understand what they needed from them. Polling during elections was something new in India in the early seventies among the print media, and although many journalists had heard of it, most were extremely skeptical of putting any faith in pollsters. What made it even trickier was that the Election Commission of India, the national governing body in charge of administering elections throughout the country at all levels, was yet to make things clear on how to disseminate polling data and results based on surveys. For the most part, journalists could post editorials and opinion pieces based on sample data, but the rules around how polls could be conducted by private parties, whether they could be used as tools to influence an election, and to what extent they could be used for campaigning by the parties were still up in the air. It was a new challenge for them as well, and like the media, the government and political parties were also on the learning curve.

Manik and Kedar quickly got approvals from Swaroop to travel with the polling firm to the five states where elections were being held. It gave them an opportunity to interact with their counterparts in other regional and national publications. They would be on the road for about a month, spending a week in each of the states where elections were taking place. Although this new project kept him busy, Manik was still upset and angry with the decision of the newspaper not to publish what they had uncovered as part of the investigation into the professor's death. He knew that Kedar had spoken to the Roys after the meeting with Swaroop. But nothing had changed.

Manik was looking forward to the weekend before their upcoming month-long tour of the states. He needed time to pack and organize his things. He had already asked Subodh and Avik to take care of his apartment, collect his mail, and keep him informed of what was going on at work.

Everyone at work was well aware that Kedar had handed in his resignation and that he would be leaving after the elections. With Harish and Kedar both leaving soon, Manik knew that things would be different. They were the ones in the senior staff that he was closest to, and he would have to find a new mentor to work with. Swaroop hadn't spoken to him about whom he would be assigned to once his election assignment with Kedar was over. Manik had already sensed a change in Kedar. He was less motivated and more relaxed now. That bothered him. The Kedar he had come to know would not give up and would continuously look for ways to get his story published. But they had not spoken much about what had happened regarding the Surinampur papers. Of course, they had been busy in meetings, and that didn't leave them much time to talk one-on-one.

Manik was also preoccupied thinking about Sucheta. It still bothered him how things had ended with her. Subodh and Avik had persuaded him to go with them to her father's prayer ceremony, as was the custom on the tenth day after his cremation. That had taken place over the past weekend. Although he did not want to go, they told him that he should for the sake of the professor. He did. There was a large turnout, with most of the professor's relatives and students in attendance. The big crowd at the ceremony meant that Sucheta didn't see much of Manik. Kedar and Rudra Pratap dropped by for a short time to give their condolences. Rudra Pratap came by to talk to Manik briefly. He told him that he had been transferred to Delhi and would be leaving the next day.

Sucheta was preoccupied with the ceremony itself and making sure everything went off smoothly. He could also sense that she was avoiding him. Just before leaving, he went over to wish her well. She politely thanked him, Avik, and Subodh for coming. Manik learned from Avik during the week following the ceremony that she had already left for Bombay and the professor's house in Calcutta was now up for sale.

All this was going through Manik's mind as he was trying to wrap things up at work this Friday. He was making sure that things were in order so he could go directly to the train station on Monday with Kedar to start their four-week tour. Before leaving, he headed over to Kedar's desk. He was on the phone with the people from the polling firm, and Manik could hear that he was finalizing arrangements to meet with them once they arrived in Ranchi, in the neighboring state of Bihar, which would be their first stop. As soon as he saw Manik walking toward him, Kedar asked him to come over and wait. Once he had finished his call, he looked at his notes. It seemed that he was going to write something and then make another call. Before doing that, he turned to Manik.

"I am sorry, Manik. I know I have been busy, and I haven't had a chance to talk to you," Kedar said.

"That's all right, sir. I was just about to leave."

"I won't keep you. I just wanted to ask whether you are ready for Monday. Do you have everything you need?"

"Yes, sir. I have readied everything at work. I need to pack over the weekend," Manik replied.

"Right. We will be traveling for a month. Please pack accordingly. Ah yes, I also wanted to make sure that you will be at home tomorrow around nine thirty in the morning," Kedar said with a smile.

"Yes. I will be," Manik replied with a puzzled look on his face.

"You will have a visitor," Kedar said.

"You don't have to come by, sir. I can drop by your place if you need anything from me."

"Oh. It's not me. I am not the one that will be visiting you," Kedar said.

"Someone else from work?" Manik asked.

"Yes. You could say that." Kedar's phone started ringing. "I need to take this call. Be at home tomorrow morning, and we will talk again on Monday. Have a nice weekend."

"Good night, sir," Manik said, unsure whether Kedar heard him, as he was back on the phone again.

Manik walked back home wondering what this was all about. He couldn't imagine anyone at work wanting to visit him besides Subodh and Avik. He had seen Anjali earlier that day, and she hadn't mentioned anything. In any case she would certainly not spring such a surprise on him. Swaroop was traveling, and Harish was still on leave following his wife's death. Manik was too tired to think about this anymore. It had been a long week, and he was mentally and physically exhausted. After a quick dinner, he went back to his notebook to start writing some music. He could hear the wind outside and knew that there was a storm expected that night. After an hour he went to bed and fell fast asleep. He was happy that he didn't have to wake up to an alarm clock on Saturday.

He was awoken the next day by a gentle knocking on his door. Manik got up and saw that it was already 9:30 a.m. He quickly readied himself and opened the door. He was surprised to see a smartly dressed chauffeur in uniform. He couldn't recall if he had seen him before.

"Manik?"

"Yes."

"Mr. Sarat Roy is waiting downstairs. He would like you to join him," the chauffeur said, and turned and walked back to head downstairs.

Manik was puzzled as to why Sarat would want to meet him. He quickly changed and ran down the two flights of stairs. He could see Sarat's car outside the gates. Sarat had gotten out and was sitting on a bench just outside the gates. His presence was an odd contrast to everything around him. People on the sidewalks were walking by in their casual clothes. Some were in their sport attire heading to the nearby parks for their morning exercise. The bench was dusty, and the road was full of leaves that had fallen from the trees during the storm the night before. There were very few cars and buses on the road. The weekend traffic in the morning was usually very light. Sarat Roy was, as always, dressed in his white Bengali attire, sitting quietly with both his hands folded and resting on his walking stick in front of him. He was trying to enjoy the sun that was now shining brightly. The storm had passed, and Manik could see that the old man had closed his eyes and was enjoying the moment. He quickly walked up beside him.

"Good morning, sir."

"Ah, Manik," Sarat said as he slowly got up. "I hope I didn't drag you out of bed. I am sorry if I did. I know it is a bit early for a Saturday, and I know people like to sleep in."

"It's fine, sir."

"Let's get some breakfast, shall we," Sarat said, pointing to the car with his walking stick. They slowly made their way to the car. Once they were settled in the back, Sarat nodded, and the driver was on his way.

"Where are we going, sir?"

"Somewhere not too far, Manik. Don't worry—I won't keep you for too long."

"It's all right, sir. I am in no hurry," Manik said.

"This city has changed, you know, and is changing," Sarat said, looking out the window.

"Yes, sir."

"It's the only constant in life—change."

The car made its way to the roads leading to one of the main avenues to the city. Manik guessed that wherever they were going was in the center of town. He could see some of the familiar landmarks, and then the car veered into a leafy neighborhood that he had passed before but never paid close attention to. It stopped at a crossing and then proceeded onto a road leading up to a white colonial building. As soon as the watchmen at the gates saw the car, they opened it, and the car parked in front of the main entrance of an elegant-looking building. There was no sign or board outside to indicate what it was, just the street number and guards, who kept the gates closed at all times. The doormen waiting outside quickly opened the car doors on either side for Sarat and Manik.

Once they stepped out, Sarat led him through the main doors into a big hallway.

"In case you are wondering, Manik, this is a club for old people like us."

"Right, sir."

Everyone in the club seemed to know who Sarat was as he led Manik past one of the many doors at the end of the giant hall. Everything inside the club was old, dark, and imposing. Even though it was sunny outside, the lights had to be turned on inside. Manik could see the beautiful decorations on the walls, the paintings, and the well-crafted seats in the hall. The door that Sarat led Manik through led to a dining area. Manik could see that it was an upscale restaurant. There were a few people there already having breakfast. Some of them saw Sarat and waved at him. He smiled back at them.

"Let's sit outside. It's too dark in here," Sarat said, indicating to a waiter that they wanted to sit in the courtyard just outside the large dining room. After going through another set of doors, they made their way to a nice table at the edge of the courtyard overlooking a well-maintained garden. Manik could see small fountains and a greenhouse at the far end.

"Never understood this place," Sarat said as they both sat down.

Manik sat across from him. "What's that, sir?"

"Anywhere you go in this darned club, it's dark. You would think that they would flood it with lights," Sarat said.

"I wouldn't know, sir."

"Oh, I know. Most of the people who come here are old fogies like me. The décor and lights make us feel even older. Well, enough of that. Let's get some breakfast, shall we?" Sarat waved at a waiter, who quickly arrived to take the order.

"What will you have, sir?"

"Bring us some breakfast. I don't want to go through the menu—some eggs, bread, fruit, and juice. Oh yes, some tea, of course. Unless you want coffee, Manik?"

"Tea is fine, sir," Manik replied.

Once the waiter left, Sarat turned to Manik and looked at him. "I know you must be wondering why I brought you here."

"Yes, sir."

"Did Kedar tell you anything?"

"No, sir. He just told me that I was going to have a visitor this morning. He didn't tell me it would be you, sir."

"Well, I think I will get to it then. I wanted to talk to you about the Surinampur papers."

"We were told that we couldn't publish anything regarding that, sir."

"Yes, I know," Sarat said thoughtfully.

"We were told the decision was yours and Swaroop's," Manik said.

"Yes, you could say it was ours. Tell me—and you can be candid with me—what do you think about that?"

"I think it's wrong, sir. I thought we put forward a compelling argument to make it public."

"Yes, you did. I am sure you feel that it was unfair."

"Yes, sir, and angry too. My professor was killed because of it, and although the police did nab the killers, we didn't let everyone know why he was killed. He had uncovered a conspiracy, and we thought it was important for the public to know the whole story."

"Yes, Manik. I must first compliment you on your efforts to catch the culprits," Sarat said.

Before he could continue any further, the breakfast arrived. While the waiter was serving, they kept quiet. Manik looked at Sarat. He had a distant look in his eyes. He had wrinkles on his aged face that showed the marks of a stressful and successful life. The waiter poured them some tea and then left them in peace to eat their breakfast and continue their conversation. Sarat pointed to the plates in front of them, and they started eating.

"You must have seen the papers, sir, when Swaroop brought them over to you and your lawyers? Don't you think that the rightful owners of the lands should be told of their existence? Even if they are not the originals, they might still make a claim for some settlement or compensation."

"I have seen some of the papers, Manik. I was in the meeting when Swaroop brought them over. I do know what's in them. Tarun and the lawyers told me in great detail what the impact of publishing them would be."

"And what do you think, sir?"

"They made a compelling argument for not publishing them and causing a scandal."

"But you agreed with them, sir?"

"You know, Manik, I have left the day-to-day running of the paper to Tarun and Swaroop. I try not to interfere with their decisions. You know, when Tarun was a young boy, I was busy trying to run my business. We were never really that close, and I didn't get to spend much time with him. His mother spoiled him, of course, and they both blame me for not paying attention to him. I am getting old as well, and I have more or less handed over the reins to him to take things forward. It is only fair that he takes the decisions and, by the same token, faces the consequences of those decisions."

"So, sir, you go with every decision he makes?"

"And yet, I am here talking to you about the Surinampur papers. Things aren't always as they seem," Sarat said with a smile.

They paused and took a few minutes to eat their breakfast. Manik was wondering where this was leading. He sensed that Sarat probably did not agree with Tarun's decision to not publish the contents of the papers but had had to go along with it. Was this an attempt by Sarat to smooth things over with Kedar and him? he wondered. Manik knew that Kedar had already spoken to the Roys. He was slowly coming to the realization that it was Sarat and not Tarun that Kedar had spoken with. He still couldn't fathom what was happening at the moment. Kedar was not the kind of person who would cave in, even for Sarat. He decided to break the silence and find out.

"Kedar is leaving, sir. My understanding is that he has handed in his notice."

"Yes, he has," Sarat said.

That confused Manik even more. *So, what is this all about?* he thought.

"Tell me, how important is it for you that the content of the papers be made public?"

"Very important, sir."

"Yes, I have heard. Justice for the professor's murder. And fairness for the rightful owners, who may not be aware of their inheritance."

"Yes, sir."

"Let me ask this another way. Is it more important that *you* make the papers public or that they be made public regardless, even though it may not come from you and Kedar?" Sarat said as he looked at him directly.

Manik paused before responding. He was slowly realizing what Sarat was trying to tell him.

"But the papers are not with us. Swaroop told us that the lawyers kept them," Manik said.

"Ah. But I am sure Kedar and you must have made copies," Sarat said with a smile.

Manik chose not to answer that. Instead he decided to press Sarat further on what his view was on publishing the contents of the Surinampur papers.

"Don't you think, sir, that we should be the ones leading the story on this? I mean, the *New Eastern Herald*. If some other newspaper takes the lead, they might get the blame, but they also will get the credit, and we would lose out."

"From a business standpoint, you may be right. I don't know, Manik. That's why I asked you your opinion as a journalist as to what was more important."

"That they be made public, sir," Manik reiterated.

"Right," Sarat said with a distant look on his face.

"So, you agree that this should be printed?"

"Yes. Otherwise I wouldn't have dragged you away on a Saturday morning to have breakfast with an old man," Sarat replied with a smile.

They continued their breakfast in silence for the next few minutes. Manik had finally figured out what this meeting was all about. He was convinced that Tarun and the lawyers were not aware of this. It also dawned on Manik that Sarat had spoken about this only to Kedar and him.

"What about the implications for Kedar and me?" Manik asked.

"Ah, yes. Well, Kedar is leaving. I am sure you will talk to him about what the next course of action is. I understand that you and Kedar will start traveling soon, and that might actually help with this. Needless to say, once the ball starts rolling, you will probably be asked to move on," Sarat replied.

"Right, sir," Manik said thoughtfully, not sure what that meant; he made a note to talk to Kedar about it.

"Still think it's a good idea?"

"Yes, sir."

"Kedar tells me that you write music?"

"Yes, sir, I do," Manik replied. He was rather surprised at this quick change of topic.

"You should keep at it, you know. It's a good thing. Not many people can do that."

"Yes, sir," Manik said, wondering where this was going.

"Kedar also told me that your first choice was to work at a current affairs magazine. You applied to some, but they never got back to you. Is that correct?"

"Yes, sir."

"Which magazines, and where are they based?" Sarat asked.

The waiter came by and poured them another cup of tea. Sarat asked Manik whether he wanted anything else. Manik was already full, and they waited until waiter had taken away all the plates, leaving them with their tea and some water. Manik then went on to explain how he had applied to some magazines in Bombay. He was surprised to learn that Kedar had told Sarat how close he was with the professor and Sucheta. Sarat was also interested in learning about Manik's musical compositions. Manik realized that the old man was a good listener and knew much more than he actually let on. Sarat was easy to talk to, and even though he was successful, he wasn't arrogant. He never interrupted Manik and was not in a hurry to finish anything that they were discussing. Manik liked that, and he respected Sarat more for it.

Finally, after almost two hours, they were done with their breakfast, and Manik sensed that Sarat had spoken to him about everything that he had wanted to talk to him about. As they got up to leave, Sarat turned to Manik.

"Wouldn't it be great if you could find something in Bombay? That way you could work at a magazine and pursue your musical interests," Sarat said with a smile.

"Yes, sir. I have tried with no luck," Manik replied.

"Yes, so it would seem," Sarat said, again lost in thought, with a distant look on his face.

"But I will keep trying," Manik said enthusiastically.

"You absolutely should. Well, you will be busy with the elections and will be on the road soon. I am not sure when we will see each other again—and what the future holds. I want to thank you for all the great work you have done. I have kept an eye on you, you know, since our meeting with Harish and Swaroop earlier in January. It isn't by accident that you were assigned to work with Kedar," Sarat said with a smile.

"That was your idea, sir?" Manik asked.

Sarat smiled. "Manik. That's a gem, isn't it?"

"I am sorry?"

"The name Manik—it means 'gem' in Sanskrit. I am sure you know the meaning of your name?"

"Yes, sir. So I have been told," Manik replied.

"You indeed are a gem. I hope you live up to your name, and I wish you all the best for your future. If you don't mind, Manik, I will stay on in the club for a little while longer to read the newspapers. My driver will take you home."

"Thank you, sir," Manik said.

"No, thank you," Sarat said, putting his hand on Manik's shoulder. He gave Manik an affectionate smile.

Manik slowly walked back through the club to the parking lot and saw Sarat's car and driver waiting to take him home. On his way back, Manik replayed what had happened during the breakfast. The Surinampur papers had already started having an impact on those connected to them. Rudra Pratap had been transferred. The one police officer that would have doggedly pursued it was no longer in charge. Kedar was leaving in a few weeks, and it seemed unlikely the *Herald* would print anything on it anytime soon. But it felt good to talk to Sarat. At the very least, Manik was happy that someone like Sarat believed that the corruption should be exposed. He also wondered what that meant for Swaroop and the senior staff. If all controversial articles were to be vetted and approved by the Roys, then many of the senior journalists would probably be moving on.

As the car dropped him off in front of his building and he started making his way back through the gates toward the stairs leading to his apartment, he knew that first and foremost he had to consider his future as well. The *New Eastern Herald* had held a lot of promise for him when he joined. He hadn't had much of a choice. It was the only paper that was ready to employ him when he graduated. But with what had happened during that eventful month, he realized that he would have to redouble his efforts to find another job. As he lay on his bed thinking about his future, he started making a mental note of the magazines and newspapers that he would be applying to. He was confident that he would be getting good referrals from Kedar and Harish. The meeting with Sarat had calmed him down. He was no longer upset and angry about the paper's decision not to publish what he and Kedar had wanted it to. His own future seemed uncertain. But something told him that things were about to change. That made him feel good for the first time in a long time.

12

Epilogue

The weeks leading up to the elections and summer were quite eventful. A few weeks prior to the elections, newspaper editors and some well-known senior journalists at most of the leading national and regional newspapers in India started receiving packages in the mail with documents in them. The documents were mostly copies of land deeds, land registrations, and covenants. Along with the papers were public documents related to builders and real estate companies that had bought lands identified in these copies from the government, seemingly without the knowledge or consent of the owners. It seemed the land had been sold by successive governments without any effort to trace the rightful owners. This story was hard to ignore. The first one to follow up and investigate this was a well-known national daily. It not only published an article based on its investigation into owners who were being swindled but also took the drastic step of identifying the owners and printing some copies of the deeds.

Other newspapers across the country quickly followed suit, and it became nothing short of a nationwide scandal. There were calls for further investigation into the whole system. Many state governments instituted commissions to allay the public outcry. But in a few weeks, too many people were involved for the whole thing to be ignored or delayed beyond a certain acceptable period. The upcoming elections meant that both the ruling and opposition parties were forced to take a stance on the scandal and offer their plans and promises to address it. After a few weeks, there were many court cases by a number of owners demanding compensation.

Some newspapers tried to identify the source of the documents but were unsuccessful. The sender's address on the envelopes invariably led to an empty field or a nonexistent building. The postmark suggested that they were being mailed from post offices across different states, and there were no cameras in those establishments and no records of who was mailing them. The focus quickly shifted to the content of the papers and assigning resources to investigate them. It wasn't apparent, but if anyone had bothered to check, they would have found that there was a connection between the locations from which the documents were being mailed and two journalists from the *New Eastern Herald* who were traveling on election duty with a polling firm to cover the upcoming state elections.

Once the articles started appearing, the story became too big even for the *Herald* to ignore. They also picked up the story and ran a few articles on it. They were careful to use other newspapers as reference in their articles. The other news on the *Herald* was that its managing editor, Mr. Swaroop Pal, was going to be taking an early retirement just after the election. There was the standard statement around Swaroop wanting to spend more time with the family. A replacement had been hired. It was someone from outside. The rumor was that the person replacing Swaroop was controversial. In the news media, the new managing editor replacing Swaroop had a bit of a reputation of being a troublemaker, especially for the government and sometimes for other parts of the establishment, like the police and even the judiciary.

The elections in all the states had been eventful. It was hard to say what impact the scandal had had on voting. But it did have an impact on constituencies where candidates from the real estate business were on the ticket. Irrespective of which party they were representing, they were soundly defeated. Even the independent candidates who were favorites to win their constituencies were not spared. One of the casualties was Niranjan Sen. He lost the election despite being a well-known figure and a popular candidate.

Kedar and Manik left the *New Eastern Herald* under different circumstances. Kedar had already submitted his resignation and was supposed to leave right after the elections. But when he returned from his tour with Manik with the polling firm, Swaroop accepted his resignation with immediate effect, and he was asked to leave well before the elections. Kedar decided to move back to Bombay.

Manik was allowed to stay on but was given lower-priority desk duties that were usually given to interns and new hires. There was someone constantly micromanaging and supervising him. One day, when he returned home, Manik found an envelope with a letter from a current affairs magazine in Bombay that he had previously applied to but had never heard back from. They were interested in interviewing him over the weekend at a club in Calcutta. When he went for the interview, he realized that it was more of a formality. He was offered a position, with a nice starting salary and additional perks. They did not ask him for any references. Still being part of the junior staff at the *New Eastern Herald* meant that he only had to give two weeks' notice. Swaroop was surprised that Manik had found a job so quickly. He wasn't able to get an answer from him as to where he was going.

By summer Manik had settled into his new job in Bombay. He enjoyed working for the magazine. It was a new experience for him, and it was turning out to be a rewarding one. He had found an apartment close to a local train station that was only four stops away from the magazine's office. As he made his way to the platform, he decided to pick up the morning paper. He chose a local newspaper, not one of the national dailies. While waiting for the train, he started leafing through the pages. At the bottom of one of the pages, he came across an article that caught his eye. It was about a new private journalism school. A consortium of newspapers had decided to start an institute to train their new entrants and hires. They would be given short initiation courses before they started working in their offices. Manik was not interested in any of that. What caught his eye were the two people running the institute. They were both award-winning journalists who had recently retired from the *New Eastern Herald*. Manik smiled when he read their names. He had worked with both of them and knew them really well. He could hear the train slowly making its way into the platform.

There was another article on the Bombay underworld. The police had been successful in making a big drugs haul. They had managed to nab a number of gang members across different cities in a sting operation. There was a picture of the police commissioner displaying the cache of drugs and arms that had been recovered. Behind the commissioner were the photos of some of the suspects who had been caught in Bombay and Delhi. Beside them were the pictures of a few policemen who had arrested them. Their names were not in the paper, and the faces were not too clear. But Manik recognized one of them: it was Rudra Pratap Singh.

Just before closing the newspaper, he found the article that he was actually looking for. There was a new genre of movies that was becoming popular in India. They went under the banner of "indie movies" or "art films." These were low-budget movies that did not have the glitz, glamour, or reach of Bollywood movies. But it was a good place for new and upcoming talent to start. What he was looking for was the announcement for the first showing of a new art movie that was premiering in a small fifty-seat theater. No one involved in the production was well-known or famous by any stretch. But Manik had a big smile on his face when he read the name of the music director. The movie producers had, partly due to budget constraints and partly due to a recommendation unknown to Manik, decided to take a chance on him. He hadn't disappointed.

Once the train stopped, Manik got on, and as he looked at the Bombay skyline through the windows of the moving train, he started to think about what he was going to compose next and started humming a tune.

About the Author

Aditya Banerjee grew up in India in the seventies and eighties and moved to Canada in the nineties. He is a graduate of McGill University in Montreal, Canada, and Manipal Institute of Technology in Manipal, India. He has traveled widely and is a history buff. He loves historical fiction and mystery novels. He is also the author of *Broken Dreams: A Callipur Murder Mystery*. He now lives with his family in Canada.

Made in the USA
Columbia, SC
23 January 2025